BOOK TWO

OF THE

KATZENSTEIN KIDS TRILOGY

BOOKS BY A.G. SULLIVAN

THE KATZENSTEIN KIDS AND THE EYE OF HORUS

THE KATZENSTEIN KIDS AND THE 12 MINOTAURS

TRYPOPHOBIA – A NOVEL

TATTOOS & POETRY

THE
KATZENSTEIN
KIDS
AND THE 12 MINOTAURS

A.G. SULLIVAN

To my kids.
Never stop dreaming and believing
in what you can achieve!

CONTENTS

CHAPTER 1
OPERATION RIMON 20
Memphis, Egypt – Fall 1979

The air in the control room hung heavy, a physical weight pressing down on Sergei Belonogov's shoulders. Every tick of the clock echoed like a hammer blow in the tense silence. His gaze was locked on the flickering radio console, the only source of light besides the dying embers on a monitor displaying a wall of static. Each burst of crackling noise sent a fresh jolt through him, a spark of anticipation warring with dread. Sergei gripped the edge of the console so hard his knuckles shone white beneath the dim light.

Suddenly, the radio crackled to life, and a voice pierced through the tense silence. "Sir, we've found them! We've found the—"

The message crackled over the speakers, promising clarity, but a deafening buzz ripped through the air before it could finish. A high-pitched whine followed, so sharp it made Sergei's teeth ache. He flinched, his hands flying to cover his ears. He exchanged a desperate glance with the radio officer, both their faces etched with a mix of confusion and alarm. The transmission wasn't just garbled; it was an assault on the senses.

"Agent, come in! Repeat, what did you find?" Sergei's voice cut through the static, his tone urgent.

"We've found the bodies!" The voice on the other end was frantic, barely audible over the interference. "Sir, you're not going to believe this..."

The radio officer's fingers hovered mid-keystroke, then stilled. The incessant clicking ceased, allowing an unnatural silence to invade the room once again. The echo of the officer's last keypress bounced around the cramped space, amplifying the stillness. Seconds stretched into agonizing minutes, the silence, a suffocating weight pressing down on them. A console, ablaze with a pulsating kaleidoscope of red lights, cast an eerie glow on their faces as the transmission resumed. Radios and monitors lining the walls erupted in a synchronized frenzy, flashing incomprehensible warnings accompanied the shocking details that reached their ears.

A wave of nausea crashed over Sergei as realization struck – cold and heavy as an anchor. He forced himself upright, his gut straining against the tightness of his leather belt. The grays in his hair seemed to deepen with each passing second, mirroring the stark darkness that had swallowed his eyes. His jaw clenched, muscles straining in stark relief. He turned to the radio officer, the air between them thick with a sense of unspoken dread. "Relay to headquarters," Sergei instructed, his voice firm but laced with a tremor that betrayed his inner turmoil. "Inform them that we found all twelve bodies."

The radio officer's fingers flew across the keyboard, a frantic counterpoint to the cold dread coiling in Sergei's gut. The weight of his duty as primary emissary pressed down on him. He knew the implications of this message were catastrophic, a potential powder keg waiting to explode. Every fiber of his being screamed to bury the truth, but duty was a harsh mistress. With a steely glint in his eyes, he forced the words past the knot in his throat. "Inform them," he rasped, "That their hearts were removed from their chests."

Suddenly a voice sliced through the tense atmosphere, sharp and authoritative. "Are we ready, sir?" Sergei's gaze snapped to the open doorway, where a man stood silhouetted, his stern face etched with a grim resolve.

At Sergei's curt nod, the radio officer fell silent, his work forgotten. Sergei snatched his leather attaché case from the floor and bolted for the door. The other man was right behind him. They burst out into the open, the deafening roar of the Russian Mi-22 transport helicopter's blades drowning out everything. The wind whipped sand into a frenzy around their ankles, mimicking the whirlwind of questions swirling in Sergei's mind. His grip on the attaché case tightened instinctively.

Inside the passenger cabin, Sergei locked the door and

collapsed. Finally, alone, he spilled the horrifying details of his expedition's annihilation in Upper Egypt. Moments drifted by as his own reality blurred – a waking nightmare. Beside him, the man with the stern face and short dark hair watched Sergei. His heterochromia gave him an unforgettable stare, mismatched eyes, one hazel, the other a piercing blue cut straight through Sergei's disorientation. This was Rurik Zakharov. Just as Rurik spoke, the helicopter roared into motion, lurching upwards. The bumpy ascent mirrored the turmoil in Sergei's mind – their destination would arrive before he could gain any semblance of control.

"Can you tell me what's going on, sir?" Rurik hollered over the noise of the rotors. His lips moved, but his words merely succumbed to the racket of the turbine engine.

Wordlessly, Sergei reached for a pair of headsets hanging from a hook above them and gestured for Rurik to do the same as he placed them atop his head. He untangled the wires from around them and then pulled the microphone toward his mouth with narrowed eyes.

Rurik followed suit and needlessly leaned in closer before repeating his question. "Can you tell me what's going on, sir?"

"As my attaché, what I am about to tell you must remain between us."

Silence hung heavy between them. Rurik, a recent initiate into the elite ranks of Soviet intelligence, understood the weight of his newfound role. Every conversation, every action, existed within an unspoken vow of secrecy. Years of grueling training culminated in this moment, in this covert operation disguised as diplomacy. Their true mission, their allegiance to the KGB and Mother Russia, was a constant, undeniable presence.

Rurik nodded solemnly; his gaze unwavering. He understood the gravity of the situation, the importance of discretion in matters of national security.

Sergei continued. "The official reason? Peace has brought us here today," he said, his voice tight with emotion. "Last March, the Camp David Accords were signed between Egypt and Israel in Washington, DC. Afterward, I was able to broker a deal with Egypt to recover the body of Nikolai Yurchenko. Do you recall Operation Rimon 20?"

"Yes, July of 1970 if I recall my history correctly," Rurik's voice came through the headset filled with static. "Nikolai Yurchenko is considered to be a national hero."

"More like a national embarrassment," Sergei murmured. He snorted, but the microphone didn't pick it up. "As you may recall, during the War of Attrition, Soviet fighter pilots stationed in Egypt engaged Israeli fighters in their Soviet MiG-21's."

Rurik, his face grim, offered a curt nod. The upgraded MiG-21's, the pride of the Soviet fleet, had proven woefully inadequate. Modifications with radar, engines, and weaponry hadn't been enough. A cold dread settled in Sergei's gut as Rurik's voice confirmed his fears. "The Israelis," Rurik said, his voice tight, "shot down five of ours."

Sergei nodded. "Precisely. We never recovered Nikolai

Yurchenko or his MiG's wreckage. However, compelling evidence suggests someone might have retrieved his remains and transferred them to the Abusir region. Last week, we sent an expeditionary team made up of twelve of our best men to investigate this lead."

"Where are they now, sir?" Rurik pressed when Sergei fell silent.

Sergei averted his gaze, glancing out the window at the dust-obscured landscape below. Their descent seemed to have begun. "Rurik," he said, his voice heavy, "what we've uncovered is far more sinister than we anticipated. Eight hours ago, we lost total communication with our team. Then, just minutes ago I received a transmission, we discovered their bodies... all dead. Their hearts removed from their chests."

Before Rurik had a chance to respond, the helicopter pitched downward suddenly.

The roar of the engines grew louder as the fuselage tilted in mid-air and then swooped slowly downward. The ride had been quick and smooth, to Sergei's pleasant surprise.

"Prepare for landing," Sergei announced, his voice projecting over the helicopter's roar. "We'll be arriving at our rendezvous near Abusir, just as planned."

Rurik's nod masked the shock that had drained the color from his face. Since hearing the fate of the expedition, he'd retreated into silence. The grotesque discovery of their comrades, hearts ripped out... the image burned in his mind, a gruesome testament to unseen forces. As the ground rushed up to meet them, he didn't look away, as if facing reality head-on would provide some sort of answer.

The helicopter touched down, and both men swiftly unbuckled and exited. Sergei, in the lead, approached the waiting Egyptian intelligence officer. Dressed in tan fatigues, the officer stood beside a large military truck of the same color, its paint and mud-streaked wheels blending seamlessly with the surrounding desert. Rurik followed Sergei, head lowered against the swirling gusts of wind kicked up by the still-spinning rotors.

"Colonel Omar," Sergei gave a curt nod as they approached the truck.

The colonel nodded at them both in return, though he kept his lips tightly pursed throughout their interaction. "There isn't time to waste. I'll take you to the location. Get in."

"How far is the site?" Rurik asked as he buckled up.

"About one kilometer south of here."

With that, they were off, sand blowing up around the tires as they drove through the desert. The trip wasn't long, and soon they arrived at a vast clearing. Sergei didn't release his grip on the case throughout the entire drive, nor when they stopped and stepped out into the dust. The open space invited the heat of the sun to rain down onto the fine sand and bake it to temperatures that caused sweat to drip down the backs of their necks. In the clearing, laid out in a strange pattern that Sergei couldn't quite figure out from afar, were the distinct shapes of twelve bodies. The Russian emissary held his breath as he approached. With each step the sand swallowed the sound of his boots, leaving only a muffled crunch in his ears.

The smell hit his nose first, and he could scarcely tolerate it, his fingers involuntarily tightening around the handle of his case. Flies buzzed around the bodies. The stench was so strong that Sergei brought his forearm up to cover his mouth. He coughed into his own elbow before he saw the stone-cold, pale faces of the expeditionary team. From up close, the pattern in which they were laid to rest still made no sense to him. But it was hard to miss them—not when their shirts were all stained the same rusty color, chests bloody. Each one held the same expression: utter horror contorted their features, pulling their mouths back unnaturally and widening their eyes. Anyone who found them would know the last thing they felt was terrible, terrible fear. He had to force himself to tear his eyes from the sight, despite how difficult it was to look. He glanced down at the equally identical and crimson holes in their chests. Their hearts had once lived there, now viciously torn from their cages.

"Here, sir," his companion said, handing Sergei a spare handkerchief. He accepted it with his free hand, covering his nose and mouth to block out the odor of death.

"Have you noticed how they positioned the bodies postmortem? Do you see the pattern?" Colonel Omar walked behind them, as if he didn't want to get too close to the bodies. He spoke with an accent. "Groups of four, side by side. Their heads are each facing south, east, and west."

"Does that have a meaning?" Rurik asked.

"Facing their heads north would better symbolize

ancient Egyptian beliefs. In ancient Egyptian beliefs, the head faces toward the direction of the afterlife. But none of these men's heads are facing north; only in the other three directions, as you can see." He gestured widely. "It appears to be a deliberate attempt to prevent these men from reaching the afterlife. An attempt to confuse the dead so they won't find the afterlife... Instead, they would remain trapped between worlds."

Sergei could tell Rurik was readying another question before he opened his mouth; the telltale furrow in his brow giving him away. "For what reason—"

"Enough about that," the emissary interjected with a stern glare. Rurik looked down sheepishly, taking his cue without pressing the issue any further than he already had.

They continued to investigate the bodies, walking between the first set of four. They lowered themselves to their haunches to closely observe the men and their wounds. To Rurik's great surprise, each man bore a lapel pin on his collar. The pin was in the shape of an atom with the initials V.N.I.I.E.F. It stood for the All-Union Scientific Research Institute of Experimental Physics. With a quiet gasp, he stood up and backed away from the bodies, the realization that he hadn't been told everything suddenly washing over him. These weren't the kind of men who would be searching for a pilot's remains, but for something far more concerning. He looked around, relieved that no one seemed to have noticed his reaction.

"What do you say about these footprints?" Sergei's voice rang out loudly. Rurik shook his head and quietly gathered himself before joining the emissary crouched on the ground a short distance away.

A single trail of footsteps appearing to belong to a large, barefooted man led away from the scene. "The lone man," the colonel said cryptically.

"The lone man?" Sergei and Rurik echoed.

"They headed in the direction of the tomb of Serapeum of Saqqara," was all the explanation the colonel offered. "It is perhaps another three kilometers south of here. We can take my vehicle there."

Yet again, they drove through the desolate desert. Sergei and Rurik were quietly pleased with the chance to escape the smell, but the haunted faces of the dead were not as easy to forget when they were back in the din of the truck. The bodies couldn't be moved while they were conducting their investigation. Rurik couldn't help but stir uncomfortably at the idea of his own body being left to fester in the sun.

Arriving at the Serapeum of Saqqara, they were faced with the ancient walls of an underground tomb that projected from the slopes of an otherwise dusty landscape. They squinted through the dirt billowing around them, looking for footprints or some other sign of unusual activity. Otherwise, they might not have noticed anything amiss in the distance at all. The vehicle came to a steady halt, and they climbed out near the entry point. An ancient stairway, carved from rock and covered in sand, led down to a doorway below ground. The walls grew higher and higher on either side as one walked down them. They peeked out subtly right at the start, almost invisible. Before anyone had a chance to take in their surroundings, Sergei pointed and exclaimed excitedly, then took the stairs without so much as a glance backward. He didn't check if Rurik and the colonel were following him, all the while carrying his case closely at his side. Right at the top of the staircase, the footsteps of the barefooted man could be seen leading down toward the vault below.

At the bottom of the staircase, near the entrance of the vault, the human footprints were joined and overrun by a herd of other types of markings in the ground. They crowded the doorway. Sergei knelt down and brushed his fingers through the sand, shifting the animal prints lightly. They seemed fresh.

"They appear to be hoof prints, don't they? It appears our friend may be some kind of cattle keeper." He spoke more to himself than the others, before slowly stepping through the large doorway on his own in search of more answers.

The hallway was wide and tall enough to make the average man feel small, but the dark foreboding in the air filled the space and made it feel tighter than it should. Without having a particular reason, Sergei's heart thumped faster. It was then that Sergei snuck a look around for the others, his breath catching in his throat at the sight of Rurik entering through the doorway. The fear he'd momentarily experienced dissipated slightly—but only slightly.

"Gods," Colonel Omar uttered at the back of the group with a loud gasp, the last person to enter the space. His eyes darted around wildly.

"What is it?" Sergei approached the colonel, but he took several steps back from him, knocking into the doorframe.

"These are sarcophagi for the mummified remains of the sacred Apis bulls!" The colonel cried out. Shelves of tombs lined the walls and within them, sarcophagi. They were larger than any Sergei or Rurik had ever seen, and any they'd imagined coming across. Then again, this wasn't exactly their field of expertise. They moved slowly through the room, keeping their distance from the shelves but wanting to investigate. The tops of each stone coffin had been moved. Some were cracked in places, indicating that a great deal of force was involved in the opening of the sarcophagi. They were all empty.

"This isn't possible," Colonel Omar spoke again, shaking his head frantically. Before either of the Russians could get there, he suddenly moved from his spot at the entrance and paced toward one of the tombs. He stopped between them, then, his voice carrying a note of panic. "I know this place well; these tombs should not be open!"

There were twelve giant stone coffins in the room. Curious, Sergei walked past the colonel toward the nearest one. Colonel Omar shifted to once again stand in his path, but Sergei sidestepped him. He attempted to push the lid of the sarcophagus, a nearly impossible feat considering it was made of over a ton of solid stone. He grunted and took a deep breath, pausing to instead peruse the exterior. Hieroglyphs were engraved neatly into and covered the surface area. Impossible seemed an appropriate description. Yet, there the lids were, carelessly shifted to one side, revealing the emptiness within. Little else could be more terrifying than seeing the tombs devoid of their

contents.

Or so the men thought. As their eyes continued to scour the room, they eventually drifted down toward the dirty floor of the vault. It became clear that the ground at their feet was littered with hoof tracks. It was as if a herd of bulls had stampeded through the room and out through the exit.

"Oh Gods," the colonel gasped again. He shook his head again and then dropped it. "Something has been released upon us. The wrath of twelve Apis bulls has been resurrected!"

Sergei ripped his eyes from the ground. He saw that the colonel had paled several shades and a sheen of sweat glazed his forehead.

"Our men, why the hearts of twelve of our men?" The colonel met Sergei's eyes with a wildness in them that the Russian emissary didn't know what to make of. "The sacred Apis bulls are a symbol of strength and fertility. If these bulls have been resurrected with the hearts of your men... they are no longer mere bulls, but something more powerful, something we must truly fear."

With a slow crouch, Sergei reached into the sand and shifted away some of the hoof prints. He glanced up at the colonel, pointing at the ground. "The footprints of the lone man?"

"Yes," the colonel nodded, eyes wide with fear. "The sacred Apis bulls also symbolize the manifestation of a king. This was no accident; the birth of a new king is upon us, and with it, twelve beasts!"

Before either of them could respond, Colonel Omar stormed for the exit in his panic-stricken state. They heard his feet slapping up the stone steps in a hurry. Rurik and Sergei met each other's eyes. They quickly and silently decided to follow the colonel. They didn't want him to drive off in his truck and leave them in the desert.

The burning sun was briefly blinding as they came out of the necropolis, beating down on the sandy terrain in the distance. Squinting ahead, through windswept dust, a column of shapes took form. A dozen divots cast their shadows across the surface, heading east. By all appearances, it was the path of the hooved tracks. Rurik broke his gaze from the sight to see Colonel Omar standing stoically in the open terrain, staring out after the blurry shapes.

"The tracks are heading east?" Rurik called out to him.

"Toward the port of Suez," the colonel broke his gaze to meet Rurik's.

"The port?"

"Yes, a shipping hub that connects to shipping lanes throughout the world."

They walked to the vehicle together, the Russians trailing behind the colonel. He seemed to have a firmer grip on the situation. Whether that was due to the clues they found or his experience, they couldn't say. It was enough of a respite to know that he seemed to have calmed down now that he was no longer in the tomb. He walked faster than they did, but it was probably safe to assume he wouldn't drive off without them.

Sergei came to a halt halfway between the staircase and the truck, dropping to his haunches. Once he'd ensured the colonel showed no signs of wariness, Rurik knelt down beside him. Sergei brought an index finger to his lips, gesturing for Rurik to be quiet. There near the exit were four sets of distinct shoe prints in the sand.

"They look like... no, that's not possible," Rurik whispered, furrowing his brow.

"Like kid-sized shoes? A sneaker of some kind?" Sergei whispered back. He stood and in the same motion, brushed his boot through the sand, effectively removing any trace of them ever having been there while Rurik watched on.

When they reached the truck, Rurik murmured the question that had been on his mind for most of the walk to no one in particular. "Why would bulls want to go to a shipping hub?"

Colonel Omar narrowed his eyes. "They are no longer bulls. They have been resurrected by the hearts of men." He paused to open his door. "They are now Minotaur's, creatures with the head of a bull and the body of a man."

With that, he got into the driver's seat. Sergei and Rurik shared a glance over the top of the truck before climbing in themselves.

The engine gave a growl and started up, drowning out everything in the backseat. Rurik leaned toward his comrade and whispered, "There are a number of things you aren't telling me."

"As one of my best intelligence officers," Sergei breathed back. He looked down at his attaché case resting on his lap and tapped his hand on the case, adding, "Are you ready for your first assignment?"

Rurik nodded.

"Let us deliver what we found here to the Kremlin, and then get you fully briefed."

CHAPTER 2
PETROZAVODSK PHENOMENON
Moscow, Soviet Union (U.S.S.R.)

The KGB headquarters stood as a silent sentinel in the heart of Moscow, its walls steeped in secrecy and shadows, faintly redolent of cigarette smoke. As Rurik strode down the dimly lit hallways, he couldn't shake the feeling of unease that gnawed at him. The air was heavy with the weight of countless secrets, every step he took seemed to echo with the whispers of the past. Yet, the familiar splashes of red amidst the muted tones of the U.S.S.R. provided a grounding sense of home.

To others, the halls might have been intimidating, even haunting, but Rurik walked with a firm foot down corridors adorned with tapestries and maps he knew intimately. He quickened his pace, straightening his back, the embodiment of disciplined resolve. He oversaw a team of formidable special intelligence operators, each handpicked and personally trained by him over the past two years. His hands-on leadership style ensured that his team was as prepared as he was for the mission that had finally arrived. The assignment he had trained for, the one he anticipated with a mix of anticipation and dread, was now his reality.

As he neared his destination, Rurik's feet didn't falter in the slightest, but no amount of confidence could stop the whispering voices in the back of his mind from telling him he was going to fail.

"You're ready for this," he reminded himself. He found himself raising his inner voice more than once a day since his return from Egypt. This was an opportunity to serve as requested, regardless of the enormity of the assignment. He'd be damned if he let himself ruin it.

He walked a little faster, trying to convince himself it was conviction driving him forward rather than fear. Ahead was a large wooden door with a bronze plaque to the right of it. The plaque read:

SERGEI BELONOGOV
FIRST CHIEF DIRECTORATE

Rurik twisted the handle and entered. It took a moment for his eyes to adjust to the dim yellow lights after the muted tones of the corridors. He took his jacket off, hanging it on the hook beside the door.

"Please have a seat," a woman with a clear voice

instructed from behind a small desk in the back of the room. She spoke without expression, her gaze fixed on the papers before her. "I will inform Director Belonogov of your arrival."

To the right of the desk was another wooden door, shut at that moment. To the left, a small waiting room had been put together haphazardly with a small table littered with outdated, colorless magazines, and a mismatching armchair to either side of it. As Rurik took a seat in one of them, the woman behind the desk made a phone call and began speaking quietly into the receiver. A moment later, she asked him to stand again.

"You may enter the office now, sir."

As Rurik entered Sergei greeted him enthusiastically, gesturing to the seat across from a desk that took up most of the office. "Rurik! I take it you are well rested from our little adventure in Egypt?"

"Yes, sir, I am," Rurik nodded as he sat down.

"Good, good." Sergei walked to a small sideboard standing beside his desk and opened a small wooden box, much like a humidor. Inside, he flicked a toggle switch and began turning a dial until a static sound, like a radio stuck between two channels, emanated from the box and filled the room with white noise.

This was a practice Rurik had seen many times before, and he wasn't surprised to see it being used. The device was one of Sergei's special tools, one he had used a number of times during their private meetings. The frequencies emitted would interfere with anyone outside trying to listen in. To anyone who knew Sergei intimately enough to see him use it, the action of opening the box would signify that what he was about to share was not for prying ears. To Rurik, it was an indication that there was a chance they were being eavesdropped on by foreign adversaries at that very moment. Worse still, their own government, in its paranoia, could be listening as well—the same government that would often ignore inconvenient truths revealed by its own operatives.

By the time Sergei returned to the large leather chair behind his desk, the white noise had faded into the background for both men in the room. From his leather attaché case, he opened the flap and pulled out a nondescript file folder. Rurik read the title as Sergei silently slid the file across to his waiting hand; "Особой важности, Top Secret."

Inside, several well-thumbed papers slipped out, creased where hands had flipped through them countless times before him. The opening page read, *The Petrozavodsk Phenomenon: September 20, 1977.* Rurik glanced up to meet Sergei's gaze, scrutinizing him curiously before he returned to the pages. He began to flip through and read the contents within, adding further creases and folds to the file. While he did, Sergei was kind enough to offer him a verbal summary in a low voice, one that would most certainly have been drowned out by anyone not sitting directly across from him.

"A number of years ago, I crossed paths with a rather impressive woman named Margrit. She was the daughter of a former Nazi scientist named Edmund Himmel, and she had graduated from the Academy of Sciences in

Moscow. Incidentally, she had also been recruited by the KGB as a candidate for our East Berlin intelligence operation." Rurik's eyebrow arched, but he kept his eyes down. "That isn't all... After some time serving within the KGB, Margrit grew to trust me. She began to tell me that she had been hiding a decades-old secret, a secret of great power. She told me that for those who could harness this power, they could rule the world."

If that were true, it would be an astonishing story. Rurik couldn't help but search Sergei's face for any sign, but Sergei's features gave nothing away, and Rurik couldn't yet think of the right questions to ask to get the answers he was looking for. Between the pages of the top-secret file, several photographs showed the familiar expanse of the Egyptian desert. Rurik knew without reading the reports that these weren't the same parts of the desert he had visited with Sergei. He'd studied the lands extensively before their trip out there, and his sharp memory was determined to keep him from forgetting a single detail of it.

"I of course, thought she was mad. Delusional," Sergei continued with a shrug. "I thought she was a woman simply looking to find a way to advance her career through wild stories of supernatural things and superstition. It certainly would have garnered attention. It did in fact, in some ways. But I was wrong. Her facts checked out, and before long her story began to ring true." Rurik froze, and Sergei went on. "Indeed, once I was convinced of this truth, I authorized Margrit to assemble a team and embark on a mission to Alexandra Land in the Arctic Sea, to find evidence to support the facts. It was there that we discovered an abandoned Nazi base and in its ruins a silver sarcophagus, just as she claimed we would."

"A silver sarcophagus?" Rurik flipped backward through the file to where he was certain he'd passed images of sarcophagi different from those they'd encountered at the Serapeum of Saqqara. He found them quickly. "Well, that explains the Egyptian connection."

"Yes!" Sergei threw his hands out, his urgent exclamation startling Rurik. A photo of a silver sarcophagus fell between them, and the sight of it made Sergei clench his jaw. "Read through the file in its entirety, Rurik. You need to know everything. Egypt has a great many secrets to contend with!"

Rurik pulled out every photo of the silver sarcophagus he could find, laying them on the desk as he read bits and pieces along the way, skimming the file for the highlights of the story. "The sarcophagus was cold to the touch, made of zinc..."

The documentation of their findings was extensive, but one passage jumped out at Rurik: *'A phrase translated from the hieroglyphs that mark the exterior of the artifact seems to be the key to opening it. Atop the sarcophagus, the biggest symbol of all, in the center of the lid, is that of an eye. This is undoubtedly the Eye of Horus.'*

Rurik once again met Sergei's eyes, asking the obvious question: "Did you open it?"

Sergei needn't have answered. The look on his face said it all.

"Yes, and I'm afraid we unleashed a great and terrible

destructive power upon our world." He leaned back into his chair with a palpable sense of regret, his shoulders slouching for perhaps the first time Rurik could recall.

When Rurik didn't answer, instead turning back to the file, Sergei began to narrate the contents of it aloud, his voice numb, as only a man who had read the words over and over could.

"Inside awoke a figure made up of a dark void with red eyes, a half-man, half-beast that resembled no known creature. A soulless body of blackness that radiated immense power. It was cold. Being not fully resurrected, but a force, without a doubt, made of pure evil. We managed to contain it within our underground facility in Petrozavodsk, but on September 20, 1977, it escaped. All were lost, and a great white light shone through the skies. Sightings of this light were reported over a vast territory, from Copenhagen and Helsinki in the west to Vladivostok in the east. If you recall the news of the event, it was named after the city of Petrozavodsk, where a glowing object was widely reported showering the city with numerous rays."

"I remember. I grew up in that region!" There was a quiver in Rurik's voice.

Opening the desk drawer once more, Sergei pulled out a pre-typed letter and hastily slid it over the photos of the sarcophagus. He quickly applied a pressed seal over his signature before handing it to Rurik. "This is your assignment. Codename: Dollmaker. You and your team are going to America!"

"America?"

"Margrit was tracking a powerful artifact—the Eye of

Horus itself. She believed the power of the Eye of Horus could be used to control or even stop this dark force. She was able to trace its location to a small town in Massachusetts, but she failed to acquire it." He paused for a moment. "It is believed that the artifact may have been found by a group of kids."

"Kids?" Rurik raised his eyebrow again.

"Yes. And I fear that not only do they have the four parts of the Eye of Horus, but they are learning about its powers."

"Ah," Rurik mused. "The four pair of shoe prints we found in the sand?"

"Yes, very good. You did not miss any clues during our time in Egypt."

"No, I did not." Rurik leaned forward, bringing his voice down to a whisper practically imperceptible over the static that filled the room. "Which is why I must now ask you, was the item you were really searching for in Egypt retrieved?"

"Damn you, what are you insinuating?" Sergei stood, his tone rising in frustration. He abruptly walked over to the box and toggled the dial slightly, causing the static sound in the room to intensify. There, he stood for what seemed to be a minute, perhaps more, eyes downcast. Then, he walked over to the other side of his desk where Rurik sat stoically and leaned over to whisper something in his ear. Rurik's eyes widened at Sergei's words, his jaw dropping as he was jolted by the knowledge passed to him so discreetly, and his cheeks reddening. He knew when he had entered the room that he hadn't been told everything about this assignment, but the more he learned about it, the more it became clear that the facts were far more dire than he first believed.

"I understand, sir," he finally said. "This further complicates things. Whatever we have unleashed in Petrozavodsk and whatever was unleashed at the Serapeum of Saqqara are threats to us all. We must not allow this to escalate any further than it already has. We must not allow this thing to resurrect itself."

"As you already know, the minds of reason are shifting in the Kremlin," Sergei went on. "Paranoia and fear grow every day. There are some who believe what we have unleashed has already crossed our borders and is taking refuge in Afghanistan. There is talk of invasion and war." He gave another heavy shrug.

Rurik stood. He'd tucked the letter and photos into the file and was readying to leave. "What do you believe, sir?"

"I believe what we have unleashed is driving us to war and chaos, turning us against one another like whispers from snakes." Sergei met Rurik's eyes. "Now you know everything. This is of the utmost importance to Mother Russia, to the world! One could say we let the genie out of the bottle, and now we must find a way to put it back in."

CHAPTER 3
WINTER BREAK
Dennis Port, Massachusetts

The streets of Dennis Port were cloaked in shades of gray, a silent canvas for the gentle flurry of snow that danced down from the sky. A light dusting was underway, blanketing everything in its wake – nothing too substantial. A common occurrence for the small town whose falling foliage of autumn and amber turning of leaves began just a few months before. It was mid-December, and winter had draped its icy fingers over the town, casting a hush over the familiar streets now devoid of their usual hustle and bustle. It brought misty windows, hot drinks, and twinkling lights to signify the festive season, but perhaps most importantly, it came with a welcome break from the routine of school for four of Dennis Port's residents, a group of friends known as the Katzenstein Kids, abuzz with holiday excitement.

Behind Dez's home on Center Street, the skeletal remains of their beloved treehouse swayed in the wintry breeze, its empty branches a haunting reminder of warmer days. They creaked under the weight of the snow, as if lamenting the absence of laughter, music, and comic book stories that once filled the air. Snow fell through the wooden house's eternally open windows.

Not far down the road, at the corner of Sea and Center Streets, Mrs. Weatherbourne's house sat nestled off the narrow road, its windows frosted with cold. Things on this end of town were unusually still at this time of year, with the town no longer in season for its typical surge of tourists and beachgoers. Inside, the elderly woman slept soundly with her faithful cat Seymour curled up warmly at the foot of her bed, oblivious to the chill whispering through the walls.

Just a stone's throw away, on the corner of Sea and Mill Roads, the vintage-style two-story home of Will and the McMurphy family glowed. Electric Christmas candles illuminated the windows, their flickering bulbs casting dancing shadows across the windowpanes, a beacon of cheer amidst the holiday gloom. A bright green wreath adorned with silver bells hung on the front door, welcoming visitors.

As the snow continued to fall, Main Street lay shrouded in silence. Its storefronts flashed festive decorations that glittered and sparkled in the dim light, while holiday signs advertised *Santa's Specials* and *Holiday Hours*. Even the house behind the laundromat, where Amy Howard slept soundly, seemed to exude an air of quiet anticipation. The soft glow of her bedside lamp cast a warm light over a scattered stack of handwritten letters, each signed *Love, Mom.*

In the Goffman home over on Depot Road, Isaac stirred from his slumber, a shiver running down his spine as a cold draft ghosted over the back of his neck. The rush of air was both cold and warm, a breath that left his hair standing on end. Startled he jolted upright in bed, his heart hammering in his chest as he scanned his dark bedroom for any signs of danger.

Every shadow seemed to loom menacingly, every creak of the floorboards an ominous whisper in the night. The longer he sat there, the more certain he became that he wasn't alone, though he could see nothing in the darkness. Isaac clutched the Cracker Jack trinket hanging from his necklace, a comforting reminder that the toy gun replica was actually his Power Gem. Isaac forced himself to take a deep breath, his fingers trembling as he summoned the courage to confront whatever might be lurking beyond his bed. The gem pulsed with a quiet, reassuring energy. It didn't glow or alert him that anything might be wrong, but still, he couldn't shake the unease.

Cautiously, he stepped out of bed and made his way to the hallway, his senses on high alert. The air was thick with anticipation, and each moment stretched out like an eternity as he crept closer to the living room.

It's okay, he told himself.

By the time he reached the threshold, Isaac could hardly

hear the world over the sound of his own heart pounding in his ears. The smell of burning wax greeted him first. On the mantel above the fireplace, nine candles burned brightly in the menorah. To his surprise, the flames blazed with an unnatural, white light that almost hurt to look at directly, but Isaac couldn't bring himself to tear his gaze away. The flames danced with a fervor that sent a chill down his spine.

He scanned the dark corners of the room, but there didn't seem to be anything there. As he watched, the last of the wax melted away, the candles nearing their ends. Blobs and droplets of wax hung off the metal casing, and the flames dwindled until they barely offered light or warmth to the room.

Isaac walked toward the menorah, his brow furrowing as the candles seemed to brighten and dance until he stood directly in front of them. An unusual vigor rose from the center candle, the shamash. This was the first candle lit, the same one used to light the others. It danced brighter than the rest and captured the boy's full attention. Despite his earlier fear, his heart slowed, and a calm washed over him. The longer he watched the dancing orange flame grow and shift, the more he surrendered to the feeling. His body almost swayed, though his feet were still, and his thoughts began to drift until suddenly, the other flames grew too, until all nine were fiery red and impossibly tall.

He couldn't tear his eyes away, watching with wonder as the candle holders merged into a bright plume of fire that began to take on shapes and forms of its own. At first, they were indiscernible, nothing but strange orange scribbles that cast dangerous shadows across the walls and spat heat. Then, the flames grew outward to reveal the head of a bull with a strong brow and a furious expression. Its form was massive, eyes glowing a horrible angry red, rich in evil, and giant horns protruded from either side of its rearing head. A huge snout flared with each breath, and as it towered over him, a scream threatened to escape from Isaac's throat but never came. The sight of the bull sent him into a state of silent fear, and the gem on his neck began to glow a bright green.

Isaac knew the danger was only unfolding; this was just the beginning. From the heart of the flames, the head of the bull rose from the muscular body of a man who took up almost the entire room. It was a figure from his darkest nightmares—its eyes burning with malevolent red fire as it stood over him. Isaac had never felt so small, shrinking beneath the sinister menace of the monster. His blood ran cold as he stared into the creature's fiery gaze, his mind reeling with fear and disbelief.

When the beast spoke, its guttural roar reverberated through the room, making the furniture tremble. Isaac knew that he stood face to face with a danger beyond imagining—a danger that threatened not only his life but the very fabric of reality itself.

A minotaur.

Suddenly, a loud growl echoed from its mouth, the voice crisp like burnt wood and something else, something ancient. With it, flames burst from its flaring nostrils like a dragon. Isaac almost ducked for fear he'd be burnt, but the flames danced over his head and licked at the ceiling.

The beast cried out, blowing heat into Isaac's face, *"Duamutef, Protector of the East, surrender your soul to Set!"*

The force of the Minotaur's voice knocked Isaac back onto the floor, and an ear-shattering scream rang out through the room, seeming as though it would never end. Only when Isaac's eyes opened again and he found himself in his own bed, covered in sweat, did he realize he was the one who had screamed, and that he'd been having a nightmare all along. He sighed with relief, feeling a heaviness leave his chest as he felt the blankets shift around him and looked into the darkness of his room. It wasn't as dark as in his dream, but somehow still eerie.

Isaac narrowed his eyes. *Was it really just a nightmare?*

Glancing around the room and down toward the end of his bed, where light shone in from the hall, he caught a fading glow out of the corner of his eye. Sure enough, warm and green, the Power Gem hanging from his neck glinted up at him before darkening altogether. He gulped.

This was a sure sign that a new danger could be upon him.

◆ ◆ ◆

In the McMurphy home over on the corner of Sea and Mill Roads, Will woke feeling bright and ready for the day. Considering it was winter break, he didn't *need* to be up at the crack of dawn. There was no school day to prepare for, and no sign of his little sister jolting him awake whenever he hit the snooze button on his alarm clock for another five—okay, ten—extra minutes. None of that stopped him. Nothing could keep the spring out of his step as he followed his nose toward the smell of scrambled eggs and freshly toasted bread, his feet only too happy to oblige the journey.

It appeared the only other member of the McMurphy family who was up so early, and who was responsible for the delicious aromas wafting through the air, was his dad. Gone were the days of hunching over oatmeal and burnt toast in a last-minute rush—he whistled while he scrambled a frying pan's contents, dancing with the spatula. The whistle was soft, and the dance stayed in the hips, but it all brought a smile to Will's face as he walked over to the fridge and pulled out a carton of orange juice. He sat at the table behind his father, already set for breakfast, and poured himself a glass, setting the carton down on the table.

"Morning, Dad," he said. "Juice?"

"Will," his dad turned to face him, beaming. He dished a helping of scrambled eggs onto the plate in front of Will, adding two slices of toast so hot the butter was already melting.

"Thanks, Dad," Will managed before digging in.

His father went back to the stove, cracking fresh eggs on the side of the pan to fry them sunny side up. "Did you sleep well?"

The recollection of the previous evening was fresh in Will's mind. He didn't think he'd ever slept better. Yet not long after he'd first turned his light off and closed his eyes, his father entered his bedroom and gently shook him awake again.

"Will? Will?"

Will gave a groggy groan, blinking sleep out of his eyes. The room was dark, save for the light streaming in from the hallway. His father leaned over him, his face red and a strange look in his eyes.

"Dad?" He sat up suddenly, forcing his dad to take a step back to prevent them from knocking their heads. Will's hand flew instinctively to the Cracker Jack trinket in his top pocket, shaped like a small and intricately formed shield. It was his Protection Gem. Out of the corner of his eye, he thought he saw it glowing and quickly pulled the covers higher, keeping his hand over it so his dad didn't see. His heart started to race a little faster. "Is everything okay?"

Will's father watched him with a strange look on his face, and then his mouth broke out into one of the biggest smiles Will had ever seen. "Everything's better than okay, son," he said. "In fact, I'm sorry for waking you, but I was just so excited that I couldn't wait until morning, and there's something I really want you to have."

The words came out in a rush, and Will couldn't help feeling a little excited as he watched his dad reach into his coat pocket. It had been a long time since he'd seen so much color on his dad's face. He'd assumed that something must be wrong, that the redness was anger or alcohol, but his father was still wearing his coat, and it was blisteringly cold outside. He must have just gotten home.

"What is it?"

His dad held out his hand. In the middle of his palm, glinting up at Will, was a token that he instantly recognized. The face of the coin had the number '3' centered in the middle of a triangle. Lettering across the top read: TO THINE OWN SELF BE TRUE. Three months prior, his father had returned home from Alcoholics Anonymous with a yellow coin that had the number '24', but he only knew that because he'd accidentally come across it in his mom's purse. That was after a day of attending AA, to get the help that he needed. This one was red.

"It's my three-month recovery chip, I got it from AA tonight, you can put it with the other one I gave you."

"Dad," Will breathed. *He looked from his dad to the chip and hopped out of bed, wrapping his arms around his father's waist in a tight embrace.*

After a moment's hesitation, Will's father wrapped his arms around his son, and Will's chest was filled with an indescribable warmth. He forgot all about the glowing gem at that moment. All he felt was pride.

"I want you to have it," his dad said when they finally stopped hugging. *There was some shyness in the way he tilted his head and handed the chip over to Will. "I couldn't have done it without you."*

Will proudly took the chip, mirroring his father and tucking it into his top pocket with a grin. It was safe and sound beside his gem.

That morning, Will had taken the chip out of his pajama pocket and made sure to wear a shirt that had a top pocket too. When it sat over his heart, it felt as if it had its own magical powers. "I slept great," he told his dad over a mouthful of eggs.

"I slept pretty well too," his mom's voice came from the hall.

Both she and his sister, Beth, were already dressed and ready for the day, by the looks of things. His mom went to hug his dad, kissing his cheek softly. Will tried to ignore the awkward hesitance between them, the slow way his mom leaned in as if she wasn't sure she should, or the clumsy way his dad's arm went for her shoulders and then her waist and then back to her shoulders again in a side hug. It was to be expected. Things were healing, but that would take time. Besides, his mom was smiling, and if he knew her as well as he thought he did, she had the same spring in her step as him.

"Will, you're up early for a no-school day," she sang as she poured herself some orange juice from the carton Will left out. "What are your plans for the day?"

"I'm planning to meet up with the gang," Will ducked his head sheepishly. "We have a new winter hangout! And I wanted to give them their Christmas gifts."

"A new winter hangout? I wanna come," his sister chirped.

Will couldn't stop his face from showing his true feelings, his eyes widening in horror.

"Not this time, sweetie," his mom came to the rescue. "You're coming with me and your dad today. We have some last-minute shopping to do." Then, turning back to Will while she buttered her toast, "It's cold outside. Remember to wear a coat, and dress warm. Just a shirt won't cut it today."

"Sure thing, Mom."

"Say hi to Dez, Isaac, and Amy for us," his dad added, finally sitting down to eat breakfast with the rest of the family.

CHAPTER 4
Déjà Vu

Two sets of bicycle tire tracks, the kind with special treads for riding in the snow, and one set of car tracks led up the driveway to Dez's house. Isaac had been dropped off, and Amy and Will's faces were pink from riding their bikes against a frigid breeze. They'd both received their winter bike treads as early Christmas presents.

"Hey guys!" Will and Isaac said together.

"Someone owes someone a pack of gum," Amy grinned as she parked her bike next to Will's in front of the garage.

"There you all are," Dez's voice called from the side door, along with the happy barks of Cocoa. "I've been waiting for you!"

"Cocoa," Grandma Ruth's voice sounded from within

the house. "Our friends are here, sí? Maybe we should make them some hot chocolate to warm them up."

"What are you waiting for, slowpokes? It's freezing out here!"

They noticed what their friend was wearing.

Amy was the first to say anything. "Dez! Why are you in shorts and a T-shirt in this weather?"

"Grandmas got the fire going upstairs, and" his grin grew wider, "the furnace is warming up the basement."

"And you're letting all the heat out of the house!" Grandma Ruth appeared, peering over Dez's shoulder at the kids and beckoning them inside.

The moment they stepped through the door, hugging Grandma Ruth and chirping "Merry Christmas," a wave of heat washed over Amy and Will. Their winter clothes suddenly felt suffocating, and the backs of their necks prickled with warmth. Despite the snowy landscape outside, they quickly shed their coats and beanies. Isaac didn't seem too fazed by the heat and was crouched down on the kitchen tiles, his hand buried in the furry belly of Cocoa, who was only too happy to be the center of attention.

"Much better in here, huh?" Grandma was beaming. Behind her, a pot of hot chocolate was already brewing, filling the room with the scent of chocolate and sugar. "It will be ready soon," she said, catching Will staring. "Go on, go."

"¡Gracias, abuela!" Dez kissed his grandmother on the cheek and then hurriedly led the kids out of the kitchen.

The entrance to Dez's basement was through the coat

closet under the stairs, a nondescript wooden door in the living room filled with coats, boots, and umbrellas. At the back, behind the hanging coats, was a small wooden door with a latch. Otherwise, it looked like an ordinary wooden backing from any old coat closet. From their first visit, the kids thought it was cool that Dez had what they considered a hidden door in his house. Now, each of them stepped through space one after the other, disappearing through the door and closing it behind them.

"Welcome to The Hideout!" Dez cried, throwing his arms in the air with a huge smile as the others walked through behind him.

"Woah," Isaac murmured.

The words "Katzenstein Kids" were written in bold stenciled lettering with a Sharpie on a makeshift wood plaque and hung on the wall behind the sofa, the first thing anyone saw upon entering. It wasn't there the last time Will, Isaac, and Amy visited, and they looked up at it in wonder.

"You've made some updates," Amy remarked, glancing around the room with approval.

The sofa was already in the basement, but before the kids had cleaned things up, the room had been used mostly for storage. Everything had been covered in a layer of dust that came away quickly with soap and water, and a few random items went straight to the garbage can out front. The rest was sold in a yard sale. They'd moved the floor cushions and bean bags from the treehouse inside, along with the stereo, games, puzzles, and comic books.

In the meantime, Dez and his mom had infused a cozy

charm into the basement. There were new cushions on the sofa, throws draped over the furniture, and the addition of more board games added to the homey ambiance. Twinkling lights hung from the bookshelf, casting a warm glow onto what was once a dark space. Even the furnace had been decorated with a string of lights, transforming it from an eyesore to a charming feature.

"Yeah, after we got everything together, I found this piece of good, clean driftwood near the docks, so I brought it home and figured, you know... It looks good, right?" He grinned up at the sign with their self-proclaimed title. "Mom helped me put up the nail so we could hook it on there, so I had permission. Then she and I went shopping for some cushions and stuff."

"It looks amazing," Isaac said.

Will nodded his agreement, immediately flopping down comfortably into one of the beanbags and grabbing a comic book from the little shelf beside it. "It's awesome down here."

"So your mom helped?" Amy inquired, taking a seat on the sofa. "How is she doing?"

Isaac and Will both looked over at Dez, Will over the top of the pages of his book, instantly interested in learning more about Dez's mom.

"Yeah," Dez nodded. "Yeah, she's doing great. She's back at work at her nursing job. That's where she is now, actually. She's doing so well it's like nothing was ever wrong."

Dez reached into his pocket and revealed his Cracker Jack trinket, shaped like a small medical bag. "My Health

Gem truly saved her," he added.

"That's really great news, Dez," Amy said, genuinely happy to hear of Silvia's recovery. "I, uh, I have news too, I've been writing and calling my mom."

This piqued Will's interest, as he set the comic down on the table. "You have?"

"Yep, every week. We've been trying to make some time to hang out, so actually I might see her in person soon."

"Okay, wait," Isaac sat down on one of the floor cushions in front of the sofa. "So you and Jo are gonna hang out for real? When did this happen?"

"Yeah, tell us everything," Dez sat on another floor cushion.

Amy hesitated before sharing, fidgeting with the hem of her shirt. "The reason my mom left was because of a fight with my dad. It wasn't because of me—well, not really."

"I could have told you that," Will said softly.

"What was that?" Isaac asked him.

Will gave a dramatic cough, clapping the palm of his hand down on his chest. "Sorry, got a bit of a scratchy throat."

"Anyway," Amy interjected. "The reason my mom ran off is because she was ashamed. My dad called her an embarrassment for falling in love with her girlfriend, Cindy. And well, the rest is history."

"What? That's crazy," Dez shook his head in disbelief. "Love shouldn't be something to be ashamed of."

"Exactly," Isaac agreed. "Why would anyone want to keep their family apart? Especially over something like love. We can't choose who we love."

"No," Amy glanced over at Will, her expression softening. "We can't."

"At least Jo's in your life now," Will offered supportively. "It's great that you guys are reconnecting. I'm happy for you, Amy."

"We all are," Isaac added, smiling.

"Ah, thanks guys," Amy ran a hand through her hair shyly. Then, her face changed as she sucked the inside of her cheek and leaned forward, lowering her voice conspiratorially. "I have something to tell you guys, actually. I've... I've been having this vision."

"A vision?" Dez asked.

Isaac and Will shifted uncomfortably, Will setting his comic book down as Amy nodded.

"Of this big brown wooden door. It has a lavender wreath hanging on it. It—"

Before she could finish, Cocoa bounded down the stairs, barking excitedly. The dog ran around the room in a frenzy of joy, tail wagging happily as she hopped on and off the sofa, jumped into Will's lap, and then ran back to Grandma Ruth, who stood at the door with a tray laden with mugs of hot chocolate and homemade gingerbread cookies. Their noses were smudged, and one was missing an eye, but they all looked delicious nonetheless.

The kids sprang up to help Grandma Ruth, thanking her as they took their cups and set them on the table in the middle of the room. They also took the plate of cookies, leaving her with an empty tray.

"De nada, de nada," Grandma Ruth waved her hand as

she departed. "Cocoa, come, baby, let's leave these kids to their secrets now. Come on."

"I'll get her," Dez grabbed the panting pup and slowly walked back up the stairs with his grandmother. A few moments later, he returned to find the others deep in their hot chocolate, each with a gingerbread cookie in hand and foam on their upper lips.

"So, about that vision," Dez started, taking a seat and grabbing a cookie.

"Oh, don't worry about that," Amy withdrew into her seat, reaching for her bag. "We can talk about it later. I actually thought we'd maybe exchange gifts?"

Dez and Will brightened, Will rummaging in his bag and Dez opening a small cabinet. Isaac watched, less enthused.

Amy noticed. "Everything okay?"

"Wait for it..." As if on cue, Dez and Will handed their gifts to him simultaneously. They were the same size, wrapped in plain paper. He held them up to his ear, shaking them. "Lemme guess... Baseball cards?"

The other two boys exchanged a wide-eyed glance of mock shock.

"What's going on?" Amy asked, perplexed.

"It's the same gift every year," Isaac explained. "So I'm never surprised."

"Why?"

"Because" Dez answered. "Isaac is Jewish, so he doesn't celebrate Christmas, but he gets like eight gifts for Hanukkah. I don't even get eight gifts."

"Yeah," Will added. "So we decided that a pack of

baseball cards is perfect. They include fifteen cards, so that's two cards for each day of Hanukkah."

Amy raised her hands, counting on her fingers. When she reached fifteen, she turned to the boys. "But... That's only one—"

"Plus the gum!" Dez and Will cried out in unison.

Isaac rolled his eyes, embarrassed. "Good grief," he mumbled, then looked up at Amy with a smile. "Fifteen cards, plus the gum."

"Riiight," Amy said slowly. "Fifteen cards, plus the gum. That makes two gifts per day." Then, pulling a plainly wrapped package from her bag, she handed it to Isaac. "Well, I got you something too. I hope you like it."

Isaac's surprise was evident as he tore the packaging off, revealing a three-pack of comic books. "The Amazing Adventures of X-Men," he read, marveling. "This is so cool! Thank you, Amy!"

The other boys looked slightly put out, but Amy handed them their own wrapped packages, which they accepted with some embarrassment.

"Thanks, Amy," they said in unison.

"Actually, all three of us got you this," Isaac set his comics down and reached into his backpack. He presented a small decoupage box with pink polka dots and handed it to Amy.

The boys opened their gifts, pleased to find that Amy had gotten each of them separate comic sets so they could all read one another's copies. She was thoughtful enough to ensure all of them had at least one comic with their favorite superhero. On the other hand, she felt her eyes watering as she opened the box to reveal a small, quality set of writing materials, including ink. It was a lot like one she'd seen in Mrs. Weatherbourne's house. She quickly wiped her eyes away, but couldn't so easily get rid of the smile that made her cheeks hurt.

"Thanks, you guys," she said. "This is really wonderful. I love it."

"We figured you could write to your mom," Will ran a hand over the back of his head. "Of course, we didn't know things were so much better, but you can still use it, right?"

"Definitely," she went over to hug Will.

When Amy pulled away, they found the other two boys staring at them with strange expressions.

"Uhhh," Will mumbled awkwardly. "So, about that vision... Uh... Well, do you guys remember when we put all our gems together last summer?"

While Dez and Isaac were distracted, Amy took her seat again, the sight of the box making her smile even as she recalled the moment Will was speaking about. Her mind flashed back to the events of last summer.

"Then in the fall when we tried it again. It was like déjà vu." Amy continued.

"Something is coming," she could hardly remember the words coming out of her mouth. The boys had told her everything afterward. In fact, she'd asked them to detail everything a few times over. "We have been told the evil Deity Set is trying to be reborn."

"Why don't we all put them together again?" Will asked.

"The same way we did before."

Images of the place that they'd gone to last summer and again in the fall flashed through Amy's mind. She remembered how their gems had glowed and glowed, to a point where they were difficult to look at, and then suddenly they weren't on Cape Cod anymore.

Sand blew all around the kids, around their feet, against their arms, and into their faces. Amy closed her eyes against the onslaught, then opened them just as quickly, afraid to look away too long. As far as they could see, the kids stood in an endless expanse of sand. The vast desert surrounded them, and she'd never felt so tiny.

"Maybe we'll have another vision of some kind... Of the past, the present, or the future," Will continued. "It's not just Amy's Prophecy Gem, her ring, that brought upon visions. When all four of us combine our gems, we are transported...taken somewhere."

"Have you been reading Dickens?" Dez asked jokingly. "I know it's Christmas, Will, but..."

"C'mon, man," Will interrupted him. "Who knows? We might be able to see what's coming. You remember the last time."

"How could we forget?" Dez said, shooting a glance over at Amy. "It's a bit hard to forget randomly teleporting to an empty desert."

Amy thumbed over her ring absent-mindedly. "He's right though. What if we could see what's coming? I don't know about you guys, but I haven't stopped thinking about it."

An uneasy silence came over them, and she could tell they were scared as they all nodded in agreement.

"Like I said," Dez murmured. "How could we forget?"

"I think I know what's coming," the words spilled from Isaac's mouth so quickly that the kids had to take a moment to process them. The room grew quiet as the others gave him a chance to gather his thoughts. He repeated himself, slower, "I think I know what's coming. I... I thought it was all a dream, a nightmare really, but it seemed too real. At my house, I saw our menorah burst into a giant beast. It was a minotaur."

"Your menorah turned into a beast?" Dez repeated incredulously. "So both of you have had visions..."

Will's hand made its way to his gemstone, safely tucked inside his pocket beside his dad's sobriety chip. "When?"

"Last night," Isaac told him. He hesitated but continued anyway. "It spoke to me. Shouted at me. It said, *Duamutef, Protector of the East, surrender your soul to Set.*'"

Amy's cheeks paled, and she put her mug to her mouth, drinking until she was filled with warmth and sweetness and had no more hot chocolate left.

"Okayyy," Dez whistled. "Well, maybe that's why we went to the desert all along. We just didn't know it, or we didn't stay long enough, or something."

"Yeah, maybe," Will said. "We didn't know that we'd leave the treehouse or end up out there, so we let go so fast that we could have missed a message. I mean, there must be a reason that we were taken to Egypt, or wherever it was."

"We don't know that it was Egypt," Dez pointed out.

"We could try again. See if we can find out more this time."

Amy and Isaac, who had been looking on, both started

speaking at once, effectively drowning one another's sentences out.

"So I guess you guys agree," Will said sarcastically.

"You go first," Isaac turned to Amy, his fingers

clutching the trinket on his necklace. It had begun to glow faintly.

"I just don't know if it's such a good idea. We don't know if it's a real place we're going to or if we're in danger out there. We don't even know how it works to get there or back." She set her mug down on the table as she finished, looking over at Isaac helplessly.

"I don't know either," Isaac shrugged. "What if this time we come face to face with a minotaur? I don't really want to see the real thing. The dream version was pretty scary on its own."

"How about we make a rule?" Dez stood up, reaching into his pants pocket and tugging something out. When he stretched his hand out to them, they could see his gemstone glowing in the middle of his palm. They didn't need to look at their own to know theirs were too. "One of us lets go even the tiniest bit, the rest do too. If you don't think your hand is doing what it's supposed to, say 'Katzenstein.' We'll come back.

"I don't want to say this is a sign of things to come without knowing for sure," Will added in a whisper when neither Amy nor Isaac said anything.

Isaac looked at Dez, still standing with his hand held out, and gave a sigh before he pulled the necklace around his neck over his head and off. He held it out to Dez's. "I guess I kinda wanna know too."

Will reached into his top pocket next, joining his friends in a semi-circle. Amy looked anxiously over at her friends from the beanbag, unable to ignore the glowing of her own gem any longer. Reluctantly, she went over to join them.

"Okay, but only because we have a plan," she said. "Say 'Katzenstein,' and we all let go."

The boys nodded, putting their hands out over hers, Dez first, then Isaac followed by Will, in the same order they'd removed their gems. But nothing happened. She furrowed her brow.

"Maybe Amy's needs to be at the top of the stack," Isaac offered. "That's how we did it last time. And Amy's mood ring was glowing then even though ours weren't, so maybe that's the key to activating the gems."

Amy removed her hand silently and watched as Dez held his gem out on his outstretched palm once more. Isaac placed his hand and gem over Dez's. After one last curious glance Amy's way, Will did the same. With a deep breath, Amy placed her hand on top. The light from all four gems brightened, then faded the moment Amy's hand touched Will's. A strong tug on each of the kids' waists pulled them away from The Hideout, bellies somersaulting. Everything went dark, then everything became blurry, as if they were peering through the porthole of a ship. None of them had a chance to see anything in the murkiness before they were ripped away again, the tug on their waists too strong to ignore. The world spun, and then all four kids found themselves standing in a dark tunnel, its ceilings high and its walls narrow.

"Where are we?" Amy whispered, holding onto Will's hand so tightly she was almost certain there'd be marks left behind on his skin. It made her loosen her grip, but only slightly.

The boys didn't answer, but something appeared to

move a few feet away from them in the shadows of the tunnel. A shuffling could be heard as the shadow moved around, stirring and shifting, and then, horrifyingly, approaching. The kids could scarcely breathe as they stared into the darkness, trying to catch a glimpse of the thing that kept them company, simultaneously hoping they didn't see anything.

"Who goes there?" The figure hissed, warning the kids of impending danger.

The kids recoiled, startled to find they weren't alone. Their hearts pounded in their chests, fear and confusion clouding their minds as they tried to comprehend the situation. The figure was close now, but they couldn't make out what it was, only that it was very tall and hunched over when it moved toward them.

They all jumped back with a shout as a man's face appeared from the shadows, eyes hidden in the dark, smelly, and dirty.

"Who goes there?" The face's mouth moved, revealing crooked and yellowing teeth. "I see you… You kids should not be down here," a man coughed, a loud rattling noise that reverberated through the tunnel and sent shivers through the kids. The man spoke again, his sickly voice hissing through the tunnel like a snake. "The beasts will find you."

In fear, the kids ripped their hands free from the stack at once and were momentarily blinded by the sudden light of the basement as they found themselves face to face with one another again, their gems bright and hot.

"What was that?" Amy cried out. "Who was that man?"

"I don't know," Will said, shaking his head. "But that was terrifying."

"Did any of you see the walls?" Isaac asked, putting his necklace back on. The others followed suit, feeling more secure with the gems secured once again. "I thought I saw something on the walls."

"I wasn't looking at the walls, man," Dez rubbed his behind. "I was a bit distracted by the creepy threatening dude."

"I saw something," Will said impatiently. "It looked like a map on the walls of the tunnel."

The room fell silent for what seemed like an age. As their heart rates slowed, an eeriness settled over the basement. It didn't seem their Hideout would or could keep them hidden from whatever was out there. The boys' hot chocolate had gone cold, leaving rings on the inside of their mugs, and outside, the light suggested it was later than it had been when they first put their gems together.

"I feel like I've been there before," Will was the one to break the silence, his voice barely above a whisper. "I... I don't know how to explain it, but it's like... It's like I knew the map was there, so I knew to look for it."

"Yeah," Dez breathed. "When... when that guy appeared, it felt like I knew he was there, like I knew he would come out of the shadows."

"Like you knew he was going to warn you," Amy whispered.

"It was like déjà vu," Isaac nodded. "Logically, none of us have experienced any of this before, right? But I feel like we've all been there before, like the trip to the empty desert."

"This isn't Gorska Maika," Will said. The name hung in the air between them. "Not to bring up ghosts from the past or anything, but this feels pretty different."

"I agree," Isaac nodded. "This isn't like anything we've encountered before. We need to be cautious, and we also need to be ready for anything."

The others nodded their agreement at the unsettling statement, the weight of the responsibility Horus bestowed upon them weighing heavily. Being caretakers of the four parts of the Eye of Horus was a daunting task. They may have stumbled into something far beyond their understanding, but they knew they weren't alone. No matter what, they would face this together. Will stretched his hand out, beckoning the others to clasp it once more.

"No stacking," Amy joked halfheartedly. "We already know what happens when we do that."

"One for all and all for one!" Dez cried out. The others weren't amused, glaring at him. "What?"

"We need our own call to action," Amy snapped. "We're not the Musketeers, we're the Katzenstein Kids! Horus said our destinies were set long ago, and the gems chose us. We are the Protectors of the North, South, East, and West."

"Then let's use that," Isaac said. "Protectors of the North, South, East, and West... Unite!"

"I love that, but how about..." Dez looked between them. "Activate!"

"Assemble!" Will shouted excitedly.

Frustrated, Amy pulled away from the circle. "No, no,

no! You guys sound like a bunch of comic book characters!"

"Well, we are comic book junkies," Dez murmured under his breath.

"Why don't you choose, and we'll all go along with it?" Will offered diplomatically.

Amy narrowed her eyes, then rejoined the circle. They once again bumped their fists together in unity as she took a deep breath and then called out, "Katzenstein Kids, Protectors of the North, South, East, and West... Coalesce!"

Dez and Isaac reacted dramatically, both complaining at once, practically out of their minds at the new suggestion.

"Coalesce? Are you serious?"

"Coalesce, really? Coalesce?" Dez groaned. "What does that even mean?"

Amy stood stoically as Will leaned over and whispered to her. "... maybe we should just go with 'unite.'"

With a roll of her eyes, Amy nodded. "Fine!" With another deep breath, she called out with a little less enthusiasm than before, "Katzenstein Kids, Protectors of the North, South, East, and West... Unite!"

The boys all laughed in agreement, grinning as they repeated after her. "Unite!"

CHAPTER 5
MRS. WEATHERBOURNE

In the late afternoon, the kids embarked on a half-walk, half-bike ride to Mrs. Weatherbourne's before darkness could descend. They'd also brought along a Christmas gift for her—a set of photo frames and candles, neatly wrapped by the store clerk for an extra dollar. They got Seymour some special cat treats, too. Both gifts were snugly placed in Amy's bicycle basket, which Isaac pushed through the snow for most of the way.

They had lost a good chunk of their day hanging out at the new Hideout, not to mention their teleportation, a phenomenon they were still trying to wrap their heads around.

"Man, it's freezing out here," Dez mumbled, making

the others laugh. He had one more layer on than they did. "You guys just don't feel it because you've probably already got frostbite of the brain or something. You're desensitized."

This prompted another round of laughter.

"Sure," Will said. "Or your house is too hot, and your body just can't handle the cold anymore...Hypothermia might be setting in."

All three of the others stopped to stare at him, baffled. "What are you even talking about?" Dez asked.

"You know, the thing they do to preserve your body for space travel...like a human popsicle..." He glanced from Dez to Amy and Isaac, finding nothing but confusion etched on their faces. He realized none of them knew what he was talking about. "Am I the only one that watches Sci-Fi Saturdays on Channel 8?"

Isaac and Amy exchanged grins. "Nerd."

"Yeah, yeah," Will waved them off.

Dez pointed, chuckling. Will simply glared at him.

Ordinarily, two of them could ride on one bicycle, but the snow and ice made that impossible, special treads or not. Unable to ride two on a bicycle, they attempted it but failed, stumbling, and laughing as they went, falling and getting back up again. Eventually, they settled on taking turns between riding and walking, zig-zagging along the sidewalk until they reached the familiar corners of Sea and Center. When the sight of Mrs. Weatherbourne's house came into view, all four kids sprinted the rest of the way, Isaac pushing Amy's bike while Will pushed his own. By the time they reached the front door, they were panting and warmer from the exertion.

Then they remembered the bicycles and veered off to park them around the side of the house before returning to the front door, dusting snow off themselves.

Amy knocked, and a moment later, they heard mewing from inside, followed by the sound of the key in the lock. Mrs. Weatherbourne, wearing an apron, greeted them with a smile, but it was Seymour who stole the show with his incessant meowing and desperate pleas for attention. Ignoring their greetings, Seymour dashed between Isaac's legs, rubbing against him before darting over to Dez, eagerly awaiting a pat with his tail high in the air. There, he flopped onto his side, purring like a miniature engine with his eyes fixed on Amy, as if silently urging her to join Dez in giving him love.

"Somebody is thrilled to see us," Will remarked, chuckling.

"That makes the two of us," Mrs. Weatherbourne said, gesturing for them to come inside. "How about we get out of the cold, hmm?"

Dez scooped Seymour up into his arms, continuing to pet his belly as they followed her into the house, where Seymour hopped out of Dez's arms. He raced over to his food bowl and settled in for a comfortable meal while Mrs. Weatherbourne busied herself in the kitchen. A small Christmas tree adorned with red and gold ornaments glinted in the living room, and a tinsel ribbon hung over the mantel. A small fire blazed behind the fireplace screen.

"It's so cozy in here," Amy observed, taking her jacket off.

"How about some hot chocolate? You all look like you could use some warming up."

Before any of the others could say they'd already had some, Dez exclaimed, "Yes, please!"

"Good, because I'm already making some," Mrs. Weatherbourne chuckled. "Why don't you all grab your gifts out from under the tree? You can open them while I finish up here."

The kids retrieved their gifts, swapping out the ones they had brought for Mrs. Weatherbourne and Seymour. As they settled onto the sofa, Mrs. Weatherbourne reappeared with a tray of hot chocolate, setting it down on the coffee table.

Dez and Will unwrapped their gifts to find identical hemp cord necklaces with knotted ends, instantly recognizing them; Isaac had one.

"Since you loved the one I made Isaac so much, I went ahead and made one for each of you, too. They will hold your Cracker Jack trinkets—I mean your Health and Protection Gems," Mrs. Weatherbourne said with a smile. "And Amy, since your trinket is a ring, I've got a little something special for you. And Isaac, I didn't forget about you for a second."

Isaac opened his small box to find a hand-painted wooden dreidel inside. "A dreidel! Thanks, Mrs. Weatherbourne!" he exclaimed, spinning the toy on the table.

"You're very welcome. There's a little something in there for your mom as well," Mrs. Weatherbourne added.

"I'm sure she'll love it," Isaac replied, placing the

dreidel back in its box. "She says hi, and she hopes you have a lovely Christmas."

"Ah, it's always lovely having you kids around," Mrs. Weatherbourne said, touching her heart. "You send her my love."

"I will. She'll always have a warm spot in her heart for you."

"And I for both of you, Isaac. All of you, in fact!" She took a sip and changed the topic. "How's your winter break so far? School keeps you kids so busy; I feel like we need a proper catch-up."

"My mom's been really good. Like, really good," Dez smiled. "She's at work right now. So I have no complaints!" He gave a cheeky grin. "You haven't missed much."

"I'm so glad to hear that, Dez. You better give your mom a big hug from me."

Dez's cockiness simmered down to shyness as he blushed. "I will," he said, disappearing behind his own mug, which was big enough to hide most of his face.

"My mom's pretty good too," Will added. "My dad got his three-month chip."

"Oh Will, that is quite an accomplishment. You must be so proud."

"I really am," he nodded.

"This is beautiful," Amy suddenly gasped. She'd unwrapped her gift and held a moleskin journal with patterns that looked like stars imprinted into the cover. It had her initials, AKH inscribed on the front and a button to clip it closed.

"Did I get your initials right? Amy Kay Howard." Mrs. Weatherbourne winked at Amy.

"I thought you could use it to write some of your adventures."

"Yes, I love it!" She passed it over to Isaac to look at, who passed it on to Will, and then to Dez. They each took turns running their fingers over the patterns on the cover, opening and closing the clip, then passing it on with a grin. She could tell the boys loved it, too.

When it came back to her, Amy opened the first page to reveal the text typed out in bold:

If Lost, Please Return To ....

She smiled, already knowing she'd later be writing "The Katzenstein Kids" on the dotted line despite the name on the cover of the journal.

"It would have been a hoot if Milton could see you kids now," Mrs. Weatherbourne lamented. "He would have loved to hear all of your adventure stories."

"My mom and I reunited, too," Amy shared, putting the journal into her bag. "I figure that counts as an adventure. We write all the time, and we're talking about hanging out in person soon. I might meet her girlfriend, Cindy."

"I'd certainly say that counts as an adventure!" Mrs. Weatherbourne agreed. "You know, Milton would have been seventy-eight years old this month, and the adventures we had were countless. They didn't have to be big and heroic things, although those were quite something," she winked again. "But if you wanted it to be, finding the best place to have ice cream could be adventurous, too."

They finished their hot chocolate together, talking about everything and nothing, from school to how they'd cleaned out the treehouse on account of the winter and made a new hangout spot in the basement for themselves. At the mention of The Hideout, the kids caught one another's eye, wondering if they should share the adventure they'd gone on that very afternoon.

"What is it?" she asked, not missing a beat.

"We teleported," Amy confessed.

So, they told her—most of it. They took turns sharing details about how they'd put all their gems together and had been transported out of The Hideout, about the dirty figure in the shadows and his creepy warning—super creepy, according to Dez. How it hadn't been the first time they'd traveled somewhere that definitely wasn't Dennis Port. When they were finished with their story, Mrs. Weatherbourne had a curious expression, almost as if she had expected them to share what they had.

"What happened the first time?"

"The first time," Will started. "We went to a desert but came back almost immediately because none of us expected to go anywhere in the first place. The second we let go, we were back in the treehouse."

"We think it was Egypt," Dez added.

"Yeah, we tried it twice, and both times we ended up in a desert," Will explained.

"Then just last night, my family's menorah turned into a minotaur in my living room and told me to surrender my soul," Isaac said quietly. "It used my son of Horus name."

"I didn't think anything of it until now, but my gem was glowing when my dad woke me up," Will told them. "It could have been around the time that happened to Isaac. At first, I thought something might be wrong, but he was so happy that I pretty much forgot about my gem."

"And... and," Amy stuttered. She looked over at the crackling fire. "I've been having this recurring vision of a wooden door with a purple lavender wreath hanging on it."

When they were all finished, Mrs. Weatherbourne sat back in her armchair. Her expression gave nothing away as she looked at them all. "My, my," she finally spoke a moment or two later. Everyone had finished their hot chocolate by that point. "If you've learned anything by now, it's that everything has meaning. It's all a part of your destinies. The desert, the creepy man and the lavender wreath... it must mean something. Just like last summer, you followed the clues, and they lead you to the Eye of Horus. As a matter of fact, your vision of a lavender wreath reminds me of a time I shared with Milton, maybe twenty years ago or so. It was our anniversary, so we decided to spend a week in Newport, Rhode Island, because we'd always wanted to tour the luxury mansions that dated back to the Gilded Age. We found a charming bed and breakfast in Portsmouth, only twenty minutes away, and had a fabulous time exploring the famous Breakers Mansion and Marble House. And in the evenings, we returned to Portsmouth to enjoy dinner overlooking Narragansett Bay." She smiled wistfully, then shook her head, as if to shake away the memories and return to the present. "The reason I'm sharing this story with you all is because, as you recall, Milton was a man who believed destiny led him. Well, we noticed an over-the-street banner while in Newport promoting a local Lavender Festival that very weekend. Of course, we attended. It was wonderful; we had fun cutting fresh lavender stems, they served delicious appetizers, and we had a taste of freshly made lavender lemonade."

"It sounds like a lovely time," Amy murmured.

"It certainly was. Well, we'd been having so much fun that we lost track of time, and it was dark by the time we made our way back to the bed and breakfast. Talk about being in the right place at the right time. As we drove through the quiet backroads, we came upon a house on fire. It appeared to have just started, and no more than a few seconds later, Milton had pulled the car over and quickly sprinted into the burning house. I couldn't believe my eyes when, moments later, he came out carrying a young girl in his arms. Then, he raced back inside, this time emerging with an elderly woman. And then, like a page out of destiny, it couldn't have been more than thirty seconds after he rescued those two people that the entire house exploded in a giant blaze."

Isaac gasped. The kids looked at each other, wide-eyed and astonished by what they were hearing. Milton and Marjorie were living heroes in their eyes, but they still couldn't believe how much they'd done to help other people—strangers, even—throughout their lives.

"They said the fire hit the gas line, which caused the explosion," Mrs. Weatherbourne continued. "My Milton, he wasn't just my hero; he was their hero that night. We both made sure the girl and woman were okay having suffered some burns, and once the fire department arrived to take care of them, we simply climbed back into the car and went on with our evening." She glanced over at Amy. "It was such a wonderful time in Rhode Island. The wreath reminded me of it. As Milton always said, we have a predestined path we all follow. On that day, if we hadn't seen the banner for the Lavender Festival, if we hadn't attended it, we may never have been on that road that evening. We wouldn't have been there to help those people."

"Thank goodness you were," Amy said sincerely.

Mrs. Weatherbourne nodded, then leaned in seriously. "Like Milton, you kids have to always be ready. Learn all you can about your powers and stay steadfast. Remember to let the powers guide you, let Horus guide you."

"Do you really think something is coming, Mrs. W?" Isaac asked.

Mrs. Weatherbourne softened at the use of her abbreviated name. "I think you have been chosen, and when there's no hero to save you, you must become the hero yourselves. Just last summer, you were a bunch of curious kids who discovered Milton's secret. Look at you now. You've done incredible, heroic things, but like all stories, this is just the beginning, and I do believe your adventures are nowhere near their end."

Dez and Will had fastened their trinkets to their hemp necklaces and were holding them around their necks, perfect mirrors of Isaac. They straightened their shoulders at Mrs. Weatherbourne's words.

"Have you told your parents yet?" She asked.

"My mother knows everything," Isaac said. "Well, almost everything."

Dez tilted his head. "My mom knows enough. I mean… When you cure cancer, you're pretty much not in Kansas anymore." He cleared his throat.

Will seemed reluctant to answer but eventually said, "My parents don't know anything."

"Yeah, me too," Amy caught his eye. "I haven't told anyone."

Mrs. Weatherbourne nodded. "Things will happen as they're meant to. There's no such thing as too late." Seymour meowed from the kitchen. "Although, I don't want to keep you. It's beginning to get late, and it looks like Seymour and I are ready to settle in for the evening."

"Thanks for having us, Mrs. W," Will said with a smile as they prepared to leave.

"It was nice seeing all of you. Be careful out there." The kids stepped into the snow, shocked by the sudden cold breeze on their warm cheeks.

"Bye, Mrs. Weatherbourne," they chorused on their way to the bikes.

"Bye now," Mrs. Weatherbourne called after them before turning to go back inside, the door shutting behind her.

CHAPTER 6
BACK TO SCHOOL

The holiday season passed without any new visions or nightmares—or, as Dez put it, without a hitch. With the excitement of a new year, 1980 behind them, the kids returned to school with the hope of a normal year. The school corridors buzzed with a cacophony of teenage chatter and slamming lockers. Shouts of greetings and playful shoves filled the air, punctuated by the squeak of sneakers on polished floors. Teachers, armed with stacks of papers and determined smiles, weaved through the energetic throng, their voices rising above the din to remind everyone to hurry to class before the late bell.

"Cool, History," Dez grinned. "I don't know if you guys saw, but we have a whole section in our textbook dedicated to the Egypt empire this semester."

"Cool!" Amy and the boys agreed.

As it turned out, History class started off with an unexpected twist as they swung open the familiar oak classroom door. Instead of the usual sight of Mr. Rice hunched over his cluttered desk, a new figure stood beside him. This woman was a stark contrast to their rumpled History teacher. The new teacher was dressed almost entirely in black, a tailored suit with a light blue dress shirt peeking out beneath the collar.

"I think that's the new teacher," Amy shared as they took their seats. "I heard some other kids talking about her at the lockers."

"I wonder what that's for," Dez whispered to the others, gesturing toward a white glove covering her right hand.

"Maybe to avoid getting chalk on her hand when she uses the chalkboard?"

"Kids, kids," Mr. Rice's deep voice broke into their quiet conversation. The rest of the class, which was buzzing with the voices of kids as they all found their desks and settled down, came to a sudden silence. "Can I get everyone's attention?"

The room full of kids looked up at their teacher.

"Welcome back to my class. I'm sure you rested up well over the winter break and are all ready to get back to learning. Am I right?"

The class gave a discordant murmur that resembled something like agreement.

"Good," Mr. Rice nodded. "Some of you may have

already met Ms. Fleming, but for those of you yet to attend Social Studies today, this is your new teacher. Please give her a warm welcome."

Several kids cried, "Welcome!" There were some whistles and one or two wordless cheers thrown in, but the applause was the loudest. Ms. Fleming smiled.

Mr. Rice seemed mildly embarrassed as he continued, unable to keep from smiling at his class's enthusiasm. "Well, maybe Ms. Fleming can take a moment to tell you a little about herself."

Ms. Fleming stepped forward with a smile, "Well, hello, everyone…I recently moved to Cape Cod from Philadelphia! Home of the Liberty Bell, something we will be covering in our Social Studies class together. I live alone, well, just me and my dog, Drax. He is a German Shepherd. Thank you for your warm welcome; I am looking forward to getting to know each of you over the next few weeks."

Mr. Rice stepped forward to join Ms. Fleming. "As you all know, every spring I help organize an eighth-grade class trip. After some discussion, Ms. Fleming will be joining me in sponsoring this year's class trip, and it's coming up very soon! If you've been paying attention, you'll know that we were vying for New York City to be this year's destination, and it's my pleasure to deliver the news that that's where we'll be headed this year!"

The class erupted in cries of excitement. Two boys in the back of the class started doing a deep chant: "Big Apple! Big Apple! Big Apple!"

"Settle down," Mr. Rice raised his voice above the din.

As the classroom settled down, a student none of the

kids had seen before walked into the room and found her way to an empty seat while Mr. Rice reclaimed control of the class. She had blonde hair, neatly tied back into two pigtails that hung over the front of her shoulders. Several people watched the girl, and whispers about who she was and where she'd come from echoed up to where the kids sat.

"There are exactly forty spots available to attend this year's eighth-grade class trip to New York City. Ms. Fleming and I have organized five days of travel by coach bus, meals, and a four-night stay at the famous Roosevelt Hotel. If you want to attend, you'll need to get permission from your parents, and the cost per student is $100. The school's PTA will be contributing the rest."

Ms. Fleming took a stack of papers off Mr. Rice's desk and split it up into piles, setting them down on the desks at the front of the class. "Take one and pass them back."

The itinerary and a permission slip, requested to be signed by a parent or guardian, made their way back to the kids, and they each took one before passing the pile back.

It didn't take long for Will, Dez, Amy, and Isaac to erupt in a symphony of cheers as they devoured the itinerary. Will, practically vibrating with excitement, was the first to erupt. "This is going to be the BEST. TRIP. EVER!" he declared, throwing his fist into the air.

8th Grade Class Trip Itinerary

Wed, April 16:
Bus ride to NYC
Roosevelt Hotel Check-In

Thu, April 17:
MET (Metropolitan Museum of Art),
Central Park, Cathedral of
St. John the Divine
Dinner in Upper Manhattan

Fri, April 18:
Statue of Liberty & Ellis Island,
Time Square, Wall Street
Dinner in Lower Manhattan

Sat, April 19:
Rockefeller Center & Broadway
Empire State Building
Dinner in Midtown Manhattan

Sun, April 20:
Bus ride home

Isaac, his eyes wide with wonder, scanned the list, his voice tinged with awe. "Central Park...and the MET? I've always wanted to go there!"

Dez, ever the movie buff, bounced on the balls of his feet, practically vibrating. "Dude, Empire State Building? We're going to the final resting place of King Kong himself!" he exclaimed, throwing a dramatic arm around his imaginary ape companion.

Amy, rolling her eyes but unable to contain a smile, swatted Dez's arm playfully. "It was just a movie, Dez," she chuckled.

"Yeah, yeah, I know," Dez mumbled, a grin still

plastered on his face. "But it's still gonna be epic!"

Despite their individual highlights, a collective sense of excitement crackled between the four. No matter which destination piqued their interest the most, they all knew this class trip was bound to be legendary.

◆ ◆ ◆

Lunch period came after history class, and the kids couldn't wait to have a moment alone together, practically racing toward the cafeteria. They grabbed their sandwiches, yogurts, and fruit juices, hastily making their way to an empty table to discuss the upcoming trip over their meals, all while avoiding the eyes of lunch ladies who might try to convince them to take something they didn't want. They didn't speak while in line, having agreed before they returned to school to be extra careful about who might be listening.

"G-Man got the mystery meat," Dez cried out as Isaac placed his food tray on the table.

Will looked up and took notice of the plate of Salisbury steak on Isaac's tray.

"Looks like the lunch lady
sold you on the mystery meat," he snickered at Dez across the table.

Isaac shrugged his shoulders. "It's actually pretty good."

"You know what's pretty good, actually better than good… this upcoming class trip," Dez added as he pulled the itinerary out of his notebook.

Only a moment after Dez had placed the class trip itinerary on the table, a young girl walked over.

"May I join you?" She asked softly, a slight accent in her tone.

When they looked up, they saw the girl who had walked into their history class and taken a seat near the front. She had blonde hair, tied back into two neat pigtails. Mr. Rice had briefly introduced her, but none of the kids had been paying much attention.

The kids exchanged glances. Isaac shrugged, and then Dez, who hadn't taken his eyes off the girl since she arrived, eyed her appreciatively. He was the one to nod and say suavely, "Sure."

"Thanks," she smiled and took a seat. "My name's Myra."

"You're French-Canadian, right?" Dez asked, suddenly remembering something Mr. Rice had said.

Myra nodded, her pigtails bouncing.

"You were in our history class, so I'm guessing you're also fourteen?"

She nodded again, opening her mouth to say something more when two other girls arrived. They had similar features to Myra's, with angular features and wide eyes framed by the same long dark lashes, all a similar shade of turquoise. Like Myra's, their long blonde hair was also tied into two pigtails.

"Whoa, are you guys related?" Will asked, his eyes taking in the tallest of the three. Her hair was the longest, and she looked older than the other two. When they met each other's eyes, he quickly averted his gaze.

"Hi, I'm Daria," the shortest one said with a smile.

"These are my sisters," Myra gestured. "Daria's two

years younger than me and Olivia…" Her voice trailed away as Olivia turned on her heel and walked away from the table with a roll of her eyes. "…couldn't manage so much as a hello, I guess."

Will felt a lump in his throat as he watched Olivia's shapely form walking away from them.

"She seems a bit tall for the eighth grade," Amy remarked, looking after Olivia.

"She is," Myra shrugged. "She should be in the tenth grade, but they didn't want to separate us, so they are allowing her to attend this semester here… in some of the advanced classes."

"Hmm," Amy shifted in her seat, sitting up straighter so she looked taller in her chair. She hoped her body language wouldn't give away anything about her internal feelings, but it was hard not to feel threatened after seeing the way Will looked at Olivia—or rather, pointedly *didn't* look at Olivia.

Two voices fought for dominance in her mind. One asked, *what would he have done if she hadn't been there?* The other reasoned that *she couldn't blame him when it was hard not to take notice of her mature body and long, blonde hair.*

"We're foreign exchange students," Myra went on. "Olivia is still kind of getting used to being here."

The group nodded, Amy half-heartedly.

"That's cool!" Dez said. "So are you guys at least psyched about the New York class trip? Big Apple, here we come!"

Isaac pointed his thumb at Will with a wiggle of his eyebrows. "That means New York Yankee territory!"

"I know what you're thinking," Will put both his hands to his head, protectively holding down the top of his Boston Red Sox baseball cap. "But no way. This is my lucky hat! I'm wearing it regardless!"

The table erupted in laughter, and the conversation shifted to the upcoming trip. Amy, though still a bit shy, found herself laughing along and sharing her own excitement about visiting New York for the first time.

CHAPTER 7
TO THINE OWN SELF BE TRUE

After school, Amy and Will rode their bicycles to Sea Street and Mill Road, stopping when they reached Will's house and parking in front of the side door. Will took Amy's hand and led her inside, their school bags slung over their shoulders.

"Hi, Mrs. McMurphy," Amy said as they passed the kitchen. Will's mom was reading the newspaper at the kitchen counter with a cup of coffee in hand.

"Hey, kids," she looked up. "How was the first day back at school?"

"Hey, Mom. It was good! We were told about the eighth-grade class trip."

"Oh? And where is it going to be?"

"New York City," Amy and Will said in unison.

"Can I go, Mom? Please?" Will walked over and handed the itinerary and permission slip to his mom.

She gave it a quick read and then smiled. "This sounds like it will be really good for you. All those places with rich history!"

"So I can go?"

Kathy put the sheet underneath her newspaper. "Let's wait until your father gets home, and we'll talk about it as a family, okay?"

"Sure," Will kissed his mom on the cheek. "Amy and I are going to do our homework and hang out in my room."

From behind the living room wall, they heard giggles. Will stepped to the side and craned his neck around, peering down at the floor where his little sister was crouched. Her hand was over her mouth, doing a poor job of hiding her laughter. Will couldn't help snickering along with her.

"It's not like Amy hasn't been here a bunch of times already, you know," he said with a shake of his head. Then, he took the stairs two at a time with Amy behind him.

"I got some lemonade, Will," his mom called after them. "It's in the fridge if you two want some."

"Thanks, Mom!" Will called back down as they got to his bedroom. There, he flopped down onto his bed, dropping his bag on the floor beside it.

Amy dropped hers on the floor at the end of the bed and then sat down, cross-legged. She tilted her head, glancing down at the covers with some shyness. "I saw the way you were looking at those girls today."

"Don't be stupid," Will rolled his eyes. "Dez clearly has the hots for Myra!"

She looked on with a smirk tugging at the corner of her lip. "Oh, but you didn't deny it."

Will had to keep from rolling his eyes again. He hopped off the bed and clicked on his radio cassette player, grabbing a tape off the shelf and clicking it into place. As the music started playing, he looked over at Amy, and they shared a smile.

"Chic," Amy started bobbing her head enthusiastically. "I love Disco…I love this song…"

Will's smile grew wider. "I got it for you. But you can't tell Dez and Isaac. I would never hear the end of it... they hate disco."

The truth was, until Amy had come into his life, he wasn't the fondest of disco either. But as Amy jumped up off the bed and began dancing around the room, he thought it had definitely grown on him. She'd grown more comfortable with him since they first met the previous summer, and they'd been seeing each other so much that he barely noticed she'd grown over that time, too. He watched her dance, relieved that they—all of them—remained close.

The Katzenstein Kids, united, he thought.

"Good times, these are the good times!" Amy sang the lyrics as she danced around his bedroom. She made her way over to him, taking his hands in hers and attempting to pull him in to join her, but he resisted, laughing. She released him with a smirk and sang the rest of the song, finishing her dance.

"Boys will be boys... Girls will be girls!"

The song slowly came to an end, then faded out. Amy breathlessly went back to his bed, plopping down. Will went over to join her when her expression changed.

"What's up?"

"Nothing," she shook her head, avoiding his eyes.

"Something's been on your mind all day, Amy. I can tell."

She poked him in the chest. "You know me too well, Will McMurphy." She poked him again, on a particular spot over his shirt pocket, where she felt something hard. "What's that in your pocket? A coin?"

Will reached into his pocket and pulled out his father's three-month chip. "Oh, it's my dad's chip; the one he earned from AA for being sober for three months."

He handed her the chip, and Amy took it, running her fingers along the face of the coin. "TO THINE OWN SELF BE TRUE," she read the inscription. "I can't believe that your Protection Gem really worked. It's so cool, and I'm so happy for you."

"Me either. My family's on a good path again, and things feel right."

He handed the coin back to him, and he tucked it away again before reaching over to open a small wooden trinket box sitting on his dresser. Amy craned her neck to see what he was doing, but before she could see anything, he had already retrieved what he was looking for; another chip like the one he'd had in his pocket.

"Here," he handed it to her. "I want you to have this one; it was the first one my dad gave me. It's called the beginner's or start-over coin. You can keep it for luck. It was my dad's first one, for being sober for a full twenty-four hours. Now we both have one."

This brought a smile to Amy's face. She tucked it into her own top pocket and leaned in to press her lips to Will's, lingering for a long kiss. When she pulled away, her cheeks were warm, and she could see the color start to form in Will's face. He grinned from ear to ear.

"How about you?" He quickly changed the topic. "How are you and your mom doing?"

Amy glanced down at the ring on her finger, her lips curving the slightest bit. "The Prophecy Gem saved us, too. Since I found all the letters that my dad had been keeping from me and reached out on my own, we've grown a lot closer. Even my dad seems to accept that I'm talking to her again. Things were kind of hard between us for a while, but I think it was mostly because my dad felt so guilty about everything." She gave him a sad look. "To think that all that time, I was longing for her and thought she had abandoned us."

"I know," Will shook his head, reaching for Amy's hand. "What your father did was wrong... He should never have hidden all her letters from you."

"I agree. I guess he was hurt and embarrassed. I mean, he still loves my mother very much. But she had to be honest with herself, and the truth was that she fell in love with Cindy."

"Now she can be who she was born to be," Will smiled.

"Yeah! And I have my mother back. I'm so happy."

"You have two moms if you think about it."

Amy laughed, but just as quickly as it started, it stopped, and her expression became grave. They weren't allowed to close Will's door when they were hanging out in his room, but she got up to check that no one else was upstairs before she came back over and sat closer to him on the bed.

"Okay, you're right," she eventually said in a low voice. "There has been something on my mind. I had another vision."

"Was it the one with the brown door and the lavender wreath?"

"No," she shook her head frantically. "Will, I'm worried. I'm worried about you. I'm worried about all of us. Last night, I woke up in the middle of the night, and my Prophecy ring was glowing green. I took hold of it in my hand, and that's when the vision occurred..." Her finger absent-mindedly stroked the gem on her finger as she spoke. "I saw us; well, I saw you, Dez, and Isaac... You were all looking down at the ground at... at a body. A dead body!"

Will didn't say anything, waiting for Amy to say more.

"I think it was me," she continued, emotion slipping into her voice. "I didn't see me watching. I must have been the one on the ground."

"Perhaps you were standing outside of the vision?" Will offered, gently rubbing his hand up and down Amy's back in what he hoped was a soothing way.

When next she spoke, she didn't address the possibility that she could have been outside the vision, that she wasn't the body on the ground. "I'm worried, Will. All these signs, all these visions..." They met each other's eyes. Moisture threatened to spill over her waterline. "I can feel it. Something horrible is coming."

Will took her hands in his, curling his fingers through hers and holding on tightly. "I'll protect you, Amy," he said earnestly. "I'm the protector, remember? I won't let anything happen to you."

Amy's eyes welled up with tears, a mixture of fear and gratitude. His words were a balm to her wounded spirit. "I know you will, Will," she whispered, leaning into him slightly. "I trust you."

The warmth of his hands, the strength of his grip, they were a tangible reminder that she wasn't alone. They stood there for a long moment, their hands entwined, finding solace in each other's presence. It was a silent promise, a vow that transcended words.

As the last rays of the setting sun bled through the window, casting long, dramatic shadows across the room, a quiet sense of hope bloomed in Amy's heart. It wasn't just Will's silent promise, but his steady presence beside her. With Will by her side, a familiar warmth radiating from him, she felt a knot of anxieties loosen. He was her confidant, her rock – the one person who understood the unsettling visions that plagued her and the unease that gnawed at her after the night's terrors.

In that cocoon of tranquility, bathed in the golden hues of twilight, Amy noticed a shift in Will's posture. He leaned in slowly, his gaze meeting hers with a tenderness that sent a familiar flutter through her stomach. The air crackled with unspoken emotions, a silent conversation passing between them. Then, as if guided by an invisible thread,

Will's lips met hers in a gentle kiss.

It was a kiss brimming with unspoken understanding and a promise of unwavering support. Amy surrendered to the familiar comfort of his touch, her anxieties momentarily melting away. She reciprocated the kiss, pouring all the unspoken emotions – the fear, the hope, and the unyielding determination – into it. In that shared moment of tenderness, a silent vow was exchanged. They would face whatever darkness that loomed ahead, together.

CHAPTER 8
NEW YORK OR BUST

As each winter month faded into memory, Dennis Port experienced a gradual thawing, a subtle shift in the air that whispered of the impending warmth of mid-April. The familiar hues of gray persisted, but with the promise of spring upon them, sporadic bursts of blue and green began to grace the horizon. Days stretched longer, suffused with the restless energy of anticipation for the coming summer.

For Will, this day marked the culmination of weeks of anticipation, as the class trip had finally arrived. As he exited the family car outside Wixon Middle School, amidst a throng of excited classmates and bustling parents, he couldn't help but feel a flutter of excitement mingled with nervous energy. His backpack slung over one shoulder, he clutched his most prized possession: his sleek new portable cassette player, a recent Christmas gift, which promised to make the impending nine-hour bus journey more tolerable.

"Ready to go?" His dad asked, his hands clasped in front of him, a gesture Will knew he made when he was trying to contain his excitement. Behind his dad, his mom hovered with the camera in hand, capturing the moment. *Parents,* he internally rolled his eyes. But he couldn't keep the smile off his face even if he tried. "Yeah, ready!"

Outside the main entrance to the school a single coach-style bus large enough for forty students, two chaperones, and a driver stood surrounded by a pile-up of cars. Excited students were dropped off, some loud and neurotic parents attempted to say goodbye and told their children to be safe, and a few equally antsy faculty members crowded the middle school parking lot. This was possibly the most popular student trip the school had ever arranged, which made it chaotic for the teachers, however thrilling it might have been. In the middle of it all, Amy, Dez, Isaac, and Will had found one another and were sharing a grin of anxious anticipation, itching to be let loose, while their parents' exchanged pleasantries over their heads. Amy was accompanied by both her moms, Jo and Cindy, while Will was being seen off by his mom and dad. Isaac and his mother, Anne, had driven with Dez and his mother, Silvia.

"You're looking so good, Silvia!" Anne said with a smile, taking the other woman's hand and squeezing it.

"You really are," Will's mom, Kathy, added. "How have things been?"

While his mom caught up with he other moms, Dez

elbowed Isaac gently in the bicep to get his attention and then gestured ahead when Isaac looked up in shock, rubbing his arm. Approaching them were Olivia, Myra, and Daria, walking side by side. Their height differences made their age gaps clear, with Olivia standing tall and Daria being the smallest of the three. Walking slightly behind them was a tall man wearing a gray brim fedora hat with a long feather tucked into the band, a strange contrast from the scene around the bus. They stopped short of the gathering of children and the man took turns hugging each girl, oldest to youngest, before returning to his car.

The girls waited for the car to depart from the parking lot and then started making their way over. Upon realizing they were coming his way, Dez's cheeks began to color, and he mumbled under his breath, "Incoming, incoming... Damn it."

Silvia heard him and spun around, turning to see what the panic was all about. She hardly had time to take the girl in before Myra's soft voice rang out.

"Hi, Dez!" The girl giggled. "You excited or what?"

Dez could feel his mother's eyes on them and knew his cheeks must be red. "Hey Myra," he said. "You have no idea! It's gonna be a long bus ride, though."

Will mouthed to Isaac, *"Hi Dez!"* and the boys laughed together while the group of mothers watched on. Silvia had a glow in her eyes as she quickly realized her son had his first childhood crush, and she and the other adults shared knowing looks.

"Okay, kids!" Mr. Rice's booming voice sounded out above their heads. He was accompanied by Ms. Fleming, both holding clipboards at the door to the bus. "It's time to wrap up your goodbyes. Make sure you place all your luggage over here," he pointed to the side of the bus where two storage doors stood wide open, revealing the interior luggage compartment. A couple of duffels had already been tossed in—the kids assumed they belonged to the teachers. "Once you've placed your luggage, please start forming a single line as we call out your names. We won't be opening up the luggage compartment again until we arrive in New York City, so please be sure to bring any items you may want on the bus with you. That includes snacks, drinks, and items you may want to entertain yourself with, such as books or games."

Ms. Fleming stepped forward. "We will be calling your names in pairs. You may remember the questionnaire you previously completed when you handed your permission slips in. We will be pairing you based on the answers you gave. The person you are paired with will be your travel buddy for the entire trip, and that means they will also be the person you share your room with once we arrive in New York."

Will looked at Isaac, mouthing, *"I picked you."*

Isaac nodded and whispered back, "I picked you, too."

Amy looked over to catch the exchange and couldn't help feeling disappointed. A part of her would have enjoyed rooming with Will, but she knew that would never be allowed anyway.

"Dude, I'm a free agent," Dez chuckled. "This could go either way!"

As the first names were called, Kathy gave Will a hug,

which he was reluctant to return in embarrassment. Dez and Isaac happily returned their moms' hugs, and Amy stood awkwardly to the side of Jo and Cindy, bidding them both a quiet farewell. Jo smiled but didn't push her, giving her a gentle rub of the shoulder instead of a hug goodbye. They stood to the sides, watching as the kids lined up neatly to depart.

Each teacher took turns calling out the names listed on their clipboards, one after the other, until, as expected, the kids heard the names, "Will McMurphy and Isaac Goffman."

Isaac pumped his fist in the air excitedly, and Will laughed at the wrong moment as the stern Ms. Fleming walked past the pair of them with narrowed eyes.

"I will be keeping an extra eye on the two of you," she reminded them sternly.

Will looked back at Isaac and whispered, "Did you notice, she is still wearing that white glove on her right hand."

"Ya, it's weird!" Isaac whispered back.

Amy was paired with a girl named Sarah, whom she had never interacted with before, and Dez with a boy named Peter, who sat near him in social studies.

"Olivia, Myra, and Daria," Ms. Fleming called the last three names. The foreign exchange sisters were all paired together.

"This bus is so cool," Will told Amy as she boarded. He and Isaac were already comfortably seated in cushioned seats near the back that could recline and were comfortable enough to sleep in.

Isaac pointed at a closed door near the back. "It even has its own onboard bathroom."

"Impressive," Amy laughed as she took a seat next to Sarah, a brunette girl in the window seat. She stood up on her seat so she could join her friends in waving to their moms before the bus filled up, then flopped back down into her seat. She still couldn't believe both Jo and Cindy were here, wearing tie-dyed shirts, flowy pants, and holding hands. "I guess that means we're officially on our way to the Big Apple!"

"Whoo, whoo!" The bus erupted into cheers. At the front, Ms. Fleming and Mr. Rice gave a gentle, "Settle down, settle down," but they couldn't hide their own excitement. It wasn't every day they got to go to New York City.

The bus started up with a loud growl, and the whole vehicle shuddered before it pulled back and away, beginning their nine-hour journey. Sarah, Amy's travel buddy, didn't seem to interested in talking, instead putting on a pair of headphones and turning her music up loud enough that Amy could almost make out the lyrics. She caught herself wondering if all the hullabaloo she'd heard about going deaf from listening to music too loudly was real or if it was parental scare-mongering.

Oh well, she thought. *This is why I brought my journal.*

When the words on the pages started to blur, which admittedly wasn't long into their road trip, Amy turned around in her seat to see what Isaac and Will were doing. There were two rows between them, and only one other person looked up at her. Isaac had his head buried in one of the comic books she'd gotten him for Christmas, and beside him, Will was quietly jamming to music through his headphones, drumming his fingers on the window to the beat and bobbing his head along.

Curious, she asked over the seats, getting one or two looks from other students. "Whatcha listening to?"

Isaac glanced up and then nudged Will with his shoulder, causing Will to turn and shift the headphones off one of his ears. Isaac subtly gestured toward Amy with his head, and Will looked over.

"Whatcha listening to?" She repeated, attracting more attention. "My favorite song... I hope."

Color rushed to Will's cheeks, and he ran a nervous hand through his hair. *Not now,* he thought. *Please don't tell everyone I'm into disco now...*

To his surprise—and relief—Amy simply smirked at him and turned back around. He didn't need to look at his best friend to know that Isaac was grinning beside him. Will was ready to settle back into his seat and replace his headphones over his ear when, like clockwork, Dez climbed over the back of his seat to join the other two boys in the back and turned to Will with a grin of his own.

"Dude," he whispered sardonically. "I hope you're playing my favorite song, too."

Will raised his middle finger at Dez, and both the other boys burst into laughter at his expense. The two boys in the seats next to theirs stood up and walked down the aisle. Will, Dez, and Isaac looked on as Myra and Daria took their places, sitting beside the boys. Out of the corner of his eye, Will caught Amy taking notice, glancing back over her seat.

"Hey Dez," Myra leaned over. "What are you guys laughing about?"

"Oh, nothing. Just messing with my friend, Will-bo!" He looked over at Will. "Hey, do you guys remember that day last summer we all went to the beach, and you thought it would be funny to tell Amy my hand grenade story?"

Daria whispered to Myra, "Hand grenade story?"

Meanwhile, Will and Isaac exchanged an anxious look, realizing their friend was gearing up for some sweet revenge.

"You two want to hear the tale of the Brown Ninja?" Dez asked the girls, ignoring the fact that Will's cheeks darkened with embarrassment yet again. "Relax, Will; it was legendary."

Myra and Daria listened closely, and Will dropped his head, giving into the newfound interest in hearing his tale of the Brown Ninja. Even Isaac and Amy leaned in so that they could hear every word. Dez gave a grin and began his story with a flourish of his hands.

"Once upon a time, Will wanted to be a ninja warrior."

"This was a long time ago," Will interjected. "I was just a kid, for the record."

"Right, *for the record,*" Dez nodded. "So, one day, Will was looking through his clothes for the perfect ninja costume, but all he could find were brown clothes instead of the traditional black. He found a knitted brown ski mask, brown pants, a brown turtleneck shirt, and brown shoes. He thought, 'Why not just be a brown ninja instead of a black ninja?'"

"So, he dressed up and headed outside and into the woods behind his house. He knew that a contractor was clearing trees nearby to build a new house, and he could hear the backhoe moving back and forth, digging up the dirt for the foundation. Will had an idea. It was time to test his ninja skills, and he was going to give himself a challenge: he snuck up through the woods and approached the construction site. In the clearing, he saw the backhoe and the large, scary guy driving it. He decided that every time the backhoe and the man were facing away to dump dirt in their own ever-growing pile, he would sneak out from his hiding spot and remove one of their wooden survey stakes. Then, he would climb up the backside of the dirt hill he was hiding behind and place the survey stake on top of the hill, like a flag on a mountaintop. A marker of his victory."

By this point, at least four rows of other kids were listening to the story with great anticipation. Dez continued, "Well, Will started his mission, watching carefully as the driver did his work, and predictably, the backhoe eventually faced away from him. So he ran out, grabbed one of the stakes, and ran back to his spot. He must have grabbed three or four stakes before the backhoe driver finally noticed anything amiss. But Will wasn't worried. After all, he was the Brown Ninja! As he was about to sneak up the mound with his fifth stake ready to be planted in the earth, he heard jingling coming from the direction of the backhoe. He stopped dead in his tracks and peered around the side of the mound, and to his horror, he saw the larger-than-life backhoe driver running toward him with an angry look on his face. He had a huge ring of keys clipped to his jeans, and it bounced and jingled with each stride."

Everyone listening gasped collectively. One or two cried out, "What happened next?"

"Will was freaked out! This guy was about to turn him into mincemeat, and he was only twenty feet away and gaining. The guy was even yelling at Will," he put on a deep voice and made himself taller. *"I'm gonna kick your ass!"*

Myra giggled, and Dez met her eyes as he went on with a grin. "Will quickly jumped up and ran for the woods, but this guy was right on his tail. Will had to bob and weave to create some distance between them, running and running through the thick brush, but at some point, he reached a dead end. The brush was too knotted to climb under and too high to climb over, while fallen trees lay everywhere, so he did all he could... He dove right into the middle of the thicket and lay flat and silent. The scary, burly backhoe driver got closer and closer; Will could hear his footsteps stomping through the leaves as he approached, and when a big boot landed on the ground next to his head, he thought he was done for! Fear in his throat, Will could hardly breathe as his eyes rolled upward to get a glimpse of the man who was surely about to take hold of him. Only when Will's eyes looked up, he saw the man looking ahead, *over* Will's head, scanning the woods in front of him."

"What?!" One of the kids cried out. "How is that possible?"

Dez chuckled. "That's exactly what Will thought. He was shocked. The backhoe driver stood inches away from him but couldn't see him! As the scene unfolded, Will thought to himself, how is that possible? After a while, the man reluctantly began to walk back toward the backhoe, mumbling under his breath."

At this, Dez looked over at Will, beaming with pride.

Will repeated one of the questions the backhoe driver had mumbled with a bit of amusement: *"Where the hell did that little punk go?"*

A few kids laughed at that, and Dez went on. "Will laid flat and still. He couldn't believe the man didn't see him, and he waited until the sound of jingling keys faded before he moved again. A smile formed across his lips, hidden beneath his knit ski mask. All he could say was, *'I must be a real Brown Ninja, invisible to my enemies!'"*

Everyone who'd been listening cheered at the end of the story. Will's original coloring was barely visible beneath the blush that covered his face. Echoes of questions came his way, and he tried to keep up with them.

"How did you do it?" Someone asked.

"It was just camouflage," Will laughed. "I was wearing brown, and the thicket was brown. I got lucky."

"Was it true? Are you really the Brown Ninja?"

"Yeah, it's all true," he blushed deeper. "Like I said, camouflage."

Dez sat back, folding his arms behind his head. "You're like a superhero. You can thank me later."

The three boys in the back shared a smile, and in the background, sliding back down into her own seat, Amy smiled, too.

Isaac turned to Will. "Well, that was fun. Now we only have eight hours to go."

CHAPTER 9
THE ROOSEVELT HOTEL
Manhattan, New York

After the grueling nine-hour bus ride, 45th Street in New York City unfolded before the kids like a majestic corridor. Towering hotels, adorned with flags from nations around the world, lined the bustling street. Throngs of people crisscrossed the roads and sidewalks, creating a vibrant tapestry of urban life. As the Roosevelt Hotel, proudly displaying the U.S. flag, came into view, Mr. Rice stood, signaling their arrival. The bus pulled into a dedicated drop-off zone, marking the end of their journey.

"Welcome, everyone, welcome," Mr. Rice exclaimed loudly, his voice laced with excitement as he addressed the groggy students. "This is the historic Roosevelt Hotel, named after former President Theodore Roosevelt. Can anyone tell me which president he was?" When no one answered, most kids still waking up from naps, he repeated himself. "Anyone?"

A few students stirred, their attention caught. After a moment of silence, a voice piped up: "Number twenty-six?"

"Yes, that is correct! You may all start disembarking in an orderly fashion, from the front to the back of the bus," Mr. Rice announced, gesturing toward the exit. "Please ensure that you haven't left anything behind. You can dispose of your trash to the left as you exit."

The kids followed his instructions, clearing their seats and piling out of the bus in a sleepy but orderly procession. Their driver had disembarked first, and the luggage compartment had already been opened. He was gesturing to an area where the kids should stand and wait when they were off the bus and finished throwing their trash out.

As the students gathered outside, Mr. Rice continued his impromptu history lesson. "What do you think, kids?" He gestured at the tall building with endless rows of windows. "The hotel first opened in 1924. It's nineteen stories, and its style of design is known as Italian Renaissance Revival."

Dez, Isaac, and Will joined Amy and the gathering of other students, followed by Ms. Fleming. There were some murmurs of approval, and one student shouted, "It's super cool, Mr. Rice!"

Mr. Rice smiled. "The Roosevelt is one of several large hotels that were developed in this area, more specifically around Grand Central Station. Can anyone tell me what

Grand Central Station is?"

The same student responded, "A train terminal!"

"Yes, very good, a train station... But more than that, it's the world's largest train station, with sixty-seven tracks and access to the New York City Subway, which is an underground subway system much like the 'T' we have in Boston."

Mr. Rice looked around and noticed all the students were off the bus. He paused to do a quick headcount with Ms. Fleming. Seemingly satisfied, Ms. Fleming said, "All right, kids, don't forget to take your bags from the luggage compartment and then go line up at the hotel entrance." A few of the students laughed. "Can we start unpacking in the order we boarded?"

"Of course," Ms. Fleming added.

Finally, the only two bags left were the duffels that went in first. Ms. Fleming and Mr. Rice retrieved them, and the driver shut the luggage compartment. He spoke quietly to Mr. Rice, and then the teachers led the students into the hotel lobby. A few students gasped.

"Now that's something you won't see on Cape Cod," Mr. Rice said.

The lobby's tiled ceilings were raised high above their heads, and ornamental designs decorated the trims and cornices. A burgundy-carpeted staircase led to an open area where a shimmering chandelier hung above a circular table surrounded by burgundy armchairs. There were various smaller seating areas with small tables and two armchairs on either side of them. Small lamps glowed from their centers, and the room had potted plants in the corners and hanging off some pillars, purifying the air. It seemed each decor choice infused the hotel with luxury, and the kids whispered among themselves, speculating about the building's glamorous past and the types of people that would have stayed there in its heyday.

"I bet this place has seen its fair share of big celebrities, people like... I don't know, those black-and-white film stars," someone said.

"Politicians probably. Senators and congressmen and stuff. You know, because it was the president's hotel and everything."

"A bunch of rich people with status," one girl shared.

"Status?"

"Yeah, status," she repeated without elaborating.

"You must be the Wixon Middle School students," a man's voice sounded from behind them. He was wearing a burgundy suit with a white dress shirt and had a bronze name tag pinned to his breast pocket. "I'm the hotel concierge. Welcome to the Roosevelt Hotel; we're very excited to host you all."

The teachers introduced themselves. "Thank you, we're very happy to be here. It's been a long trip."

"I can imagine," the concierge nodded. "I'll guide you to your rooms on the sixth floor. Please leave your luggage here; we'll take the elevators, and I will have the bellhops follow with the luggage."

Magically from behind a corner, two younger men appeared, they wore burgundy suits and bellhop caps, both wheeling hotel bell carts forward. They smiled at the kids and began packing the bags onto the carts while the concierge led everyone else to the elevators, the teachers right behind him. The gold doors of the elevators opened, and groups of kids filled the elevator cars. Excitement filled the cars as the thrill of upward motion took hold. At the sixth floor, the kids exited the elevators into a burgundy-carpeted hallway lined with decorative doors for each of the hotel rooms.

The teachers had a quiet talk with the hotel concierge while the students retrieved their luggage from the bell carts, which arrived moments later as promised. As names were called, the hotel concierge opened room doors, and kids in groups of two entered rooms. The last nine hours of being on the bus seemed to catch up with them, and they were all in need of some rest.

Will and Isaac, Dez and Peter, and Amy and Sarah went their separate ways, entering their assigned rooms. Not long after everyone had settled into their rooms, they were called back into the hall by the teachers.

"Did everyone settle in okay?" Ms. Fleming asked, eyebrows raised questioningly. There were some nods. "Good, I know we have all had a long day, and you all must be ready to have some dinner by now. The concierge has just gone down to let the hotel restaurant know we're on our way, and then after dinner, we'll all retreat to our assigned rooms. The bedtime curfew is nine p.m. Any questions?"

Will rubbed his stomach, whispering to Isaac. "I'm starving."

After a moment's silence, Ms. Fleming nodded. "Then follow us."

Dinner was a subdued affair, but the food was delicious. The students eagerly dug into their plates of roasted chicken, perfectly seasoned and tender, alongside creamy mashed potatoes drizzled with rich gravy, and vibrant green beans sautéed with garlic and herbs. The elegant ambiance of the dining room, with its high ceilings, crystal chandeliers, and white linen tablecloths, only enhanced the dining experience. The exhaustion of the long journey had caught up with them, leaving them too tired for much conversation. However, hushed whispers circulated about the exquisite flavors and the sophisticated atmosphere, with some students expressing their awe at the grandeur of the hotel restaurant.

Outside, they could see and hear the hustle and bustle of the streets of New York City coming to life. Yellow cabs honked, delivery trucks rumbled, and sirens wailed in a never-ending symphony of urban noise. The skyline filled the large windows from frame to frame, a sight none of the students had ever encountered before. Skyscrapers and office buildings pierced the sky above, their windows glinting in the evening dusk. There wasn't a moment where it quieted down, from the moment of their arrival in the metropolis all the way until they returned to their rooms.

They could see much of New York from the sixth floor. Before she went to sleep, Amy stared out her window at the twinkling lights of the city. The skyline glowed and sparkled brighter than she'd ever seen in the movies. Even that high up, the sound of blaring car horns could be heard from the buzzing streets below.

◆ ◆ ◆

Later that evening, the clock displayed a surreal 1:13 AM, its illuminated hands a stark contrast to the pitch-black sky outside. Amy awoke with a gasp that echoed in the silent room. Her heart hammered against her ribs. She whipped her head towards Sarah's bed, fearing she'd startled her roommate, but Sarah remained blissfully asleep under a rumpled heap of blankets. Relief washed over Amy, momentarily calming the frantic thrumming in her chest.

Trying to quell the adrenaline rush, Amy sank back into her pillow. But sleep, a traitor once again, abandoned her. Behind her closed eyelids, the embers of the nightmare flickered, refusing to be extinguished. Though the specifics remained frustratingly elusive, the chilling essence of the dream lingered – a shadowy figure lurking in the room's periphery, its sudden lunge the catalyst for her frantic awakening.

Unease settled over her. *Was it just the strangeness of a new city, a new room, playing tricks in her mind, or was something more sinister at play? Was she truly being watched?*

Unable to bear the suffocating darkness any longer, Amy threw back the covers and padded towards the window. The cityscape sprawled beneath her, a tapestry of twinkling lights against the inky canvas of night. It felt like hours had passed since she drifted off, yet the relentless energy of the city seemed unchanged. *Was this the land of perpetual twilight, a place where time itself defied definition?*

A shiver danced down her spine. *It had been months since her last vision*, the unsettling premonitions that had plagued her since the discovery of her Prophecy Gem. Now, on their first night in the Big Apple, they had returned with a vengeance. Not just one, but two vivid flashes had assaulted her sleep. The first, a recurring image of a brown door adorned with a lavender wreath, the second, a horrifying tableau of Will, Dez, and Isaac standing over a lifeless body — a body that, in a moment of terror, she'd feared could be hers.

Taking a deep, shaky breath, Amy tried to rationalize the fear that constricted her throat. She was safe, here and now. Her eyes, adjusting to the darkness, traced the outlines of the unfamiliar room as she made her way back to bed. But the seed of unease remained, blooming into a silent question in the quiet of the night: *Could this be a harbinger of things to come in this vibrant, yet unsettling, city?*

CHAPTER 10
THE BIG APPLE

The following morning, the hotel arranged a delicious breakfast buffet in the hotel restaurant to ensure the students had an early start to their first day in the big city. Well-rested and full of excitement, everyone was up bright and early and was rushed downstairs by Ms. Fleming and Mr. Rice to begin their day of touring Upper Manhattan. After filling their bellies, the teachers led them to the lobby entrance.

"Now kids," Mr. Rice called for everyone's attention. Several kids had mouths full of food. "Please remember all the rules we went before we left. Stick with your travel buddy at all times and make sure to stay close to Ms. Fleming and myself. If in doubt, or you find yourself lost, please do your best to use the city markers and make your way back to the last official spot we visited on the itinerary, as those will be the first places we will look for you. Everyone understand?"

"Yes, sir," the students chorused.

"Good. We're starting the day with a walk to Grand Central Station to explore the New York City Subway! We're all going to take the subway to Central Park, and then we'll be visiting The Metropolitan Museum of Art, also known as the MET. Any questions?" He scanned the students' faces, and when he was sure no one had anything to add, he continued instructing them. "This afternoon, our second stop will be the Cathedral of St. John the Divine, and then we have dinner reservations in Upper Manhattan. Please line up in two rows, side by side with your travel buddy. One of you behind me, the other behind Ms. Fleming." With the formalities out of the way, his excited tone from the previous day returned, and he raised his voice slightly for the next question. "Are we all ready to tour New York?"

Several of the students gave hearty cheers, which made him smile wider.

"Then let's go!"

Another cheer, and they were off through the hotel doors, exiting out underneath a burgundy canopy. They were hit with the sound of the city at full blast. A doorman waved at some of them before they turned left, and the sun shone down on them as they left the shade of the Roosevelt Hotel. New York was somehow even noisier than it had been over the course of the previous evening:

people shouted incomprehensibly from various directions, cars honked and hooted even though it seemed like the traffic wasn't moving so early in the day, and a buzz coming from everywhere as people spoke to one another brought it to life. The sidewalk was wide enough for them all to walk on with space for other pedestrians, too, all of whom avoided the rows of students, although most people turned back for another look as they passed by, only to find the students looking right back at them with equal curiosity.

The walk to Grand Central Station was only a few minutes. They walked to the end of the street, then took another left, and there it was, a massive building that was wider than tall. Atop the building was an analog clock with Roman numerals carved out of stone, some Roman deities, and behind them, an American eagle. Oak leaves carved out of stone adorned the top of the building's architecture, and latticework arched windows were spaced along the outer wall. Extending from the front of the building over 42nd Street was a viaduct that overshadowed Park Avenue.

"That's the Pershing Square Viaduct," Sarah murmured absently beside Amy. "They use it to recognize holidays like Christmas with lights and stuff.

They turned and crossed the widest marked crosswalk any of them had seen, walking beneath the viaduct. One or two kids pointed and stared upward, quickly reprimanded by Ms. Fleming.

"Kids, no stopping on the road," she called. "Eyes forward, please. Safety first."

Grand Central Station was just as massive on the inside,

and none of the kids were prepared for it. People rushed back and forth throughout the building, yet it was less crowded inside than outside. The back wall had a board of departure times in full view from all directions. Up ahead, Amy watched Dez and his travel buddy, David, spinning in a circle with their arms spread. They must have asked the students closest to them to give them some room because everyone dispersed. There was more than enough space too. Isaac and Will started up next, and Amy couldn't help it; she joined in.

"Kids, kids, come on," Mr. Rice called, laughing at the students who had started doing circles. Amy wasn't alone in joining the boys, but Sarah looked on like she thought they were crazy. "We're going to be taking the subway next, so we'll be heading down one of these passages here." He gestured to a wide side passage that led them downward and deeper into the terminal, then led the way for everyone to follow him.

When they reached the bottom of the passage, they were in another square room with high ceilings. This one's ceiling was painted, making the students "ooh" and "aah." Mr. Rice leaned in to say something softly to Ms. Fleming, and then they stopped walking forward.

"We have a bit of time to spare, so who wants to see something cool? I need two volunteers. You don't have to be travel buddies."

Dez's hand shot upward without hesitation, and then, further behind him, Will put his hand up, too.

"All right! Dez, Will, come up to the front, please."

Amy and Isaac peered over the heads of other students,

watching Mr. Rice quietly speak to Will while Ms. Fleming spoke to Dez. Then, bewildering the students who watched them, the two boys ran to opposite corners of the room. They were perhaps fifty feet apart. There, they stood facing the corners of the rooms at exact distances from one another in diagonal directions. They looked back at the teachers, both of whom gave them a thumbs-up from where they stood with the other students. The boys faced the corners again, and for a few moments, they appeared to be speaking to the walls.

"Whoa, cool!" Will suddenly shouted, his voice echoing throughout the chamber. From where she stood, Amy saw him duck his head the way he did when he was embarrassed, then he went back to talking to the wall.

Ms. Fleming and Mr. Rice both laughed.

"Does anyone know what Dez and Will are doing right now?" He looked around at the kids. "No one?"

By this point, the boys had returned to the group, both slightly pink with excitement—and then run back.

"Dez, would you like to let the class know what you were doing?"

"Will and I were talking to each other," Dez grinned. "It's like a phonic illusion or something."

"Indeed," Mr. Rice nodded. "There are some who believe that this was intentional, but whether accidental or otherwise, this area is the whispering gallery of Grand Central Station. There are a few places around the world with whispering galleries where you can do something similar to this one; with one person being across a room or in a different area entirely than the other person, the two can converse, and their voices will travel clearly."

"Awesome," and "Cool," rang out among the kids.

"We don't have time for everyone to have a turn, but maybe two other pairs. Let's go with travel buddies this time."

The next two kids chosen raced across the room to the four separate corners and began whispering to one another from their distances. Two exclaimed excitedly, much like Will had, but not nearly as loudly. Amy smiled at the memory, looking over at him. She couldn't tell if Will reacted from the back of his head. When the kids came back, they were as breathless and pink as Dez and Will had been.

"Thanks, Ms. Fleming and Mr. Rice," they said as they took their places back in line.

"That was so fun," Amy heard a girl cry out.

They continued until they were underground in an area all of them could recognize. The ceilings were lower, and the pillars were tiled with the number **42** on them, indicating their street stop. Subway trains zoomed into and out of the tunnels, and people waited to catch theirs, with barely enough breadth for passengers to hop off. In the case of the students and their teachers, they were given more space than the average person. It might have helped that there were too many for one person to push past. The kids stayed close to their teachers, who led the way through entranceways and onto their train through two separate doors, breaking the group up between two cars. Without their travel buddies, the kids were all mixed up.

Slipping past their classmates, Will and Amy found

refuge in the back of the subway car. They shared a smile, their hands intertwined around the grab bar, just as the train lurched forward. But their peaceful moment was shattered by a trio of rowdy teens.

"Yo, B-town, nice Red Sox cap," the biggest one sneered, cornering them.

Will rolled his eyes, a smirk playing on his lips. "We're just visiting from Massachusetts."

The local teens hand lashed out, knocking Will's cap to the floor. "Wrong place, wrong time, B-town. This is Yankee territory."

Will felt the familiar warmth of his Protection Gem. He knew he was safe, but he didn't want a fight. Amy retrieved his cap, whispering, "Let's go."

The local teen then shoved Will as they tried to leave. But Will, shielded by the gem's invisible force, didn't budge.

"What's up, B-town? Why so stiff?" the teen taunted, pushing harder. He recoiled, nearly falling into his friends.

Their confusion morphed into anger. Suddenly the teen noticed Amy's glowing Prophecy Gem. "What's that?" he demanded, seizing her hand.

Instantly, both Amy and the teens minds were transported to a dark, dilapidated apartment. There they witnessed a man beating the boy with a leather belt, the boy's cries echoed "No, dad, no, stop!" filled the air. Amy reluctantly recognized what she was witnessing, the teen did as well.

The vision ended abruptly, leaving them facing each other in the subway car. Will leaned into Amy's side. "Are you, okay?"

Amy nodded, then looked into the local teen's eyes. "You need to get help. Nobody should be treated like that." A wave of calm washed over the teen. "I'm sorry," he muttered, turning away and motioning for his friends to follow.

Will replaced his cap, looking at Amy. "What happened?"

"My Prophecy Gem," she explained, "It showed him a vision. I think it might have saved him. Do you think anyone noticed?"

"No, I think we're okay." Will replied.

As quickly as it began, it came to an end as the train screeched to a stop. Will and Amy discretely rejoined their classmates having arrived at their stop. The teachers quickly led them out of the station and out into the sunshine. The whole thing passed by in a blur, and the kids were glad to be reunited with their travel buddies at the end of it.

"That was insane," Dez told Amy.

"More than you know," Amy added.

In a few short paces, they were given a walking tour of Central Park, although Mr. Rice reminded them that they didn't have time to explore every pathway in the park. The entrance into the park was over an arching bridge that felt magical, with a pond beneath whose surface was broken every so often by fish below and frogs above. "This is called Gapstow Bridge. Pretty, isn't it?" He pointed to the field on the southwest side of the park.

"That over there is called Sheep Meadow. Does anyone

know why that is?"

The students looked out over green fields that seemed to stretch as far as they could see. People were picnicking on outstretched blankets, and a group of four kids played with a Golden Retriever and a frisbee.

"Because they used to have actual sheep here?" Someone asked, their voice laced with uncertainty.

"That's right! This meadow was designed to give city folk the feel and taste of pastures out in the country since they didn't have much of that themselves. The sheep used to keep the grass manicured, but the entirety of Central Park was man-made. It was believed that looking at the grass and animals, before it became a walking and playing space as we now see it, would be good for mental health."

They walked on, past several other monuments, but stopping wasn't on the agenda. The walk over to the Bethesda Fountain and Bethesda Terrace in the center of the park was a bit long for Ms. Fleming and Mr. Rice's liking, so the students settled for marveling at it from afar. Their last stop before they left the park was another fairytale location: a wide stone staircase curved out to welcome them through to a garden that was hidden along a steep hillside.

Before they took the steps, Mr. Rice stopped everyone at the entrance. "This is known as a Quiet Zone here in the park, so we want to keep our voices down. People enter this enchanting area to escape the world outside for a while, so I thought it might be nice for us to stop by. Also, I know you're all doing Shakespeare this year, so maybe you can get some extra English credit." He winked. "This area is known as the Shakespeare Garden and is filled with botanical samples that he mentioned in his works. It was a tribute dedicated to the bard in 1916 and modeled after Victorian-era rock gardens."

◆◆◆

At the MET, Dez, Isaac, Will, and Amy were reunited.

"Okay, kids, we can spread out a bit more here, but we're all to meet back here in two-hours," Mr. Rice told them at the museum entrance. Various security officers watched over the kids closely, and it occurred to them that the teachers had arranged for them to have a day of freedom in the museum. Hardly anyone else was around.

Will set an alarm on his watch for just under two-hours and then he and Isaac quickly went to their friends, while their travel buddies went separate ways, most likely to reunite with their own friends. The teachers watched the kids split off with some amusement, splitting up themselves to stay with, or at least near, the groups.

Amy and Dez were waiting for them at the entrance to the Medieval Art Gallery.

"Cool weapons, anyone?" Dez wiggled his eyebrows.

The boys didn't even answer Dez, walking on ahead into the gallery. Amy dragged behind, watching and listening.

"Whoa, check out this chainmail and armor!" Dez called. A jingling sound followed, and Amy looked up to see him shaking the silver back and forth. He was about to go for the helmet when Isaac smacked his hand to Dez's back.

"You can't touch the stuff, man. We'll get in trouble."

"Oh, right. Sorry." Dez continued to look through the Medieval Art Gallery, occasionally murmuring something in awe, though his exclamations were seemingly to no one in particular. "A single ball flail! Imagine actually fighting with these things."

Isaac, making sure no one was around, straightened the chainmail, causing the minor ripples that Dez had left in the vest to disappear. Then he walked off in his own direction, pausing when he came to a gallery full of European sculptures and artwork. At first, he didn't notice it at all and was ready to walk past the passage leading into it, moving on to look at a battle-axe, but something caught his eye, and he turned back to the exhibit, entering it without his friends. He heard Dez give another excited cry as he turned away, something about a Viking battle-axe, perhaps the same one he'd been interested in. Isaac ignored it, entering the gallery and making his way to the black sculpture, standing in stark contrast to the white wall beside it.

As he approached it, Isaac realized it wasn't black at all, but bronze. Part of its form was unmistakable, one he had been face to face with quite recently, though only as a fiery vision: it was a minotaur that appeared to be in some kind of tussle with a Greek hero. Both the characters were extremely detailed and muscular, with little sign of clothing on their forms apart from the helmet the hero wore on his head. The hero towered over the beast, whose body was bent in a defensive position that was almost horizontal, a leg around the hero seemingly the only thing that kept it from falling to the ground. Their bodies together created a triangular shape with the hero as the peak. He was poised to end the beast's life, a blade in his right hand, pulled back and ready to be brought down.

Beneath the sculpture, Isaac read the title:

Theseus Slaying the Minotaur

"Quite something, isn't it?" Isaac jumped at the sound of Ms. Fleming's voice. He turned to see her standing slightly behind him. It was just the two of them. "It's French, dating back to somewhere between the 1700s and 1800s," Ms. Fleming continued.

"Who was Theseus?" Isaac asked, looking back toward the sculpture.

"According to Greek mythology, he was a legendary hero, one of the early kings of Athens. Like most Greek heroes, he was famous for getting rid of the bad guys; villains, and wild and dangerous beasts, such as centaurs, and this was perhaps his most celebrated, certainly his most famous, adventure. It was the day he slew the terrible and fearsome creature with the body of a man and the head of a bull, the Minotaur, who dwelled in the mysterious labyrinth at Knossos. Haven't you heard that story?"

Isaac shook his head. He knew of legends that included minotaur's who hid in labyrinths. However, he couldn't recall ever having heard their source.

"Well, before Theseus entered the labyrinth, no one had ever come out alive. At least, that's the belief. But I'm no history teacher," she gave a high-pitched laugh, and Isaac wondered if he had ever heard it before. "Anyway, are you going to be okay in here?"

Isaac nodded. "Yeah, I'm okay. Will has an alarm for us to all meet back at the front."

"Good," Ms. Fleming nodded, and with that, she turned and left him on his own again.

Isaac continued to read the plaque beneath the sculpture. According to it, Theseus was believed to be either the son of a powerful king or the son of the Greek deity Poseidon. There were differing tales of why the tribute was sent, but King Minos of Crete chose seven young men and seven young women to sacrifice to the terrible beast, and seeking an end to the barbarity, Theseus volunteered to be one of the next seven men to enter the cavern. The journey was more complex than he thought it was going to be; the cavern was more than a dark tunnel that led them to a monster, but rather a labyrinth that got deeper and wound around and around in what seemed like endless circles. Theseus had to search levels and layers of a maze to find the monster and battle it to the end.

When he was done reading, Isaac gave the sculpture one last glance, paying extra attention to the beast's features. He had to restrain himself from reaching out to touch the statue, in particular, the horns, which appeared to be so sharp from afar. *Would they pierce my finger until I bled?* He shivered at the thought, knowing that the real thing certainly would pierce him if given the chance. Isaac reached down, and through his shirt, he could feel the comfort of his Power Gem dangling from his neck.

Suddenly feeling on edge, he decided to move on, looking at other, less scary sculptures of Greek deities and their mostly human children. He passed Perseus, holding the slain head of Medusa, with tendrils of hair carved to look like snakes. Hercules was entangled in some strange and exaggerated depiction of a struggle with Achelous, a river god that transformed from man to bull to serpent. There were other, more boring pieces of art, at least as far as Isaac was concerned, like tables elaborately carved and designed in the mid-seventeenth century, and he walked past those fairly quickly. The truth was he was unsettled by the statue of Theseus slaying the Minotaur and in a semi-hurry to get out of the exhibit and return to his friends. He simply didn't want to admit that yet.

Back in the Medieval Art Gallery, Dez had explored his fair share and was ready to move on when he realized that Isaac was missing. "Yo, where did Isaac go?"

Amy and Will were about to leave the gallery together. They looked around the room but couldn't find Isaac anywhere.

"I think he might have gone into one of the passages earlier," Amy offered. She pointed in the direction of one of the arched doorways. "I saw him around there last, not long after we came in here."

"Okay then," Dez shrugged. "I guess I'm gonna go and find out what was interesting enough for him to ditch us."

Will chuckled. "Meet us in the American Wing."

"Sure, man," Dez walked off.

"The American Wing?" Amy asked when he was gone, looking curiously at Will.

"I know you like art, and I saw a bunch through the door. Come on," he held his hand out to her, and, cheeks deepening in color, she placed hers in his as he led her to one of the other passages they'd already passed by.

At the entrance, Will came to a sudden stop, and Amy bumped into him, giggling as she pulled back. He put his index finger to his mouth to shush her, smiling as he poked his head through the door and looked around.

"Looks like it's just us so far," he grinned and walked in. They could hear the sound of other students entering the Medieval Art Gallery behind them. "Hurry."

With that, he tugged on her hand, and they ran into the exhibit until they found themselves beneath a glass ceiling, in an area modeled after a courtyard. There were potted plants and stone benches set between sculptures and paintings.

"What is this place?" Amy asked. Neither of them expected an answer, but a male voice came from above.

"This is one of our most recently updated exhibits," he said. They glanced up to see a museum attendant walking down a set of stairs to their level. "The museum itself was established in 1870, and the American Wing was added in 1924, but this skylit courtyard was actually only added this year."

Amy's eyes lit up. Still holding Will's hand, she walked over to one of the stone benches and sat down. He took a seat beside her, and they sat together for a few minutes, looking around the room. The museum attendant smiled at them before leaving them to enjoy the silence. Amy found it peaceful, *I always feel safe with you*, she mouthed, glancing around at the carefully carved white stone sculptures of women in fancy gowns and the domestic paintings that didn't have a theme beyond being American. There were paintings of ships on the water, paintings of flowers, and paintings of men gathered in plain rooms around large tables.

After some time, Amy wanted to see more than she could from the bench and stood, Will following her. They began walking through the exhibit, out of the natural light and into artificially lit areas where paintings were carefully hung on the walls. They walked quietly together; Amy keenly aware that Will's fingers were intertwined with hers. She imagined they were older, visiting the city without their teachers and peers, and that this was a date. Will did too.

"Wow, this one's beautiful," Amy walked over to a painting of a contemplative woman sitting at a writing desk. She was pale, with auburn hair tied in a messy bun, and there were papers scattered before her.

"The Letter," Will read the title on the plaque beneath it. "She looks kinda like you."

Amy laughed and let go of his hand to give him a playful slap on the arm. "No, she doesn't."

"Ok she doesn't," he argued, smiling. Then, he leaned in to kiss her cheek and watched as it turned even pinker.

They had walked through most of the American Wing and were on their way back to the entrance when they heard Dez's voice. "Man, I have no idea where those two went. They said to meet them in the American Wing."

"This is the American Wing," Isaac said. "It's bigger than I thought it would be. Is that a skylight?"

"Yep, it is! And it's new!" Amy called. She and Will had found their way to the same spot where the museum attendant had been when he came across them in the skylit courtyard.

"There you are!" Dez said, bouncing up from the same bench Amy and Will had been on. "What are you? The lady of the house?"

They all laughed, Amy and Will rejoining their friends in the courtyard.

"Guess what?" Isaac asked, continuing without waiting for anyone's guess, to Amy's amusement. "We found the Egyptian Art Gallery."

"What are you waiting for? Let's go," Will said excitedly.

It didn't take long to get there. Towering above them stood the Temple of Dendur, a Roman structure from Nubia. According to the plaque beneath it, an emperor paid to have the structure carved and then dedicated it to the Egyptian goddess Isis—the mother of Horus, the kids knew from their summer research—and her siblings. Two stone figures stood guard beside it.

When the kids walked into the room, they were first greeted with the most obvious sights of several different hieroglyphics of varying sizes and tablets with Egyptian symbols carved into them; some on tables, some in glass cases, and some standing freely on their own platforms because they were too big for any other display. With all that they knew, the kids felt at home right away. One or two other students walked through the exhibit, unaware that the four sons of Horus had entered it, the chosen Protectors of the North, South, East, and West. The defenders of the children of men felt their excitement rise as they began checking out the cool artifacts.

There was an undeniable energy circulating about them, one they each felt, a sensation coming from around and within them. The gems on their chests felt alive, as if they were trying to communicate with their wearers in some way.

"Please tell me I'm not the only one feeling that," Dez murmured quietly. Alongside the energy came something else; the feeling of being watched.

"No," Amy shook her head. She glanced around the room, checking if anyone was looking their way. "Our gems?"

"Maybe we should keep our heads down here," Will said. "We don't want to attract any unwanted attention, right?"

"Good plan," Isaac nodded. "We're... linked in some way to this place, to the things from this ancient past... Let's explore quietly."

They nodded and walked together. Amy noticed a large, colorful tapestry filled with Egyptian deities. Hieroglyphics were elaborately interwoven between the different figures. Her eyes rolled upward until she reached the top, and her eyes widened. "There he is," she whispered.

The others followed her gaze up the long tapestry, Will speaking first. "Horus!"

"That must be Set he's battling," Amy added. "And now he has returned to rise again."

They admired the image in all its glory: Horus battling Set, as inscribed in the tale of the Sacred Drama, each holding long spears and pointing at one another, with Set in his traditional smiting pose. The Eye of Horus was woven into the fabric, too, near the bottom. Internally, the kids knew this Horus was only a symbol of the real Horus, the one they saw and heard in their own minds.

Will nodded solemnly. "Don't worry. We *will* stop him."

Turning away from the tapestry, the kids noticed that they were no longer alone in the Egyptian Gallery. Olivia, Myra, and Daria were watching them from a short distance away. If anyone else had seen them there, they might have looked like they were reading one of the tablets in a glass display. As it was, the kids decided to move on, walking in a different direction from the foreign exchange students without saying anything to one another.

"I hope they didn't hear us," Amy said quietly when the girls were no longer in sight.

Will tilted his chin, gesturing to keep walking forward until they crossed into another area of the Egyptian Gallery. A long wall display protected by glass lined a large part of the room. Dez and Isaac walked over to it while Amy and Will remained near the entrance.

"Do you think they'll follow us?" Amy whispered. They were careful to stay hidden behind an alcove at the entrance. Someone would need to enter the room to see them.

"I'm not sure," Will responded. "I figured we could wait, and you know, if we see them walk past, we'll know for sure."

"Guys, check this out!" Dez cried out.

With one last glance out of the area, satisfied that the

girls were nowhere in sight, Amy and Will went to join the other two. They were still standing at the long glass display. Inside it, inscribed on papyrus, were the ancient scrolls of Imhotep.

"The Book of the Dead," Will read the title. "That sounds scary."

"I didn't know it was a real thing," Isaac said. "I heard it mentioned once in a horror movie. Look at this," he pointed to the description beneath the title. *"The Book of the Dead of the Priest of Horus, Imhotep.'* It was written by the Priest of Horus."

Dez smirked. "Well, at least we know where it is now if we need it later."

"This place is starting to give me the creeps," Amy admitted, glancing around yet again.

"Yeah, let's get out of here," Will said. "We have enough to worry about."

Mercifully, the alarm on his watch started beeping, warning them all that they had a few minutes to get back to the entrance of the MET.

After the MET, the class climbed onto the coach bus waiting for them outside.

"The bus will be taking us to the Cathedral of St. John the Divine now," Mr. Rice told the students from the front of the bus as they began their journey. "It's known to be the largest cathedral in the world."

The trip wasn't long, though the sun hung low in the sky by the time they arrived. It was then that they realized the word "large" was used only because there couldn't possibly be many descriptions to adequately describe the size of the cathedral. It was huge, with sharply pointed towers peeking out the sides and back, and a flower symbol marking the center of the building. A staircase, as wide as the building itself, led up from the street.

They stepped out of the coach bus onto the sidewalk, and Will gazed up at the building in awe. "This is so cool," he said to Isaac. "Maybe I should be an architect someday... So I can design cool buildings like this one."

"You should," Amy appeared at his other side, overhearing what he'd said. "You have a wonderful imagination."

"It's a Byzantine-Romanesque style of architecture," Mr. Rice told him. "And I quite agree with Amy. You could absolutely be an architect with your imagination, Will."

Will ducked his head low, thanking his teacher with some embarrassment. Then, the kids followed the teachers up the stairs and into the cathedral. Mr. Rice paid the admission fee for everyone and, after declining the guided tour for an extra fee, began giving one of his own.

"The cathedral is probably the oldest building any of us have ever been in, with its construction beginning in 1220. It was built in several stages, starting once as a simple brick church dedicated to the evangelist."

Will glanced up at the tall ceilings and the windows with their black frames, finding it hard to believe that such an elaborate building started so small. He found the details of the building distracting, wandering through passage entrances and then rejoining the group before they moved too far. He missed parts of what Mr. Rice said until they were moving beneath a crossing tower in the shape of a dome.

"The construction of the church was finished earlier than expected with the completion of its wooden crossing tower, in the 1520s. But there was a devastating fire in 1584, and then the rebuild was completed around the 1600s when this dome shape came into place."

The sound of their footsteps echoed along the walls as they walked through the stone passages. Mr. Rice stopped speaking, appreciating the architecture.

"That's all for now, kids. You're welcome to explore for..." He checked the watch on his wrist. "Let's say thirty minutes. Then we'll be on our way to Upper Manhattan for dinner."

The cathedral was one of the quietest places they'd ever been. It was mostly empty, too, which made every sound seem louder, as there was nothing to absorb the noises echoing up and down the halls. Amy, Dez, Isaac, and Will were glad for a relaxing venue to visit after the excitement and eerie energy they'd felt at the MET. Will and Amy sat on a bench where the sun shone through one of the tall windows, and Dez and Isaac played balance beam on a lined pattern that ran across the floor beneath their feet. As the minutes ticked by, Amy watched Will taking in the cathedral, a smile pulling at the corner of her mouth as she thought about *Will the architect.*

"Come on, everyone," Mr. Rice called from somewhere inside, rounding the class up to leave the cathedral.

With some disappointment, the kids got up and raced outside, joining the rest of the students at the very back of he queue as they all boarded the coach bus once more. Mr. Rice counted their heads as they climbed aboard.

"Does anyone remember where we are headed this evening?" He asked.

"Upper Manhattan!" Dez's roommate, Peter, called from somewhere up front.

Mr. Rice smiled. "Yes, and what will we be overlooking during dinner?"

"The Hudson River!" Peter answered again before anyone else could, redeeming himself and then climbing onto the bus himself.

"And can anyone tell me what event during the American Revolution was on the Hudson?"

"Something to do with Rock Hudson?" Sarah asked.

"No, no, not that... I can give you a hint. It had something to do with George Washington."

"The Battle of Long Island," a student called lazily, the next to enter the bus.

"They don't often answer questions," Isaac murmured to Will.

"I know," he nodded.

"Yes, very good," Mr. Rice exclaimed. "Another question for you all: who's hungry?"

Several students made noise, some whistling and others shouting variations of "yes." Will and Isaac realized they were trailing behind. Ms. Fleming, who the kids hadn't noticed was missing from the group, crept up behind the boys just as they began to pick up their pace.

"You two better catch up," she said. "We wouldn't want to leave you behind."

CHAPTER 11
OUT OF THE SHADOWS

E vening fell fast over the Roosevelt Hotel, sneaking up on the tired eighth-grade class of Wixon Middle School—in a satisfied, accomplished sort of way. The hustle and bustle of the city that never slept played out like a concert beyond the walls of the historic hotel, endless echoes of sirens, car horns, shouts, and whistles swallowed up by an ever-hungry night. Inside the hotel, all seemed calm and quiet. Isaac and Will slept soundly in their assigned room, undisturbed by the creak of the floor beyond the door or the dark shadow cast below it as a strange figure stopped right outside. The knob turned slowly, round and round, until it stopped with a click as the internal locking cylinder limited it from going any further.

It spun back as if whatever was on the other side let go of it, snapping back into its original place. Then the knob turned again, this time with violent velocity. With an ease that could only come from a source of great strength, the locking cylinder inside snapped with a gratifying click and the door swung open with a low whine. The dark, shadowy figure stretched its arm out and pushed it wide, its large body crossing over the threshold and entering the room unbeknownst to the boys in their beds.

The drapes were open, moonlight shining down on and illuminating Isaac's small figure as he breathed contentedly, his chest rising and falling in a steady rhythm. He did not feel the presence of the big otherworldly beast that stood above his bed. If anyone were in doubt about the strength of the savage and powerful creature of legend seeing its huge and bulging muscles would strike all uncertainty from their minds. With the head of a raging bull, long protruding horns, and a flaring snout, and the strong beefy body of a man, it leaned in over the boy. Its breath was hot and moist, but Isaac slept on. The narrow eyes in its head burned like orange embers filled with pure evil. It wielded powerful arms and hands tipped in long clawed fingers that resembled kitchen knives made to slice through skin and even bone. Its legs staggered on two rock-hard hooves, and it had a bull's tail, tipped with fur. It looked like it had walked straight out of Isaac's horrible vision in the flames of his family menorah, but this minotaur was all too real, filled with rage and a divine and insatiable hunger for human sacrifice. This was a being made of flesh, with blood pulsing warmly through its veins.

The creature growled low in its chest at the sight of the glowing green gemstone on Isaac's chest. It tilted its head, green mirrored in its eyes. The Power Gem was reacting to the danger above the boy. The minotaur raised its massive hand, readying itself to snatch both the gem and Isaac's head right along with it. The impossibly sharp claws glinted in the moonlight. As its arm struck downward it was intercepted by another boy's arm.

"Watch out!" Will screamed, one hand between the minotaur and Isaac's head and the other gripping his Protection Gem tightly in his fist.

With an enormous amount of energy glowing green from his shielding arm, Will turned and raised his arm up redirecting it back at the minotaur, sending the beast flying backward. Its form crashed loudly into the wall causing dust and debris to fly out in every direction. Barely a moment later the minotaur rose quickly to its hooved feet, horns swinging. Will felt his heart skip a beat in fear as the beast grunted, the threatening sound echoing in their small hotel room.

A mouth filled with razor-sharp teeth opened up and the voice it released was deep and haunting: "Sons of Horus reborn, surrender your souls to Set!"

The minotaur leaped out at them from the corner of the room, its claws extended, prepared to take their gems and their lives if necessary. Isaac leaped from his bed and stepped toward it, the boy who was once fearful of participating in the simplest of quests out of concern for his worrying mother showed no fear at that moment. The comforting strength of his Power Gem radiated through him like an electrical current. He raised his arms and crisscrossed his hands over one another in a defensive stance, and with a focus of energy he delivered a devastating burst of energy down upon the vengeful minotaur just as the beast was about to collide with his small frame. The minotaur crashed into the green glow as if it were a solid barrier, its reared snout coming to a sudden stop against what appeared to be an invisible wall. It roared angrily when it realized it was being held at bay. Behind Isaac, Will positioned himself with one hand cupped on his friend's shoulder and the other wrapped tightly around the Protection Gem, making the energy shield Will had brought forth between them and the beast impenetrable.

With another furious roar, the minotaur slammed its big hands down on the glowing light emanating from Will's shield, but it couldn't touch either of the boys. When it roared, their shield couldn't keep the beast's warm awful breath from reaching them and they both grimaced as it hit their senses. The beast tried again, slamming its clawed fists down harder, and was suddenly tossed upward and back, thrown like a horned ragdoll into the already crumbling wall its body had smashed into before. Plaster rained down from the ceiling as the building suffered under the weight of the mythical creature. More dust filled the air, creating a smoky effect that the boys couldn't see through, and the room shook like an earthquake, drawers opening and books clattering to the floor from the sheer force of the impact.

Isaac and Will's hearts raced as they stared into the dust,

keeping their focus on the bubble of energy protecting them both. As the dust settled they squinted into the corner where the minotaur had landed only to find that it was gone. Neither of them moved.

"Where did it—"

Will's question was cut off by the sound of a man screaming somewhere beyond their room, a horrible sound that made both boys drop their hands immediately. The power of their combined shield died down, and the room darkened without its green light. The damage from their tussle with the minotaur was partially hidden in shadow and partially exposed by moonlight. Beyond their room, they heard the man howling again in obvious pain. With one last glance at each other, they raced out of their room and into the hallway. The door on the other end had been thrown open and its shattered wooden pieces were hanging in barely connected tatters from its broken hinges. Lying on the floor beneath it was their teacher.

"Mr. Rice!" The boys cried out, running to his aid. They both landed on their knees with hard thuds beside him.

Their teacher was conscious, looking up at them through narrowed eyes. His voice strained from pain and his breathing labored, he mumbled, "It was a great beast... nothing I've ever seen... You must get the other students to safety. Forget about me!"

The other students must have heard Mr. Rice's screams because along the hallway the doors to their rooms began to open and the curious and frightened faces of the other kids peeked out at the carnage in the hall. Mr. Rice clutched his side tightly, but blood spilled out between his fingers in gushes seeping into the burgundy carpet.

Ms. Fleming opened her door on the opposite end of the hallway; she was wearing pajamas and a serious expression. "I called 911! Everyone, just stay in your rooms and close the doors. Help is on the way!" Some students hurriedly disappeared back into their rooms shutting their doors as she walked down the hall. She gave another call to the stragglers. "Back in your rooms!"

The last of the doors shut with Isaac and Will remaining where they were. Ms. Fleming glanced up and down the hall, then quietly told them, "Stay with him. And be careful. Hopefully, whatever it was doesn't come back this way."

Surprised, the kids nodded their understanding and Ms. Fleming returned to her room, shutting the door behind her.

"Maybe she's just getting dressed," Isaac offered weakly.

Will turned back to their history teacher. He didn't have time to worry about why Ms. Fleming was behaving so strangely. They could see that Mr. Rice was gravely injured and seemed to have also sustained a head injury, with blood slowly beginning to drip from his nose and ears.

"Get Dez," Will said urgently. "We need his Health Gem."

Isaac turned to leave and the kids were surprised to see Dez already cautiously making his way over, looking over his shoulder at Ms. Fleming's door.

"Get your gem," Isaac called. "We need it now!"

Dez's hand reached up to his chest, to where his hemp necklace should have been and found it missing. "I don't have it. Let me check my room!"

He returned to his room for several minutes while Isaac and Will waited helplessly. When Dez finally came back he wore their same helpless expression looking down at Mr.

Rice moaning in pain on the floor. They turned to look at him expectantly, and he shook his head.

"I looked everywhere... it's gone."

"The minotaur must have gotten it," Isaac snapped angrily. "He came for mine, too. We have to find him; we can't just let Mr. Rice die."

"I agree. Let's go after it," Will nodded. "Dez, you stay here and find Amy. Isaac and I will try to track down the minotaur."

"Did you say *minotaur*?" Dez gaped at the other two.

"Yes, it was a minotaur!" Will stood up. Isaac followed suit, hopping to his feet.

"But how can you be sure?"

"Dude, don't tell me you never read *The Invincible Iron Man*, April #24? Trust me... That thing was a minotaur!"

With that, Isaac and Will ran the length of the hall and through the broken door. They continued down the stairwell, making it down one flight when both of them winced.

"Do you smell that?" Will asked.

"Yeah, it smells like a wet dog."

"It must be from the minotaur. I could smell it in our room as well."

They sped up, taking the stairs as fast as they could until they were six stories down with no sign of the beast other than the stench it left for them to follow. At the bottom of the stairwell there were two doors: one led to the lobby, and the other continued down to the basement. In silent agreement, they chose the basement and fear began to set in. The basement was darker, dimly lit with a narrower hallway. Will had to fight the urge to hold his nose closed between his thumb and fingers. When they reached the bottom there were even more basement stairs taking them deeper underground, so they kept going until they finally reached the end.

"We must be three stories underground," Will murmured.

"Stay behind me and be ready," Isaac told him.

The two began to explore the dimly lit rooms of the third basement level with quick, yet cautious steps. The air down in the basement was thick and warm. Most of the doors in the space were closed with padlocks attached. But one door looked as if it had been forced open, part of the lock on the ground and the metal handle bent. Isaac gestured to be quiet, pressing his index finger to his lips, and then they peered in finding an incinerator room. When they were sure it was empty, they stepped inside.

The machine buzzed away in the corner, and it smelled faintly of garbage. Heat came from the ventilator behind it and there was a bag of trash to the left of the incinerator. In the far corner, they could see an iron door.

"This must be how he got in," Isaac murmured. He pushed the door open, revealing a long dark tunnel. "We have to follow it."

Will opened his mouth to respond and then stopped. In the distance somewhere behind them in the stairwell they heard a call. They froze, listening intently. Just when they thought it wouldn't come again, someone cried out.

"Will! Isaac!"

"It sounds like Dez," Will whispered.

With a shaky breath, Isaac retreated from the tunnel, tugging on Will's arm. "Either way, we have to leave. If we can hear it, it's possible others have, too."

Will stared down the tunnel for a moment longer before allowing Isaac to pull him back. They shut the iron door and then made their way back up the stairs and out of the basement, moving quickly but carefully. Their only worry going down the stairs had been the minotaur. The fear of being caught, of anyone discovering the secrets they carried with them was perhaps stronger at that moment.

They were about to climb the sixth flight to the sixth floor when Dez cried out from the top of the stairs, "Will, Isaac! I found it." Behind him stood Myra, Daria, and Olivia. "Well," Dez corrected himself with some excitement. "Myra found my necklace."

Myra nodded, approaching the three boys.

"Where?" Will asked her.

"I found it near the stairwell," she said quietly.

Isaac furrowed his brow at this. "I guess he must have dropped it?"

Will didn't break his gaze from Myra's but stayed quiet. It seemed pretty suspicious that the minotaur would go out of its way to steal the gem and then carelessly drop it. Surely, a beast like that would have noticed losing it, especially if it was important enough to take? Besides, from his memory the minotaur was going to take a lot more from Isaac than his gem. Though, he kept his suspicions to himself.

"Let's get the girls to a safe place," Isaac said quickly, moving on from the topic of the minotaur. "Dez, you know what you have to do."

The boys led Myra, Daria, and Olivia to their rooms. Behind them, Dez knelt down on the floor next to Mr. Rice, growing weaker and weaker by the minute. Pressing the palm of his hand to Mr. Rice's forehead, Dez shut his eyes and a green glow started to shine through the back of his hand, getting brighter.

"What's he doing?" Myra asked.

She was about to turn to check when Isaac opened the door to their assigned room blocking her vision.

"Taking care of Mr. Rice until help gets here," he said forcefully. Then he gestured for the girls to enter their room while Will did his best to shield them from seeing anything.

CHAPTER 12
THE LABYRINTH

The paramedics arrived on the scene and prepared Mr. Rice for transport on a stretcher. He was no longer moaning in pain because he was unconscious. Dez, Isaac, and Will were huddled around the door to Dez's assigned room, taking turns watching through the keyhole as his still body was carried away by two EMTs dressed in blue. The blood around his ears and nose had dried, much to the kids' relief. A woman walked behind them ensuring everything went smoothly. Another official lingered near the broken door speaking quickly into a radio clipped to his shoulder; he looked like he might have been a policeman or detective, but the kids could only speculate.

"Looks like he's going to be okay," Dez said quietly.

"Mr. Rice will be okay, but he's going to talk eventually. There's no hiding this mess!" Isaac retorted.

"I think we will be okay," Dez added calmly. "He was really out of it when I was healing him with the Health Gem."

"Dude," Isaac shook his head. "That was a real-life minotaur. That thing was trying to get my gem and it wanted to take my head with it. If it wasn't for Will, I would've been dead meat."

Will backed away from the door, glancing over at Peter's bed. The other boy was fast asleep. According to Dez, the kid would sleep through a bomb. "My Protection Gem started to glow, and it woke me up." He lifted the necklace out from under his shirt so the others could see. "Look, it's still glowing bright."

"That's weird," Dez furrowed his brow. "Shouldn't it stop if the danger is over?"

Suddenly, goosebumps covered Will's entire body, the hair on the back of his neck and all down his arms standing on end as he glanced between his two best friends. Panicked, he cried out, "Where is Amy? I just noticed she hasn't been here this whole time?!"

Dez smacked his forehead with a groan. "I can't believe it! Between hunting for my gem and those girls suddenly showing up with it, I completely forgot to about Amy!"

For the briefest second, Dez's statement made Will pause, but then he swung open the door and quickly made his way to Amy's room. He looked back only to make sure the detective wasn't interested in him before picking up his pace. Dez and Isaac were right behind him.

At her door, Will had to stop himself from pounding on it. Instead, he raised his fist and calmly knocked twice. From the corner of his eye, he noticed his gem was still glowing and tucked it back underneath his shirt. When no one came to the door for several moments, he tried the knob and gave a sigh of relief when it swung open, but his heart sank when he realized what that could mean. The Minotaur could have accessed Amy's room just as easily. After all, his and Isaac's room had been locked and that hadn't stopped the minotaur from entering. He tried not to think the worst even as he glanced around the room and saw that she and her roommate were nowhere to be found.

"No, no, no," he whispered, shutting his eyes as panic flooded through his system and made his heart pound harder than anything else had that night.

"Sarah?" Isaac's voice broke into Will's spiraling thoughts. He opened his eyes. Isaac was crouched down on his hands and knees, his head under Sarah's bed. "Sarah, is that you?"

"Som... Som... Something..." Her low voice cracked and trembled when she tried to speak.

"It's okay. Take it easy," Isaac murmured, trying to soothe her frayed nerves. "Are you okay?"

Sarah nodded weakly, her breaths coming in short, shaky gasps.

"Are you hurt?"

She shook her head, eyes wide with fear.

"Okay, that's good. Take a breath. Where is Amy? Have you seen her?"

She took a deep shaky breath. "Something took her...

Something horrible took her!"

Will, Isaac, and Dez stared at her in disbelief, their worst fears confirmed. The Minotaur had kidnapped Amy.

"Students! All students, please come out of your rooms!" Ms. Fleming's firm voice rang out from the hallway before they could get any other answers out of Sarah. "Attention, all students please come out of your rooms into the hallway. I have an announcement for everyone."

Dez and Will joined the other students in peeking their heads out of the door to look up and down the hallway while Isaac helped Sarah out from under her bed. Ms. Fleming stood at the end where Mr. Rice was attacked. A sheet had been placed on the floor to hide the blood, and yellow tape was stuck around the door. There were also yellow numbered plastic markers in a few spots on the floor as the officials conducted their investigation. Ms. Fleming was flanked on either side by a police officer, both fully geared up in their uniforms. It wasn't unusual that their social studies teacher carried an air of authority about her, but standing between the two policemen made her look as if she were the one in charge.

"Is everyone accounted for?" Ms. Fleming raised her eyebrows expectantly, scanning the hallway for any signs of unaccounted students.

As Sarah opened her mouth to say something, Isaac gently nudged her shoulder with his own and was the first student to cry out, "Yes!"

Each student down the hallway followed his lead, doing the same, including Sarah. The boys could tell she was perplexed, but there was no time to explain. Things were already a mess and if the police found out Amy was missing, they knew it would only get worse.

"I just got word that Mr. Rice will be okay. Amazingly, he was not more seriously injured," Ms. Fleming told them all, her voice calm but tinged with concern. "However, I'm very sorry to say that the class trip has officially been canceled."

Many students groaned at this news, while others who had somehow missed all the commotion gasped in surprise. Dez caught Peter's baffled glance as he surveyed the mess in the hall.

"Yes, I know how disappointed you all must be, but some kind of wild animal is currently loose in the city. This poses a safety risk for us all. The hotel concierge has already begun reaching out to all your parents on our behalf to let them know you are okay and that we will be heading home tomorrow, earlier than planned." She gestured at the officer to her right. "This is Officer Daniel with the New York City Police Department. He has some words as well."

Seeing the police officer step forward in his official uniform made it all the more real for the kids and they paid close attention to everything he said in his distinctive New York accent. "Hello kids, as Ms. Fleming said, my name is Officer Daniel, D-A-N-I-E-L. I want to assure all of you that you are not in any danger; we have armed officers, NYC's finest, checking each floor as we speak and patrolling the streets around the hotel. We also have animal control and our local park rangers on the case and they know what they're doing when it comes to this sort of thing. Most importantly, I want you to remember there's nothing to be afraid of. Whatever this wild animal was, I'm sure it is more scared of you than you are of it."

"I doubt it," Dez mumbled under his breath.

"Sheesh, at least we have *some* good news," Will said softly. "They think it's all down to some kind of wild animal."

"Currently, we have detectives in route to the city zoo to see if anything escaped and our animal control friends are contacting the shelters too, just in case. But until we know more I must advise that all of you remain sheltered here where we can ensure your safety until you depart. Stay in your rooms, keep your eyes and ears open and let us know immediately if anything seems out of the ordinary. Do that and you should have nothing to worry about." He winked from under his cap.

"All right, students. Let's listen to Officer Daniel,"

Ms. Fleming cut into the whispers of the students. "As he said, please stay in your rooms for now and we'll let you know if anything changes. I'd also like you all to be respectful and cooperative with the police officers and hotel staff as they work to ensure our safety. I will see all of you in the morning. Pack up and be ready for the bus home and lock your doors. Goodnight."

Some students mumbled *goodnight* as they turned back to their rooms following Ms. Fleming's and Officer Daniel's instructions.

"We're going to find her," Isaac said to Sarah. "Give us some time."

Sarah glanced between the three boys, her eyes drifting down to the glow shining through Will's shirt. He put his hand over his chest, and she retreated to her room like all the other students without another word. The boys closed the door after her and Will led the way back to his and Isaac's room before anyone noticed anything amiss. He assumed it was a safe bet now that Peter was awake. Who knew; the other boy might have been wondering where Dez was right now. There was no yellow tape across their door; the police hadn't figured out that the wild animal had been in there. They slipped in without so much as a glance in their direction. The authorities were busy with more important things than three stray boys.

"We must act," Will said as they entered the room. "We need to search for Amy. The Minotaur must have kidnapped her for her gem and there's no telling what he'll do to her to get it off her finger!"

Dez surveyed the damage of Isaac and Will's battle under the moonlight, tiptoeing around piles of debris. "Holy..."

"Yeah, like I said, he wanted my gem *and* my head," Isaac said. "Will's right. We have to find Amy. And fast."

"We also have to be careful of Ms. Fleming," Will added. "She has been all over us this entire trip."

Isaac nodded, recalling how Ms. Fleming had come out of the shadows in the European Arts section of the museum. More than once she'd snuck up on him and Will. Isaac absently wondered if any of the others had a moment with her like that, where they'd been alone with her.

"Let's wait it out," Dez suggested. He sat down on the

edge of Isaac's bed. "They'll wrap up in the hall soon, right? They can't expect kids to sleep while they're running up and down."

"Dez, they slept through a minotaur attack, and no one has noticed Amy is missing except for us and Sarah. I think it's safe to say all expectations are out the window." Isaac flopped down onto Will's bed. "But I do think that we should wait it out like you said. What other choice do we have?"

Will grabbed his backpack and walked over to sit in front of the door. He peeked out every so often to check the status of the hallway while rifling through his backpack. He pulled out a few schoolbooks and some stationery, then said, "Okay, I'm ready."

"Ready for what?" Dez asked.

"To find Amy. I got some rope, a battery-powered flashlight, a set of matches, a Sharpie and some glue and tape. Just in case. I also got all four of us some rations."

This brought a grin to Dez and Isaac's faces, both of whom didn't think they'd have a reason to smile again so soon. Neither of them had a chance to say anything when Will spoke up again.

"The coast is clear!" He frantically whispered. "Now's the time!"

Will threw the door open, stuck his head through it, and looked both ways to make sure no one was in the hall further than he could see with the door closed. Satisfied that the coast truly was clear, he gestured for Dez and Isaac to follow him and darted out of the room, under the yellow tape, and through the broken door, down the stairwell with the boys right behind him. They descended as quietly as they could, taking the steps two at a time so as not to lose pace until they reached the lower basement stairway. They opened the door that would lead them further downward wincing when the stench of wet dog hit them square in the face.

"What is that?" Dez asked, covering his mouth with his elbow as he coughed into it.

"The Minotaur," Will answered grimly. "It smells like a wet dog. I guess there's not a lot of ventilation in the basement. I couldn't smell it anymore on the way down, but earlier we followed its smell down the stairs to the basement."

"Nasty," Dez remarked.

The other two boys, despite the situation, couldn't help chuckling. They nodded their agreement and continued into the dark passage. Will stopped to rummage in his backpack and then pulled out his flashlight clicking it on and lighting up the way ahead for them.

"Smart," Isaac commented as they closed the door to the basement behind them and continued down toward the incinerator room.

"These stairs just go on forever," Dez whispered, his voice softly echoing off the walls. "How deep *is* this place?"

"When Will and I came down here earlier, we figured we got about three stories down before we found the incinerator room."

"Whoa," Dez murmured.

"We're here," Will whispered back. "Come on, it's that

room over there."

Dez and Isaac followed the flashlight toward the incinerator room door. It was still open, just as they'd left it. Will shone the light into the corners of the room and the boys peered inside. All was quiet. There were no signs of movement or noises of any kind. In the back, they could see that the iron door was still shut so they went over to open it and then entered the passage.

The walkway wasn't what they would have called large, but it was big enough for the three of them to walk through side-by-side, and it was clearly big enough for the Minotaur to have walked through with Amy. The walls were made of large stone blocks and the ceiling was constructed of a brick archway that curved over their heads. They had been walking in a straight path for some time before anyone said anything.

"Today at the MET," Isaac started. "I read that minotaur's were known for hiding in labyrinths. There was this sculpture of a Greek hero named Theseus who slew one, but there were other stories of ancient warriors walking into the labyrinth and needing to navigate their way through a complex maze of tunnels to find the beasts. Then, when they found one, they would fight to the death in an effort to defeat it. In Theseus' case, no one had ever come out alive before he killed his Minotaur."

"Do you think we can defeat it by outwalking it?" Dez groaned. When Isaac looked sharply at him, he said "What? We've come down nine stories and you guys didn't come into this tunnel before. There's no telling how far *this* passage goes. And worse, we could get lost down here."

"I don't care!" Will suddenly cried out in frustration. "We have to find her. We're the Katzenstein Kids! How can we call ourselves that if we complain instead of doing something? How can we call ourselves that *without* her?"

Dez and Isaac exchanged a quiet look but said nothing, nodding somberly. Will turned away from them and continued down the passage. The rest of the walk was mostly quiet. The kids kept walking until in the distance the light caught something white, and they hurried toward it. As they got closer, it appeared to be the end of the tunnel, nothing but a wall with the number *34* painted on the stone. It soon became clear however, that it wasn't a dead end at all, but an intersection where two tunnels branched out to the left and right. If it weren't for Will's flashlight they would have missed it.

"Which way do we go?" Dez asked.

"I can't really smell the minotaur anymore," Isaac murmured. "Can you?"

"It all smells the same down here."

Will looked left and without a word began walking in that direction. Dez and Isaac followed. As far as either of them was concerned there was no point in trying to reason with Will until they found Amy, so they followed his lead through the seemingly never-ending passage. Unlike the last one it didn't feel like they were walking in a straight line. The passage turned and curved, became steep and then went downhill while the boys followed its winding path, walking past several tunnel entrances they deemed too small for the minotaur to fit through.

"If we have to crouch there's no way that thing got

through," Isaac stated reasonably.

By the time the winding passage had straightened out again it felt as though an hour or more had passed. They were no longer entangled in a maze of passages and tunnels too small to explore popping up on either side of them; they only had one path to follow. Dez released a huff of air through his nose every so often and Isaac brushed it off as exertion from the long walk, but it occurred to him that it could just as easily have been Dez's way of quietly complaining so Will didn't bite his head off again.

"Damn it, are you kidding me?" Dez exclaimed, pointing ahead. "The worst things keep happening! It's the same intersection, the one with the numbers *34* painted on the block."

Will shone the light upward, and sure enough the wall up ahead was the same one that they'd come to before.

"It must be 34th Street," Will said. "Let's go right this time. Last time we went left and just ended up back here. None of the tunnels along the last path were big enough for the Minotaur, so we can rule them out."

Will shone the light to the right, illuminating another seemingly endless passage and the three continued on their way. Before long they came across a steel door that had been forced open, its surface marred with dents that looked as if something big had slammed into it much like the one in the incinerator room.

"This must have been the route the Minotaur took," Will whispered excitedly. He shone the flashlight into the area making sure that they were alone and then the kids made for the door, certain they were now headed in the right direction.

The door had been damaged so Will gave a heave and then a grunt as he struggled to get it open on his own. Dez and Isaac joined in, Will holding the flashlight in between his teeth and Isaac counted.

"On three. One... Two... Three!"

They pushed together and the door shifted open with a rusty screech against the ground enough for them to shimmy through sideways. Isaac went through first, followed by Will, and then Dez passed the backpack and flashlight through the space before joining them on some concrete steps.

"Here you go," Dez handed Will his things, clicking the flashlight off. "I don't think we need that anymore."

"Wow, this is so cool," Dez said, glancing up. A dim string of lights hung from the ceiling lighting up a much larger tunnel than the passages they'd traversed thus far. "It looks like we're in a subway tunnel. The steps seem to lead down to an old track."

"Well, I got to tell you," Isaac called out, "Subway tunnels make for the perfect minotaur hiding place, they probably lead all over the city.

"Now which way?" Dez asked.

He wasn't pleased about having to put the flashlight away. Lighting their way through the tunnels had given him a sense of control and he already felt that slipping away. Ahead, it appeared there were two paths to choose from yet again, both of them running parallel with the old subway track: the one on the left cast in shadow and seemingly abandoned with dirt piles lining its entrance and the other lit up by the hanging lights on the ceiling.

"Look!" Will pointed at a spot near the tracks on the left and then ran ahead. He reached down into the dirt and picked up a silver hair barrette with a small glittery flower on it. For the first time since they learned Amy had been taken, Will lit up. "She must have dropped it on purpose for us to find. She wanted us to know she was taken this way." He pointed to the darker of the two passages.

"I wouldn't have expected anything else," Dez said with a sigh. He rolled his eyes and began trudging forward. "Here we go again."

With a mix of relief and disappointment, Will tugged the flashlight out of his backpack and flicked it back on lighting the way forward once more as the boys walked into the darkness along the old tracks. They didn't have far to go before they came to another lit area.

The walls on either side of them opened up to reveal walls and ceilings covered in white subway tiles. All three of them recognized the look of them from when they'd visited Grand Central Station. Rows of numbers lined the walls.

Dez walked up to one of the rows. He hadn't seen it from afar, but a faded white arrow pointed toward the numbers. "What do they mean?"

Will stepped off the track to join Dez, his shoes crunching against small stones on the floor. "20th, 18th, and 15th S-T-S.," he read. "They must be streets. New York has lots of numbered streets. The arrow is telling us we're headed towards those streets."

"But Amy could be anywhere down here... This place is

huge. Hundreds of miles of tunnels and passages."

"The perfect labyrinth," Isaac muttered grimly.

"Hey guys, check this out!" Isaac called from a few feet across the track. He had climbed onto the platform and was standing behind a tiled pillar, in front of a large board.

"What is it?" Will called over the sound of his footsteps as they ran over to Isaac, clattering and echoing against the tiles eerily.

"It's a map of the New York City Subway system," Isaac told them with some disappointment in his voice. When the other two joined him, they could see why. "Dez is right. We've been down here for hours. The sun is going to rise soon and we'll all have gone missing. Just look at this map. It's just like ancient mythology," he echoed his sentiment. "The Minotaur is using this place like a labyrinth and we've run out of clues as to where he could be hiding Amy."

Will glared at Isaac, heat rushing to his cheeks. "I can't Give up!" He paced up and down running his hands through his hair while he thought. "If only we had her Prophecy Gem, we could see where she is right now."

From a dark corner of the tunnel behind them they heard a scuffling and froze, holding their breath. Will instinctively clicked his flashlight off but realized that it wouldn't help; they were all standing under the light of the tiled area like deer in headlights.

A man's voice suddenly rang out from the darkness, raspy as if he had smoked too many cigarettes in his long lifetime: "Deeper and deeper you enter a bewildering maze from which no one has ever escaped."

Will's heart pounded as he took a small step forward, the shuffle of his shoes against the tile loud in his ears. He called into the darkness, "Who are you?"

Silence. The old man did not answer.

"Have you seen anything strange lately?" Dez added.

Again, the old man did not answer and the boys feeling confident enough began to move closer. This was not the Minotaur. Will hesitantly raised his flashlight. Its batteries were running low and in the dim light they could make out a dark and dirty face of what appeared to be a homeless elderly man. To their shock he appeared to have only one eye a sunken hole covered by skin and slightly red where the other should have been.

Under the light he leaned forward abruptly making Dez, Isaac, and Will leap backward away from him. They kept moving, Will refusing to take the light off the man until they had put distance between them and him. "This is from the vision, the vision we had in the basement Hideout last December," Will cried out. Isaac and Dez nodded in agreement.

"If it's strange you seek," the elderly man called after them in his raspy voice. "Follow the Cow Tunnel built beneath 12th Avenue… There, you will find the remains of the old slaughterhouses!"

"I know which way that is," Isaac whispered as he pointed toward the map on the wall as they continued onward, following his lead.

After a few steps in the new direction, Will turned back toward the one-eyed elderly man sitting in the dirt. "Thank you," he mumbled.

The old man replied, "Knowledge comes to those who seek it. A master can only point the way."

CHAPTER 13
HOLDER OF THE PROPHECY GEM

Amy's eyes opened groggily; her lids stuck to her eyeballs as they tried desperately to hold onto the last remnants of sleep, her tongue stuck to the roof of her mouth. The room was dark, and her senses came to her quickly as she tried to adjust to the lack of light, from the damp concrete floor beneath her to the musty odor overwhelming her nostrils. It was the type of smell one might expect in a basement, but Amy could tell that this was no basement. Looking down she noticed that her legs were shackled to a metal chain. It was more like a dungeon holding her prisoner than a basement. If she moved the chains jingled, so she tried not to do too much of that. She didn't want to draw unwanted attention to herself. Her body was cold, though, a cold that went deeper than the skin and when she stretched out her stiff limbs her muscles ached dully from being on such a hard surface for so long. But it appeared she wasn't injured. A scrape here and a bruise or two there. Nothing too serious.

From another room somewhere beyond hers she could hear a loud clunking noise. It took her a moment to realize that it sounded as if a herd of wild horses were running around, their hooves clattering on the hard floor.

Minotaur's! The memories came rushing back to her all at once.

After such a long and eventful day, it hadn't taken long before she started to drift off. It was in that in-between phase of sleep—where she felt the world fading away yet she still had a sense of her immediate surroundings—when she was snatched from her bed and carried into the depths of the underground by a huge hand. The Minotaur's clawed fingers had wrapped themselves around her waist, stealing her away in the night like she was little more than a rag doll. Amy kept her eyes shut for most of the journey, terrified that the beast might look down and notice she was awake. Part of her wanted to scream as they passed by the other students' doorways, and another part feared the beast's fingers might reflexively crush her, whether it meant to or not. Not to mention what it might do to anyone who tried to help.

The minotaur had taken her down three flights of stairs when she heard a terrible scream coming from a man somewhere behind them, all but confirming her worst fears.

They must have traversed for more than an hour through tunnels whose directions she couldn't keep track of in her exhausted and scared state when she felt herself beginning to lose consciousness again.

The Minotaur forced its heavy body through a metal door and for the first time since they'd entered the basement, they entered a dimly lit area, and a quick peek revealed an old subway track.

A sudden thought occurred to her. If anywhere is a good place to leave something behind as a clue for the others to find me it would be here, where it's less dark. She knew she didn't have a moment to waste. The Minotaur moved quickly. In a last-ditch effort she gave a lazy stretch in the Minotaur's hand, a movement she could easily have made while sleeping, but a calculated one. Her hand knocked her hair barrette free of its tendrils and it fell into a small pile of dirt near the tracks. She closed her eyes again as the Minotaur picked up its pace.

Amy couldn't remember the rest of their venture, nor could she escape the fear that bled into her memories of their twisting and turning descent into pure darkness. She had been kidnapped. But why? Amy's brow furrowed as she went through the possible reasons, and then fearing the worst, glanced down at her hand.

"Thank goodness," she breathed a sigh of relief at the sight of the mood ring on her finger. "I still have the Prophecy Gem."

Somewhere inside, a voice whispered that this was destiny—that everything she and the others had seen had brought her to this place. Whatever the Minotaur's were after, this was only the beginning.

BOOM! A large wooden door between the room Amy was in and the one adjacent burst open, slamming into the wall with a loud crash and making her flinch. In its opening stood three massive bulging beasts—minotaur's in every sense of the word, with threatening orange embers for eyes, giant horns pointing sharply out of their heads, flaring snouts, and sure enough hooves for feet. Amy looked on in disbelief; there were three as if one wasn't enough to deal with! Their entry brought a foul smell into the room, like a musty basement frequented by a pack of wet dogs. The stench made her grimace as she squinted up at the beasts from her position on the floor. She resisted the urge to cover her face with her arm. The last thing she wanted to do was anger or offend them in some way. Who knew what they needed her for, or what they would do if they found her less than useful?

Amy gulped down the lump that formed in her throat at the thought.

The largest of the three beasts stepped forward from the middle and spoke, much to her surprise, in a deep and thunderous voice. "Holder of the Prophecy Gem, your God calls upon you to serve!" Amy's heart pounded. The Minotaur's horns were so long that they almost touched the ceiling and she realized that she was in real danger. "Set, God of War and Chaos, Ruler of the Desert, Power over the Lands, Thunderstorms, Eclipses, and Earthquakes, calls upon you to reveal the location of the Was Scepter!"

Its breath smelled worse than its body, slamming into her face like a slap of hot stinking wind.

"I don't know what that is," she said, looking between the three Minotaur's.

"Tell us the location of the Was Scepter!" The beast repeated, a growl deep in its throat. It didn't believe her.

"I don't know what that is!" She cried out louder, looking between the three Minotaur's. Apart from their size it was difficult to tell the difference between them. "I can't help if I don't even know what that is!"

I wouldn't help you even if I did, she thought to herself.

The Minotaur to the left of the biggest one stepped forward with two heavy stomps that caused small pebbles on the floor around its hooves to shudder upward and bounce back down with a soft rattle, reaching out toward her. Reflexively, Amy threw her body backward, the chains clanking against the concrete as she tried to put distance between herself and the beast. It had a particular goal however and it clawed at Amy's hand before she knew what was happening, grasping for the Prophecy Gem on her finger. In the instant the beast made contact with the gem it glowed a blindingly bright green and shot a bolt of green energy through the Minotaur's arm, causing it to pull away with a cry of pain. Its beefy body spasmed twice, as if it had been electrocuted and it took several steps back again.

Amy glanced down at the ring. It was still glowing green.

The first Minotaur looked on angrily. "You fool," it shouted at its companion. "We have been resurrected from the Underworld. We are powerless against the Eye of Horus!"

"Yes, Draconis," the second one bowed its head in shame. "I should know better..."

Draconis, Amy thought. *The big one is Draconis. He must be the leader.*

The leader turned back to Amy, leaning in menacingly. "Are you willing to surrender your soul to Set, my dear?"

He saw the way she curled up even further against the wall and his eyes seemed to twinkle with pleasure, fiery cruelty blazing in their depths. "Oh yes," he nodded gleefully. "Soon Set will come for all the children of men," taking a deliberate pause, "and women, as he did for the Four Sons of Horus: Imsety, Duamutef, Hapi, and Qebehsenuef."

The mention of Qebehsenuef steadied Amy. She was scared—no more than that, she feared for her life—but at that moment a calm fell over her because she knew the beast standing before her was wrong. Horus' sons lived on; she herself was a part of the spirit of Qebehsenuef, Protector of the West and Holder of the Prophecy Gem. Deep down she knew that she was being watched over by Horus himself, and more importantly her friends Dez, Isaac, and Will must already be searching for her. They would find the breadcrumb she'd left for them; she knew they would.

They must be close, she reassured herself with a steadying breath, simply staring Draconis in the eye with a new sense of resoluteness.

The big minotaur grew impatient, pointing his clawed finger down at Amy's face. She dared not flinch or blink. "Use the Prophecy Gem! Reveal the location of the Was Scepter!"

Amy stayed silent.

Draconis growled deeply, his voice thundering through the room when he repeated himself. "Use the Prophecy Gem! Let it reveal the location of the Was Scepter!" At Amy's quiet defiance he added, "You seem to not care what becomes of you; perhaps we could find someone you do care about to help convince you to cooperate."

The thought of her friends being on the way suddenly wasn't so comforting.

"That seems to have gotten your attention," Draconis said, his clawed fingertip digging into her chin and forcing her head back so she had no choice but to look up at him.

From the tunnels far beyond the room the soft rhythm of steps could be heard. The third minotaur spoke for the first time. "It must be the others. Maybe they found what we are looking for?"

Draconis pulled his claw back and Amy hissed as it scratched her without piercing her skin. He gave her one last threatening look and then gestured to the others. "Watch the girl."

He walked carefully out of the room with slow and deliberate steps that quieted his clunking hooves and made Amy think he didn't want anyone to know he was coming.

♦ ♦ ♦

"Over here," Will said excitedly aiming the light at the wall up ahead. It reflected faintly off of the faded white numbers and letters painted on the tunnel wall. "12th A-V."

Dez and Isaac were close behind him, all three pausing to check out the final painted marker. These tunnels were definitely larger.

"Eww, what's that smell?" Dez asked, wrinkling his nose.

In unison, Isaac and Will answered, "Minotaur!"

"Damn," Dez chuckled. "Smells like expired milk!"

"The one-eyed elderly man did say these were cow

tunnels," Will murmured. "They sure look big enough to fit multiple cows through."

They started walking again when up ahead a shadow flitted along one of the tunnel walls. Instinctively, Will clicked the flashlight off. The boys moved off to the side hiding in the shadows of the same wall the marker was painted on.

"We have to be ready this time," Will said to the others. "Form a defensive position."

They lined up in a row with Isaac taking the point, leading the way with one hand extended outward, ready, and waiting to deliver a burst of energy powerful enough to send a minotaur flying. Will took the middle, interlocking one arm through Isaac's free arm and offering the other to Dez who took the signal to grab hold of Will's free arm with his own. Both he and Will needed the connection of touch to use their powers—Will to shield and Dez to heal.

"Katzenstein Kids," Dez whispered. "Protectors of the North, South, East, and West..."

Isaac and Will joined him in whispering the final word, *"Unite!"*

With that, they began to move forward slowly toward the direction they'd seen the movement. At the end of the tunnel, they came to a large double door that resembled a set of saloon doors, wooden and curved, cut into a wall of oak slats. As the wall came into view, an old and faded metal sign read:

ABATTOIR ROW AHEAD

"These must be the remains of the old slaughterhouse that the one-eyed elderly man told us about," Will said, taking notice when they approached the large double doors.

The words were barely out of his mouth when the doors flew open with a force that pushed them all back onto the ground. In the doorway glaring menacingly down at them stood the huge minotaur Draconis, his muscles bulging. He had black tattoos inked into the rough skin of his chest—symbols the kids didn't recognize—and wore a necklace of what appeared to be either large teeth or small tusks. Two other Minotaur's flanked him on either side, making it clear to the boys who the leader was.

"Kill them all," the giant beast roared.

At the word of their leader, the Minotaur's at Draconis' sides lunged forward to strike down Dez, Isaac, and Will as they lay disoriented on the concrete. The tunnel glowed a fantastic green, each of the necklaces at the center of their chests reacting to the threat above them and with a striking speed no one would have expected them to muster, Isaac threw his fist forward grabbing onto his gem with the opposite hand.

The only words out of his mouth were a desperate cry, "NOOO!"

A massive force blasted forth from his fist like a cannon, radiating such power that the air around his body seemed to distort momentarily. The blast slammed into the Minotaur's catapulting them all back into the wall of the concrete tunnel. Their leader gave a snort and a grunt shaking his head and scraping his long horns across the wall in the process. The three beasts glared in disbelief at the power of the young boy before them as they lay disoriented.

Dez and Will got to their feet each giving Isaac a hand up. They returned to their formation ready to send a second strike down on the Minotaur's if it became necessary.

Draconis slowly rose, his two minotaur comrades in tow. "Holders of the Eye of Horus," he growled. "Your powers are impressive!"

The Minotaur to his left shook its head and body, its tail flicking from side to side irritably. "These are the kids from the hotel. The sons of Horus stand reborn before us; these three and the girl hold the four parts of the Eye of Horus."

"Where is she?" Will cried out. "Where is the girl?!"

Standing tall, Draconis straightened his shoulders and flared his nostrils. In his deep and menacing voice, he said, "Destiny awaits you, as does the Underworld. Set will once again have your souls, Sons of Horus!" He tilted his head and a threatening fire seemed to dance in the depths of his red eyes. "All of this has happened before. All of this will happen again."

Then, to the boys' surprise Draconis and his two comrades turned on their hooves and raced down the tunnel, disappearing into the darkness without another word. The kids watched on listening intently as the echoes of their hooves against the concrete faded with each passing second. In the silence that followed they heard a faint sound somewhere in the abattoir.

"Amy?" Will cried, breaking free from Dez and Isaac. The three cautiously walked through the wooden cattle doors and into a hall of smaller rooms. There, they could hear that the faint noise was Amy calling out to them from behind a pair of closed doors. Will pushed on one of the wooden doors and it opened without resistance. Amy was on the floor in the back of the room, wet hair sticking to her forehead and clothes clinging to her skin.

"Will! Dez! Isaac!" She shouted at the sight of them.

The boys raced over to her. "Are you okay?" Will asked falling to his knees next to her and searching for any injuries while Isaac went for the shackles around her legs. With a burst of green light the metal shackles broke in half and fell away.

"I'm okay. I'm not hurt!" A tired Amy threw her arms around Will, who embraced her tightly.

"I was so worried about you," he whispered. "I mean, we all were but me the most."

In the background, Dez and Isaac rolled their eyes sarcastically.

Amy pulled back from Will's arms and planted a big kiss on his lips and he smiled. "My Brown Ninja to the rescue."

They all laughed at that, and Will helped Amy to her feet.

"We missed you too," Dez said.

"Yeah, we were really worried about you Amy," Isaac added.

"I was really freaked out! I thought the worst!" Will hugged her again.

The others looked on with a smirk and Amy taking

notice over Will's shoulder grabbed both Dez and Isaac, pulling them into a group hug. They laughed relieved to be together once again, relieved that they were all safe and sound—especially Amy.

When they broke free of the embrace they were all smiling.

"We've gotta get out of here," Isaac said. "It's almost morning, and we need to get back to the Roosevelt before they find us missing."

CHAPTER 14
KNOWLEDGE COMES TO THOSE WHO SEEK IT

The sun peeked over the horizon, winking at the world as the new day began. Dawn approached much too quickly, but somehow the four kids managed to sneak back into the hotel's lower level with little time to spare. They closed the door to the basement and finally back in the safety of the hotel Amy's arms drooped low at her sides as exhaustion washed over her. Most of the journey through the underground tunnels on the way up had dried her hair, but some damp tendrils clung to her forehead like vines stuck to a cliffside.

"Here," Will murmured, "rest your arm on my shoulder."

Amy gladly accepted, wrapping a heavy arm around him

and leaning against him as they made their way up the stairs and through the hallways as quietly as they could. Dez and Isaac took the lead, sidling along the walls and inching around every corner with careful movements before signaling back to Amy and Will that it was safe to proceed.

Upon reaching their room, Isaac opened the door and the four slipped in quickly one after the other. The soft click of the door shutting behind them sent a wave of relief through each of them. Dez peered through the peephole for a few seconds and finding the hallway to be empty on the other side, he retreated to the bedside. Amy was so worn out that she collapsed mere seconds later, catching the edge of a chair that Will barely managed to slide into place behind her.

"Hey, Amy," he said softly. "What did they want from you?"

All three of the boys watched her intently, noticing that she paled at the question. "They wanted to know..." A deep breath. "They wanted me to use the Prophecy Gem to tell them where the *Was Scepter* is."

"The what?" Dez and Will asked in unison.

"I'm freaking out," Isaac gasped, "There looking for a *Was Scepter*," drawing everyone's attention to the fact that he was pacing the length of the room. "Am I the only one freaking out?"

"That was WAY too close!" Dez exclaimed, his own fear echoing Isaac's. "I mean, let this sink in, we just had a fight with not one, not two, but *three* mystical ancient beasts that until now had only existed in stories!"

"Not to mention the Was Scepter," Isaac added, his

voice rising in pitch. "Who knows what kind of power that will put in the hands of the Minotaur's? We need to find it first."

"We need to keep our heads," Will urged, placing his hands on Amy's shoulders and rubbing them in what he hoped was a reassuring way. "We're all back, safe and sound. No need to panic."

Although Will was trying to put on a brave face, Amy could feel the tension in him as his reassuring massage became erratic and irregular until his hands eventually rested on Amy's shoulders, squeezing in a way that made his nails dig into her clothes. She shrugged him off gently before glancing over her shoulder. He leaped back from her, an apologetic gleam in his eyes to accompany his awkward smile.

"We just need to not panic," he repeated. "This is just like Milton's treasure, when we were trying to find the coordinates to the Eye of Horus last summer."

"Yeah," Isaac nodded fervently. "We need to put on our detective caps and figure this out!"

"It's like the one-eyed elderly man said... *Knowledge comes to those who seek it.*'"

"Right!"

Amy looked between the two boys. "The... one-eyed elderly man?"

"Oh," Will glanced over at her. "Well, down in the tunnels, an elderly man with one eye came out of the shadows just like when we put the gems together over Christmas... I mean when we teleported, it's obvious now that we all went down into those tunnels but the creepy man who spoke to us back then was there tonight! It turns out he wasn't really that creepy though. He helped us find you."

"He told us to go to the old Cow Tunnel," Dez added. "He even told us which avenue to look for."

Amy lurched forward on her chair. A split-second attempt to stand was met with joints popping, muscles aching, and bones creaking. Deciding her body wasn't quite ready to be upright, she slumped back and leaned toward the side table, grabbing the notebook and pen marked with the hotel's letterhead.

"If what you're saying is true, then when we teleport, it's not just about a vision—we're actually moving from one place to another," Amy mused, her eyes wide with newfound understanding. "This power could allow us to go anywhere on the planet."

"Exactly!" Will exclaimed, his excitement bubbling over. "Although your Prophecy Gem can help see the past, present, and future, both teleports resulted in us physically visiting new locations. Remember what the one-eyed elderly man said? 'Knowledge comes to those who seek it.' We gain knowledge when we put the gems together and teleport—when we seek to know more."

Isaac nodded in agreement. "This must be why the Minotaur's wanted you to tell them the location of the Was Scepter. They know we can use the gems to locate it."

Dez stepped forward, his voice filled with determination. "If this is true, then shouldn't we just combine the gems and teleport to the location of the Was Scepter?"

Amy hesitated, a flicker of apprehension in her eyes. "Here in a hotel in New York City? That could be dangerous." She paused, her mind racing as she considered the possibilities. "We still don't fully understand this new power. Don't forget, we don't know how to control where we go, or how to stay."

Will added, "Amy's right. The few times we tried it, we just ended up somewhere random, then as soon as we let go of the gems, we returned to where we started."

Dez and Isaac took a deep breath as they acknowledged these facts.

Amy's excitement returned. "We still have other options. I believe the clues are all around us. Let's write this all down. What do we know so far?" She asked the boys, pen poised, ready to unravel the mysteries that lay before them.

A silence fell upon the room. Glances were exchanged. One of them would open their mouth, only to inhale deeply and close it again. Isaac's urge to pace returned, but he replaced it with a rhythmic tapping of his toes against the carpet. The beat was steady, but it did not soothe them. It mimicked the ticking of a clock. Time passed them by. Time, they didn't have. Yet, none of them could articulate what they had seen. The discoveries and knowledge were vivid in their minds, playing back like a movie yet escaping explanation, sitting on the edge of their tongues.

Outside, birds greeted the crisp dusk sky. Even in New York, where the city ruckus seemed to come from everywhere the rising sun brought animals out of hiding, signaling the morning with their soft tunes. Their peaceful sounds felt jarring amidst the destruction of Isaac and Will's room, the light shining down on heaps of plaster and debris. The kids felt the morning shouldn't be so normal after the night they'd had; the birds should understand the seriousness of their situation and pick a better moment to sing. Joining the chorus was the scratching of Amy's pen on paper. Her hand hovered as the pen flew from one word to the next.

Unable to put it into words, she put it on the page. The boys noticed her hand slowing. They leaned in to see what she'd written, the words a cursive blur from afar: ***What we know so far...***

Amy had written at the very top, adding a slow ellipsis to give herself time to decide what should follow.

Dez, Isaac, and Will surrounded her, Dez on tiptoes to see over his friends' shoulders, Isaac holding his breath as Amy's hand began to write once more. He feared a stray gasp could distract her, or worse blow the page away. Dez felt a cramp in his calf but ignored it. Will stood forward, resting a gentle hand on the back of Amy's chair, afraid to touch her shoulders again.

"What do you think? Did I leave anything out?" Amy leaned back, admiring her work.

What we know so far:

1. Draconis is the minotaur leader—I only saw three of them, but they made it sound like there were more.

2. Since they've been resurrected from the Underworld, they're powerless against the Eye of Horus, which means our powers can protect us for now!
3. Set is coming!
4. They know who we are! (THIS ONE IS KIND OF IMPORTANT.)

"Looks good," Isaac hummed. "Very explanatory."

"It's missing one thing, though," Will added as he took the pen from Amy and leaned over her to reach the page. He scribbled a line beneath her list.

5. They are searching for the location of the Was Scepter!

His words were far less organized and dug deeper into the page, leaving ink splotches and unsightly stains just below her beautifully crafted list. Amy tried not to focus on that.

"There we go!" Will exclaimed triumphantly as he pulled back. "That's everything we know."

"What *don't* we know?" Dez asked.

Isaac's hand shot straight up into the air as he gasped, "Can I make that list?"

"Wouldn't be a very long list," Dez shrugged. "There's only one thing we don't know for certain."

Each of them looked at one another and at once stated in a serious whisper, "The location of the Was Scepter."

"We need to find it before they do!" Isaac insisted. The boys shared a knowing nod, and Amy looked between them with a furrowed brow.

"What is a Was Scepter?" She finally asked.

"It's a large staff," Will responded. "An ancient artifact."

"With a curved head and a forked tip," Dez added.

"And it's known to have magical powers that can be used as a weapon," Isaac finished off. "Or it can be used to create a bond between the mortal world and the Underworld."

Amy's eyebrows disappeared beneath her hair as she stared at all of them. "How do you guys know this?!"

"Do you really have to ask?" Will smiled.

"We've seen them before, in our comic books," Dez answered. "There are tons of supernatural stories that include Was Scepters."

"Of course," she whispered. "Comic books..."

The kids sat in silence for a while, absorbing the information. Amy and Dez shared a yawn as the fatigue of the night caught up to them. Minotaur's, superpowers, and ancient artifacts with magical powers were all things they had read about, impossible things entwined in fantasy and comics, but never in their wildest dreams did they ever think such things were real, let alone that they might face them. Perhaps that was another reason that Horus had chosen them. Their pure hearts and limitless imaginations made them the perfect choice, considering the extraordinary circumstances.

Amy was the first to speak again, bringing up the

elephant in the room, "I don't trust those three foreign exchange students: Olivia, Myra, and Daria. Did you notice how they just suddenly appeared in our school after winter break?!"

"I agree with Amy," Will said, equally suspicious. "Do you guys buy Myra's story that she found the Health Gem near the stairwell?"

Dez shifted uncomfortably, reluctant to agree with his friends. "I'm not sure, guys... I mean I like Myra. And why would she take it and then return it?"

Isaac gently patted Dez on the shoulder. "Dez has a point. Maybe she did find it. When was the last time you saw it?"

"I think..." Dez paused for a moment to think. "I'm pretty sure I placed it on my nightstand because I was getting ready for bed. But then there was a knock on the door and it was Myra." His eyes went wide. "Darn! She did take it! She asked to borrow toothpaste and I left to get her some from the bathroom. Then she left. But she had a chance to take it and I didn't check after she left!" Dez's shoulders slumped as he took a seat on the edge of Will's bed, realizing Myra deceived him after all.

"Sorry, Dez," Amy murmured. "She and her sisters are up to something. We need to find out who they are and who they might be working for."

A knock on the door interrupted their conversation. All the kids jumped up, including Amy. Isaac walked over to the door and opened it a crack, using his body to hide the room. The others stood behind him, helping.

"Oh, perfect, you're all up early and all together," Ms.

Fleming stood in the hallway outside. Little did she know they had been up all night. "Your parents heard about the horrible events of last evening and were very concerned, so Isaac and Amy's parents are coming to New York City today to pick you all up." The kids exchanged surprised looks before Ms. Fleming continued. "I'd recommend resting up for the long drive. Get ready and pack your things. They should be at the hotel by this afternoon."

"Yes, Ms. Fleming," the kids said in unison.

Isaac hurriedly shut the door as their social studies teacher walked away, her hair in a bun so tight it must have been painful.

"This afternoon!" Isaac exclaimed. "What, did they drive all night?"

"I'm so tired," Amy whined, slumping back down in her chair.

"Me too," Isaac nodded. "Don't get me wrong, I'm relieved we managed to save you and make it back here by morning but I didn't expect to see my mom today."

"I think we should all get some sleep," Will said. "We'll figure out our next step once we've all rested. I don't know about you guys, but I'm already packed because I never unpacked."

"Yeah, same here. Except for my toothbrush," Dez shrugged. "Sleep sounds good. Sleep, and then figure out how to find the Was Scepter before the Minotaur's do. And all while Amy and Isaac's parents are around. How hard could that be?"

CHAPTER 15
MATRYOSHKA DOLLS
Moscow, Soviet Union (U.S.S.R.) – 1977

In an area where many of the streets resembled a maze of dark and narrow alleyways more than they did neighborhoods, flanked by derelict houses whose windows were boarded up and whose doors rarely opened in daylight hours, there was a long street not traveled by everyday folks. At the end of it was a large run-down facility that could have been a house and could just as easily have been an old industrial factory or warehouse of some kind. The brick face had blackened from age, rumored to be from a fire that left soot clinging to its surface long after—a rumor no one cared about enough to disprove. Weeds and moss grew around the entrance foundations flourishing at the ground and then suddenly drooping before they could reach their full heights, leaves curling and browning. A shadow descended over the building and the people in its nearby vicinity had branded the house with the nickname *"House of the Abandoned"* —an appropriate name, considering it served as an orphanage for the less fortunate children of Moscow.

Inside a number of sleeping wards three young sisters spent most of their time dreaming of better days. They had not been there long, perhaps a month or so, yet this place was a stark contrast to the life they once had. It was easier to do so in the daytime when they had one another. More and more the nights seemed to be a time of loneliness—at least that was the case for the youngest of the three. Who could no longer find refuge in her dreams for they were no longer memories of better times. Instead, she was haunted by scenes of a more frightening nature.

The whisper of sheets brushing against a thrashing body could scarcely be heard over the cold wind whistling through the halls as Daria, barely eleven years of age, found herself in a deep sleep—a sleep so deep it threatened to swallow her whole. There was no way of measuring the intensity of her brain activity, but her eyelids twitched as the eyes beneath them moved from side to side.

She tossed and turned beneath the covers as she was pulled into another reality that lived somewhere in the depths of her subconscious, though it felt much further away than that as the vivid scene unfolded in the recesses of Daria's mind...

Playing in a field of brilliant green grass, she saw a woman in the near distance, long blonde locks swept up by a calm breeze. The woman faced away from Daria, yet Daria sensed that she knew her somehow. "Hello?" Daria called out into the distance, feeling as if nothing came from her mouth but hearing her voice echo on the wind. Nothing. Not even a turn of the woman's head to indicate she'd heard Daria. With a shrug of her small shoulders, Daria glanced around the seemingly endless green clearing, her eyes landing on a herd of cattle. Their heads were down as they grazed away at the swaying grass. Daria laughed, excited at the sight of them and suddenly darted forward with her arms spread out on either side of her body like an airplane. A rush of happiness came over her as she ran through the fields once more.

While she played, a small red bird flew down over her head chirping for her attention. She gasped at its beauty; the coloring remarkably bright. It almost shimmered. With a smile, Daria waved her hands playfully above her head and the bird played back, swooping down toward her and up again as she tried to catch the little thing. Back and forth they ran, its chirps like music and all was right in the dream world until out of nowhere a crack like a whip snapped across the sky and the sound of a sonic boom broke through the world as thunder threatened all below. A flash of lightning drew down from above.

The noise startled Daria and she paused a moment to gather herself; she noticed the cattle were no longer grazing peacefully but rather spooked by the noise from above, shifting and snorting between each other. Daria looked out across the field to find that the blonde woman appeared unfazed. More and more that was not the case with the cattle. Their snorts had turned to grunts and their shifting quickly turned to rushing as the cows began to stampede in fear stomping across the vast grassy field. They were headed straight for the young woman! "Watch out!" Daria shouted, but the woman did not move.

Hoping to somehow get her attention, Daria began running toward the woman only for the tiny red bird to swoop down at her head as if to stop her. Daria swatted her hands at the bird trying to protect her head and scare it away at the same time, but it refused to let up. The faster she ran the more aggressive the bird became in its interference, pecking and pulling at Daria's hair. "Watch out! Watch out!" She cried out breathlessly. The woman seemed not to hear anything, not Daria's loud cries, not the bird's squawks and not the stampede of mooing and bellowing cows heading straight for her. Daria felt as if she were closing in when to her horror she tripped over her own feet and tumbled to the ground rolling to a hard stop across the grass. She threw her arms out angrily at the tiny red bird who'd swooped down across her feet as she ran, looking up at the young woman in earnest.

It was too late; the stampede of cattle trampled over the woman in the distance. Daria screamed—

And woke herself from her deep sleep gasping and breathing heavily as her heart raced. When her eyes opened Daria saw her sister Myra climb out of her own bed and crawl into Daria's before she felt Myra's arms hug her tightly.

"It's okay, Daria," Myra whispered. "It was just a dream."

"Why is it the same? Why the same horrible dream since we arrived at this godforsaken place?" Daria asked. "Could it be Mother? Could Mother have been the one standing in the grassy field?"

Myra shook her head; Daria felt the movement more than saw it. "No... It was just a bad dream. Mother died with Father in a car crash. I don't think Mother ever lived on a farm," she smirked. "Nor did she seem like the type of lady to be surrounded by cows grazing in a field."

The girls giggled quietly at the thought.

◆ ◆ ◆

The next day, the three sisters worked in the laundry room together, doing their rounds. This was one of many chores they had come to get accustomed to since arriving at the House of the Abandoned only a month or so earlier.

As Daria, Myra, and Olivia focused on their chore of folding bed sheets an older girl approached, her tone dripping with condescension. "You seem a bit tiny to be working in the laundry," she remarked. "Perhaps we should get you reassigned to cleaning the toilets. We usually let the young one's clean toilets, since their small hands and arms are a perfect fit for scrubbing the inside of a toilet bowl."

Daria glanced at her sisters, who had paused their work, their eyes fixed on the unfolding confrontation. With a surge of defiance Daria stood tall, her voice unwavering. "It's not my size that matters," she retorted.

The older girl stepped closer, a smirk playing on her lips. "Of course your size matters. Look at you, how can you even fold a single bed sheet? They're ten times your size!"

Daria's eyes sparkled with confidence. "You must not have heard of the fairytale 'The Giant Turnip'," she countered.

Intrigued, the older girl nodded, her arrogance momentarily subdued.

Daria seized the opportunity picking up a large bed sheet

and tossing it towards the older girl, who caught it with a startled yelp. The sheet billowed in her hands threatening to engulf her as she struggled to maintain her grip.

With a twinkle in her eye Daria began to weave her tale. "Once upon a time, an old man planted a turnip. The turnip grew and grew and grew some more until it was enormous. The old man tried to pull the turnip out of the ground, but it was too big. So he called his wife to help. Together they tried, but the turnip wouldn't budge. So the wife called her granddaughter and then the granddaughter called the dog and then the dog called the cat and the cat called the mouse..."

Daria paused for dramatic effect, her audience captivated. "The old man, the wife, the granddaughter, the dog, and the cat all tried to pull the turnip out of the ground, but it was still too big. Then, the tiny mouse, the smallest of them all, gave one final push and finally the turnip came free!"

As she finished the story, Daria reached out and took hold of one end of the bedsheet the older girl was struggling with. The older girl, now mirroring Daria's grip, looked at her with a mixture of surprise and newfound respect.

"Sometimes, those you may least expect, even a tiny mouse can make a difference," Daria said, her voice gentle but firm. "There is value in even the smallest and least among us."

Olivia and Myra burst into laughter, their pride in their sister evident. The older girl unable to suppress a chuckle herself, finally relinquished her hold on the sheet. With a sheepish grin, she turned and walked away.

Daria, Myra, and Olivia resumed their folding, a silent understanding passing between them. They had faced down a bully, not with fists or aggression, but with the power of a story, a reminder that strength comes in many forms and that even the smallest among us can make a difference.

As the hours passed in between the splashes of water that filled the otherwise quiet laundry room the telltale sound of a vehicle entering the stone parking lot outside could be heard: a crunch of gravel beneath rubber tires. Like a dinner bell following its arrival excitement rang out in the facility; orphan children of all ages whispered amongst themselves and hurried through the hallways preparing for the green line.

Located in the main hall and used to line up the children for selection was a painted green line. The girls cleaned their hands and hurried to join the other orphan children who were adjusting the fit of their clothes, tucking in frayed edges and hand-combing soap into their hair to make it appear well-groomed.

Many had taken their place on the green line day after day and year after year. Spending a limited amount of time in the sun and never quite knowing what a healthy diet looked like, they would do what they could to seem more appealing. Some would prick their fingers, piercing the skin and apply droplets of blood to their lips and cheeks to add color, worried the toll on their young bodies would show and deter anyone from choosing them. Others who considered themselves too old never minded the green

line; the military often took boys aged fifteen and up under their wing. It was a fair break for a young man—not as fair of a break for the young women, however. Who were typically the target of Moscow's rich and elite, to be used as servants or for other seedy acts since they were considered to have little else to offer but their body or their labor in some way or another. Who were they to object.

Daria, Myra, and Olivia knew they had little chance of being selected together and for that reason, for them, the green line was never a welcoming sight. They comforted themselves with the reasoning that the arrival of a vehicle didn't always mean the green-line presentation of orphans would be to prospective suitors. Sometimes the cars were simply driving into the lot to make a delivery or for other business needs. Nevertheless, they did their best to stay close to one another, to be ready. The girls dressed quickly, putting on their favorite yellow dress—the one with pleated tops and puffy sleeves. These dresses were one of the only items the girls were able to keep from their past lives, which they kept aside for these special moments. Once dressed, they tied their hair up in matching, neat pigtails.

Commotion echoed from the front door of the facility, down the main hall. While they waited for a sign that it was time to line up the girls heard a man's voice as Madame Polina escorted the visitor into the main office. Time slowed in the silence that followed; the orphan children all sat ready and waiting for the bell.

What seemed like a lifetime passed before the main office door finally opened to the sound of the grown-ups emerging, their laughter echoing down the hall. Then, the chime of what sounded like a school bell rang. The children were quick to move single file into the main hall and lining up neatly along the green line. Daria, Myra, and Olivia hooked and curled their pinky fingers together as they hoped nothing would come between them.

Standing in wait was a man—a man who, by the clean shave and freshly laundered suit, must surely be a deliberate man. He had dark cropped hair and eyes of two colors: one blue and the other hazel. In his hand was a file, and the tightness of his jaw suggested a sense of determination as did the straightness of his shoulders as he walked down the hallway gazing intently down at each orphan. Slowly, he moved down the line of children looking at each of them carefully. His eyes narrowed as he came to a stop at Daria, Myra, and Olivia. He took a step back to look at them side by side.

"My name is Rurik Zakharov," he told them gently. "And what, may I ask, are your names?"

The girls, with some apprehension on their faces, responded from youngest to oldest.

"Daria... Sir."

"Myra... Sir."

"Olivia... Sir."

"Your file states that you are sisters. Correct?"

They all nodded. "Yes, sir."

Rurik took a long pause, sizing each of them up in detail. He added, "I don't suppose you would want to be separated from each other. Correct?"

"No, sir!" Olivia exclaimed. Her fear of being left behind as the oldest and the defiance that kept her and her sisters together this long came out before she could help it. "These are my sisters and we have never been apart. We protect each other, we support each other and we will not allow anyone to come between us!"

Just then Madame Polina approached. "Mind yourself, young lady," she said harshly. "You shall be grateful if Mr. Zakharov honors us with any choice!"

Olivia dropped her eyes. "Yes, Madame," she murmured to the floor.

Rurik took another step back, the corner of his mouth twitching as he glanced from the youngest to the oldest, the shortest to the tallest, all clothed in fancy matching yellow dresses. With a deep breath he told the girls, "Some refer to me as the Dollmaker." He walked closer to them pointing a finger at each one at a time. "The matriarch, the little mother, and the seed. I do not see three sisters; I see a set of Matryoshka Dolls."

At this, Daria cracked a smile.

Pleased with his inspection of the girls, Rurik nodded and called out, "I will take all three!"

CHAPTER 16
THE GRIP, THE GUARD AND THE BLADE

Over the next few days, the three sisters discovered why they had been adopted by Rurik. He was a KGB officer in search of the perfect infiltration team for specialized type missions, and he believed he had found it in them. He shared this information with them as they climbed into a black car with tinted windows after what little luggage they had was safely tucked into the trunk. At the time, they didn't know exactly what that meant.

"After all, does a Matryoshka doll not nest? Does it not hide that it has much more within, than one would assume upon first glance?" He laughed at his own wit and the girls said nothing in return, though they were rather fond of their newfound identities as the Matryoshka Dolls. More than that, they were glad to be leaving the House of the Abandoned behind. None of them glanced back, not even as the last of it slipped away in the rearview mirror.

Olivia kept her eyes downcast for most of the drive, watching as the painted lines on the road ahead of the car shifted and changed from white to orange and from dotted to straight—the only proof she had of time passing by. Occasionally, she'd look up in time to read the traffic markers—in time to see them leaving the city of Moscow. Daria fell asleep beside her somewhere along the way and Myra wasn't far behind.

"Where are we going... Rurik?" She eventually asked. Almost an hour had passed, and they were still on the road.

"Not very far outside of Moscow," he told her, as if he could read her thoughts. When Rurik spoke to them, he looked them in the eye—something most adults didn't do. "I am enrolling you in the Red Banner Institute. It was once known as the *Special Purpose School*, a rather apt name considering the three of you have quite a special purpose."

"We're going to school?" Myra perked up.

"A place where you will learn things you would never learn anywhere else, my dear," Rurik smiled. "The institute serves under the KGB. There, you're going to focus on learning various things. You'll learn English, the art of understanding foreign intelligence and counter-intelligence, special operations tactics, and advanced training in self-defense."

"So when you say *infiltration team*, you mean we're going to be..." Myra looked between Rurik and her sisters, leaning in closely and whispering the last word, "...spies?"

"You are already so much more," Rurik told them sincerely.

Soon enough, they arrived at the facility. The Red Banner Institute was a two-story stone and wooden building. By the aged exterior and its peeling paint, it was clear the institute had been constructed before the war. There were no signs of blackness, either from soot or mold; no signs of moss to tell onlookers no one was around to care for it; and there were no dying weeds climbing up the sides of its foundation. Instead, quite charmingly, lilac branches caressed the windows from beneath. Although the surrounding area was quiet, save for the teeming sounds of small wildlife creatures, the air of the place showed no signs of neglect. It looked nondescript from the exterior, like an ordinary house on the outskirts of Moscow—nothing like what they expected a spy-training school might look like.

"This will be your home, at least for a while." The girls watched as Rurik looked up at the building with something resembling pride on his face. He added, "As it was once mine."

The luggage was carried into the building and the girls were led away from Rurik toward their rooms by a girl who appeared to be around the same age as Olivia. She said nothing to them, simply nodding toward a closed wooden door and departing when the girls opened it. The dormitory was quartered, with four-poster beds spaced out a fair distance apart. In the orphanage, they had shared a long room with over ten other rejected children.

"There's so much more space here than we had

before," Myra was the first to say anything.

"I know we don't really know what to do with it right now, but I really think we could make this a good home." Daria had already begun to unpack her suitcase, emptying the few items of clothing she owned into the nightstand beside her bed.

"Daria's right," Olivia nodded. "I'm pretty sure if there's one thing we can agree on, it's that this place is a far sight better than... *that* place." She grimaced at the memory of the orphanage.

Myra joined Daria, beginning to unpack. "And the most important thing is that we're together."

Although the institute was tough, the girls threw themselves into their training, determined both to grow more effective in their new roles and to make a home of the school where they spent the better part of their time. Settling in meant spending their days training and their evenings studying, waking up early to complete their chores and get ready for their lessons, and going to bed with their heads swimming. In between, in minutes that felt forbidden and exciting all at once, they explored the building and did their best to learn its secrets—from the creaky wooden floor panels that gave when they stood in the wrong spot to the books that opened hidden rooms if one removed them from the shelf. They did their best not to stand out, but it was hard to ignore the pointed glances from the handful of other students at the institute, even more so the occasional whisper about the "new girls with their pigtails and matching dresses." By way of comfort, they told themselves their differences were what drew Rurik to them in the first place.

One afternoon the girls returned to their rooms to find identical notes on their beds inviting them down to the Rug Room. A room none of them had yet seen but had heard about through the whispers of other students. The notes were unsigned, all sprawled in the same black handwriting. They were quick to make themselves presentable and quick to hurry down the stairs.

It was when Daria, Myra, and Olivia reached the hallway that led to the Rug Room that their pace slowed as their nerves got the better of them.

Olivia held out her hands, offering one to each of her sisters. "We'll let go when we enter," she whispered.

Daria and Myra nodded, taking her hands. As always, they were grateful to have one another. That knowledge was enough to keep going.

When they entered the room, they noticed a distinctive woman standing in front of a lit fireplace, spitting, and crackling as wood burned away in its center. The flames cast shadows across the woman's face, lines of age glimmering in the orange light. Even so, the woman resonated with the experience of what it was to be a proper woman, holding herself elegantly, yet firmly; her movements measured, yet direct. Daria, Myra, and Olivia came to a halt at the edge of a large rug decorating the floor, unable to help but search the room with curious eyes while the woman stoked the fire. A collection of assorted swords and weaponry hung on the walls and there were shelves upon shelves of thick hardcover books.

The woman turned to them, making eye contact when she spoke her first words. "Look at me when I speak to you." Daria, Myra, and Olivia jumped, quickly looking on as they were told. Each of them had to force their gaze away from the distracting curiosities of the Rug Room. "Very good. Now, turn and walk out of this room. Count to ten, and return."

Sheepishly, the girls turned on their heels and did as they were told once again, leaving the room before returning to the very same spot. They stood straight, following the woman's example. This time, they held her gaze.

"Again!" The woman cried out.

They wordlessly left the room and returned once again, standing as they were.

"Again!" She repeated.

And again, the girls left the room and returned. This time, frustrated, the woman walked up to them with the grace of a dancer, circling them as if doing an inspection. With a newfound calmness she spoke once more. "I asked you to leave the room and return, and nothing changed. Lesson One: always smile when entering a room; it disarms those who take notice—as does your youthfulness." She lowered her voice as she leaned in close. "Both could one day save your life."

"Who are you?" Olivia asked.

The woman stood firm, ignoring the question. "Repeat after me," she told them. "I am a woman, I am a weapon, I am the grip, the guard, and the blade."

One thing they had learned in their lessons was to act

without hesitation. And so, the girls repeated after the woman.

"My name is Lady Sonechka. It means 'Wise One.' And we have a lot to teach you in the ways of wisdom." She looked between them. "Each of you will be joining me each day from now on for two hours first thing in the morning. After that, you will be attending finishing and etiquette classes as well as international studies and foreign language in the afternoons."

The sisters could hardly hold back their surprise at earning even more training, nor their excitement as they shared a grin.

"Yes, Lady Sonechka!" They said in unison.

The following morning found Daria, Myra, and Olivia up and ready for the day well before the sun. Their chores were completed earlier than ever and with nervous knots in their stomachs they skipped breakfast, with nothing left to do but wait for the hand on the clock to tell them it was time to make their way to the Rug Room. This time, they were more prepared, each stopping on the first of numerous rugs decorating the room with a disarming smile on their faces. Lady Sonechka stood waiting for them with narrowed eyes. They were awarded with the slightest twitch of a muscle in her cheek, but the smile never quite touched the rest of her mouth.

"Very good," Lady Sonechka murmured appreciatively as she walked around them, eyeing them up from head to toe. They stood straight, their chins held high. Then she asked, "Do you consider yourselves to be women of

God?"

Each girl nodded in the affirmative.

"According to Proverbs 31, one must realize that it is an honor to be called a woman of God, and as we humble ourselves before God, he graciously bestows his strength and courage upon us. I want you all to read it tonight."

With that, Lady Sonechka walked over to the wall and removed a fencing sword from one of the weapon racks. She snapped her wrist sharply and the sword cut through the air between Daria and Myra with a swish, then between Myra and Olivia, before doing the same in reverse. The blade came closer to their skin than the girls were comfortable with at times, but they did their best not to flinch, not to move an inch.

"However," the lady continued, "in God's un-availability, I will graciously bestow my knowledge and techniques upon you." She thrust the tip of the sword inches from their delicate faces. "...In the hopes that we can prevent you from meeting God too soon."

The girls watched in silence, hearts racing, as Lady Sonechka returned the sword to its place on the wall.

"We have much to learn before you and the sword become one," she told them, glancing backward with a twinkle in her eye. "Close your eyes."

They did.

"I call this chamber the Rug Room. There are eight different rugs throughout this space. Can you tell me what color the rug is that lays beneath your feet?"

The girls were silent. Olivia's eyelids twitched as she mentally chided herself. *How could she not have taken notice?*

"You have spent the past two days in this room, entering and leaving numerous times. Surely you must have taken notice," the lady echoed Olivia's thoughts. "Again, what color is the rug at your feet?"

The girls squirmed yet appeared to have no answer.

"Open your eyes."

They did, looking down at the burgundy Bokhara rug, clearly woven and embroidered out of the finest quality materials.

"Lesson Two: you must always be mindful of your footing."

A steely determination came over the girls and the hint of a smile played around Myra's mouth. They nodded their understanding and with that the lessons continued under Lady Sonechka's careful guidance and supervision. The girls proved themselves to be adept students and hard workers. Rurik was convinced that there was no better team than a family. Statements such as these brought the girls immeasurable joy and they found they wanted to exceed their new father's expectations.

Most mornings saw the girls finishing their chores as quickly as possible, excited to rejoin Lady Sonechka in the Rug Room and quietly awaiting further instruction. Their first lesson was well-learned, and they never failed to arrive with a disarming smile. It only took one training session for them to realize skipping breakfast was a mistake; a workout program had been specially formulated for them and it required fuel. They exercised until they were breathless, and their hearts pounded against the inside of their chests, until sweat dripped off their foreheads and they thought their muscles wouldn't be able to stand the strain anymore. Then, when the physical exertion came to an end, the mental exertion would begin. A quick lunch was followed by studies, mostly reading on philosophy and war until they couldn't focus anymore.

The first several days were the most difficult, but each day the girls returned to the Rug Room they returned with limbs that were stronger than the day before. And each day, they hoped that each of them would be given permission to remove one of the beautiful blades decorating the walls. They were convinced Lady Sonechka knew how badly they wanted to take the blade in hand, though they saved such talk for the late evening hours when the other students were fast asleep and they were quite certain they wouldn't be heard—both on the topic of their training and their overwhelming desire to move past the baby steps their trainer insisted they take before touching the steel.

It was weeks after their first lesson that Lady Sonechka was satisfied with the progress they had made and the strength they had developed, pacing around and inspecting them as closely as she did that first day before giving a curt nod.

"You may each take a blade," she told them.

The girls couldn't help but exchange a glance before they each took one of the fencing swords down from the wall with great excitement.

"Fencing began as a form of military training and quickly evolved into a sport in the fifteenth century," she said, prowling around them like a wildcat on the hunt for prey. "The rules and moves may seem complicated at first, but when mastered, they will become second nature. Do you understand?"

"Yes, Lady Sonechka!" They cried out in unison.

"Then follow me."

Lady Sonechka led Daria, Myra, and Olivia out to a large space where they all stood together, their fencing swords ready and poised, and their saber masks on. The lady positioned herself across from them and the girls took their own positions feet apart.

"On these grounds, fencing is an art form, and the sword is a brush. It is an extension of your arm." She swung hers for emphasis. "Beyond these grounds, when the sword is in your hand the only sport you play is one where the prize is your life."

The girls held onto her every word, heeding solemnly. They became the grip, the guard, and the blade, intending to master the art of fencing using a trio of combinations in their stances, attack maneuvers, and defense. When their trainer spoke of the blade, it was with equal parts reverence and warning and something about the power of being a swordswoman enticed them. Seeing the way Lady Sonechka handled the sword made an impact on them; for each of the girls was like three parts of the sword. They threw themselves into their training for this moment and the reading materials were endlessly fascinating. The girls were desperate to become one with the sword and to free themselves not only from the memory of the loss of their parents, but also places like the House of the Abandoned but from the chance of ever being sent back there. They had a united goal in mind. When Rurik called upon them, they planned to be ready.

◆◆◆

After nearly a year of grueling training, today was the final exercise the girls would engage in to perfect their sword techniques. Lady Sonechka led Daria, Myra, and Olivia out to a large space where they all stood together, fencing swords poised and saber masks in place. The lady positioned herself across from them and the girls assumed their stances, feet shoulder-width apart.

"Matryoshka Dolls ready?" Lady Sonechka called out, her voice ringing with authority.

The three sisters, Olivia, Myra, and Daria barely had time to nod their assent before their mentor charged forward. "Fierceness is essential in mortal combat!" she declared.

The sisters moved in unison, anticipating the attack. Olivia was first to meet Lady Sonechka's blade, the sound of steel-on-steel echoing through the training hall. "I am the blade," she retorted.

Lady Sonechka, undeterred, circled to the left, where Myra's sword awaited. "I am the guard," Myra declared, parrying the blow.

Impressed but not finished, Lady Sonechka spun to her right, facing Daria. "I am the grip!" Daria cried, her sword meeting the Lady's in a shower of sparks.

Lady Sonechka paused, taking stock of their flawless defense. They had anticipated her every move, preventing any attempt to outflank them. But had they considered the final element? She stepped back, a challenge in her eyes.

Olivia, eager to prove herself, surged forward, leaving

herself open. With a blur of motion, Lady Sonechka was behind her. "There must be no hesitancy in using any method to bring about the complete and utter destruction of your enemy," she proclaimed, raising her sword for the final strike.

But before the blow could land the sound of metal on metal erupted again. Myra's sword blocked from the left, Daria's from the right. Olivia, having recovered her position, added her voice to the chorus. "In combat, it is essential to make the enemy think one thing while you deliver a strike from another direction!"

Lady Sonechka lowered her weapon, a smile gracing her lips as she removed her mask. "That's the end of our exercise," she announced. "You have all learned what I have taught you very well. And I see you finished your required reading of Sun Tzu's *The Art of War.*"

The sisters, breathless but beaming, removed their masks and exchanged proud glances. They had mastered the art of combat, but more importantly, they had learned the value of teamwork and strategy. The lessons of the Matryoshka Dolls would serve them well, both on and off the battlefield.

"Final lesson," Lady Sonechka expressed, "Everyone has their place and everyone has their value. Together, you will always be stronger than apart." *"Like the Fairy Tale about the Giant Turnip,"* Daria reminded herself.

Lady Sonechka clasped her hands together, her eyes scanning each of the girls in turn. "Remember, you are more than mere students. You are a team, a unit. You must always watch each other's backs, anticipate each other's moves and act as one. Understood?"

Daria, Myra, and Olivia nodded in agreement, their determination shining brightly in their eyes.

"Good," Lady Sonechka said, a hint of pride evident in her voice. "Now, let's debrief and discuss what we've learned today."

As they gathered around Lady Sonechka in the Rug Room the sisters couldn't help but feel a sense of accomplishment wash over them. They had come a long way since their days at the orphanage and now, under the guidance of Lady Sonechka, they were beginning to realize their true potential. They knew they were ready for whatever challenges lay ahead, and together, they knew they could overcome anything.

"It's time for you to return the swords to their places.

Today was your final lesson, tomorrow we will discuss our final test: the Trials of Misha. But for now, rest and reflect on what you've learned today."

Reluctantly, the girls returned the swords to the wall, their minds are still buzzing with the thrill of their training session.

With their training session complete the sisters bid farewell to Lady Sonechka and made their way back to their dormitory, a sense of excitement and pride at how far they'd come building within them. They were one step closer to fulfilling their destiny and nothing was going to stand in their way. And with Lady Sonechka's guidance, they were more determined than ever to succeed.

With that thought in mind they settled into their beds for the night and drifted off to sleep, their dreams filled with visions of the adventures that lay ahead. For the Matryoshka Dolls the journey had only just begun, but with each other by their side they were ready to face whatever the future held, including their final test: the Trials of Misha.

◆◆◆

Outside the heart of Moscow where winter's icy grip lingered, Daria, Myra, and Olivia, stood on the precipice of their ultimate test since arriving at The Red Banner Institute. They had honed their swordsmanship under the watchful eye of Lady Sonechka, a master of blade and spirit. Their training complete, they now faced a trial that would determine their worthiness to bear the mantle of spies.

The sisters were abruptly awoken in the dead of night. With a sense of urgency, they were whisked away by a helicopter, its rotors slicing through the frigid air. The journey was swift and silent, the landscape below a vast expanse of snow-covered wilderness. As the helicopter descended, their hearts pounded with anticipation.

With a final farewell from their pilot, the sisters were left alone swords in hand, in the desolate wilderness. Their instructions were simple: walk one kilometer west through the forest, their, the helicopter will be waiting to pick them up. The biting cold pierced their layers of fur-lined clothing, but their determination burned hotter. They ventured deeper into the woods, their eyes scanning the surroundings for any sign, any clue.

A marking on a tree caught their attention – the silhouette of a grizzly bear, its claws etched into the bark.

A shiver of unease ran down their spines. Further along the path they stumbled upon the skeletal remains of a human, picked clean by an animal. The sisters exchanged uneasy glances, their grip tightening on their swords.

As they pressed forward, the forest grew denser, the snow deeper. They noticed bear tracks in the snow, some small, others larger. The realization struck them like a thunderbolt – they were heading towards a bear's den. The tracks of bear cubs confirmed their suspicions. They knew that if they continued they would face the wrath of a protective mother.

Daria, the youngest, spoke with a voice as steady as her blade, "We have been given clues, sisters. The bear, the bones... they are warnings. We must change our path."

Myra, the strategist, nodded in agreement. "We were told to walk west, but not to our deaths. To the south lies another path; we can turn west once we clear the bear's den. We must trust our instincts."

Olivia, the oldest and most courageous, drew her sword. "These are our trials, our final test. I say we go forward. If danger finds us, we shall meet it with steel."

Myra and Daria pause, they look into their older sisters' eyes and remind her, "Don't forget our lessons, a battle not fought is a battle won."

Olivia takes their words to heart, "You are right, we need to stick together." With newfound resolve, they turned south, leaving the bear's den behind. The forest seemed to hold its breath, the only sound the crunch of snow beneath their boots.

Olivia, Myra, and Daria pressed on through the dense

forest, swords drawn. The air crackled with anticipation; their senses heightened. A twig snapped, a rustle of leaves. Then, a blood-curdling roar shattered the silence.

A monstrous mountain lion, its eyes blazing with predatory hunger, lunged from the dark shadows. Its massive frame dwarfed the sisters, its claws extended like daggers. Time seemed to slow as they instinctively reacted, forming a triangle of steel.

"I am the blade!" Olivia cried, her sword flashing in the moonlight as she charged forward, her agility belying her youth.

"I am the guard!" Myra declared, her broadsword raised in a defensive stance, her unwavering gaze locked onto the beast's every move.

"I am the grip!" Daria roared, her strength evident as she anchored their formation, her sword deflecting the lion's swipes with a resounding clang.

The battle raged, a whirlwind of fur, steel, and primal fury. The sisters moved as one, their yearlong training seamlessly blending into a deadly ballet. Olivia's swift strikes drew blood, while Myra's shield-like defense repelled the lion's ferocious attacks. Daria, the unyielding foundation, held firm, ensuring her sisters could unleash their full potential.

The mountain lion, though fierce, was outmatched. Weakened by their coordinated assault, it let out a final, desperate roar before collapsing to the ground, its lifeblood staining the snow. The sisters stood panting, their bodies bruised but their spirits unbroken. They had faced their most formidable foe yet and emerged victorious.

With a renewed sense of purpose, they resumed their journey, following the helicopter pilots' cryptic instructions. The forest thinned as they turned north, the distant whir of helicopter rotors growing louder. They emerged into a clearing, the helicopter waiting for them, its engine idling.

As they climbed aboard, a figure stepped out of the shadows, her silhouette familiar yet unexpected. It was Lady Sonechka, her eyes filled with pride and warmth. She embraced each sister in turn, her voice thick with emotion.

"You have done well, my Matryoshka Dolls," she said. "You have passed the Trials of Misha."

The sisters listened intently as Lady Sonechka explained the true nature of their test. The grizzly bear, a symbol of untamed nature, had been a test of their wisdom and restraint. By avoiding a futile battle they had conserved their strength for the greater challenge that lay ahead.

The mountain lion, she revealed, was no ordinary beast. It was a hunter, a creature of darkness sent to eliminate those who crossed its path. The sisters had not merely defeated a predator; they had protected themselves and each other through the knowledge they learned.

"Your journey is not over," Lady Sonechka concluded. "But you have proven yourselves worthy of the path that lies ahead."

With a newfound understanding of their purpose, the sisters settled in on the helicopter, their hearts filled with both gratitude and determination. They had overcome the trials, faced their fears, and emerge stronger. The road ahead was uncertain, but they knew they would face it together, united by the bond of sisterhood and the unwavering spirit of warriors.

CHAPTER 17
THE COVER STORY
Manhattan, New York - 1980

The elevator dinged softly as it reached the sixth floor of the Roosevelt Hotel and Rurik stepped out into the quiet hallway. His footsteps echoed softly as he made his way toward room 629. With a light tap he announced his presence before slipping inside unnoticed.

Rurik entered the room and removed his gray brim fedora with a long feather tucked into the band. Olivia, Myra, and Daria all jumped off the bed where they had been chatting.

"Dollmaker, we have failed to obtain the four parts of the Eye of Horus," Olivia's voice carried a tone of disappointment.

"Actually, sir," Myra interjected, her expression grave.

"I had one in my possession, but I returned it."

Rurik settled into an armchair, observing the trio perched on the side of the bed with a measured gaze. He gestured for Myra to continue, intrigued by her revelation.

"I had the Health Gem in my hand when we were attacked by a mysterious beast," Myra recounted, her voice tinged with lingering unease. "It was the same creature that's been making headlines."

Daria chimed in, her eyes alight with the memory. "Mr. Rice, one of the chaperones intervened but he was gravely injured. We returned the gem, realizing the danger it posed." She exchanged a glance with her sisters before continuing. "But we were also able to witness its power..." Her voice filled with wonder. "One of the Katzenstein kids healed Mr. Rice of all his wounds with a single touch."

The other girls murmured their own awe, nodding.

The Dollmaker listened intently, processing their account before speaking. "So our intelligence was accurate; the gems possess formidable powers. While I share your disappointment, I understand your actions. Our mission remains unchanged: infiltrate, obtain the Eye of Horus, and track these beasts back to Set before chaos ensues."

Olivia interjected; her tone urgent. "Sir, the Katzenstein Kids are involved and aware of the presence of the beast as well. They possess knowledge of the Eye of Horus and may hold vital information about Set's plans. We must continue to track them."

"Very well," the Dollmaker conceded, a glimmer of anticipation in his eyes. He clasped his hands together as he considered the new information. "If everything we have learned is true, then this beast you encountered is one of twelve Minotaur's I have been tracking since my visit to Egypt. And if Set truly is the mysterious being that has been released upon us, much of what has happened makes more sense. After all, he is the god of chaos and war. Paranoia, fear, and chaos is everywhere. Our motherland is engaged in war in Afghanistan, and tensions are growing all around the world." He shook his head. "We must do all we can to stop Set and his army of Minotaur's, to bring an end to the storm he has rained down upon us."

"Yes, sir," the girls said in unison.

"That's what we're here to do," Myra added. "We've compiled a folder on what we know of the four kids," she handed him a brown file, "and we know they are familiar with how to use the pieces of the Eye of Horus. We believe they are also seeking answers about the Minotaur that attacked the hotel last night. We believe the Minotaur intended to take the Health Gem. If we hadn't gotten it first, this night may have gone quite differently."

"Do you believe your cover has been compromised in any way?"

"No sir, and we've also devised a plan."

The sound of a ringing phone woke the Katzenstein Kids from a much-needed nap. Dez, Isaac, Will, and Amy rubbed the sleep from their eyes and blinked at each other before anyone realized what woke them. *Ring-ring-ring,* the phone continued. Amy was the first out of bed, her eyes wide. The sound of her voice put an end to the trilling ring of the hotel phone. It had been knocked onto the floor in the altercation with the Minotaur, so she crouched down to answer it.

"Hello?" Amy's eyes widened, and she covered the mouthpiece to tell the others, "It's the front desk! Our parents are here."

The boys hopped out of bed and began gathering the suitcases, thankful they'd had the sense to pack before passing out.

"Thank you so much. We'll be right down," Amy told the front desk operator.

"We should check in with Ms. Fleming," Isaac suggested as they were heading out.

With one last wince at the sight of their room they closed the door behind them. Someone was bound to assume the beast created the havoc. By then they would be long gone. It was hard not to feel guilty, but the truth was it wasn't their fault.

Finding Ms. Fleming didn't take long. She was already in the hallway, pacing up and down as if on patrol. When she saw them, she practically swooped toward them.

"Good afternoon," she said, taking in the kids and their suitcases. "What have we got here? All packed and ready to go back home?"

"Yes, ma'am," the kids echoed.

"The front desk called to let us know that our parents are at the front desk. We're headed there now."

Ms. Fleming eyed the door to their room and gave a brisk nod. "All right, if you've got everything, off you go. Give your parents my regards."

"Yes, ma'am," they said again.

Their teacher watched them step into the elevator and disappear behind its automated doors with a gentle ding. Before they knew it, they were stepping out into the hotel lobby with all its plants and shades of burgundy.

"Ahhhhh!" A cacophony of parental exclamations slammed into them from the open space. To the kids' surprise an excited Jo and Cindy, as well as Isaac's mother Anne, raced over to embrace them.

In the rush of hugs and hurried greetings, Amy cried out, "We all heard you were coming but we couldn't believe you were going to drive all the way here!"

Jo brushed her daughter's hair behind her ear. "I think I can speak for all of us, including Will's mother and father, and your mother as well Dez, that when we heard what happened we all knew we had to get to New York as soon as possible."

Cindy added, "That's right. When we got the call, we teamed up and hit the road first thing this morning."

"At the crack of dawn," Anne nodded.

"What call?" Amy asked curiously, looking between the women.

Suddenly, appearing through the Roosevelt Hotel's fancy glass doors like a movie star on the red carpet, was the Cape Cod Daily's own Mike Kelly, dressed in a polyester brown suit and swaggering. His hair was slicked back. "What call, you ask?" He called out. "My call, of course! You didn't think I would miss a news story like this, did you?" Mike offered a charming smile, his white teeth dazzling. "Not when my young friends are involved."

The kids knew then that they would all come together

in a spirited outpouring of gossip. They all had tales to share of the past twelve hours of adventure.

Taking charge, with more than one unnecessary wink, Mike grabbed a suitcase and spun on his heel. "I think it's best we wrap up and finish this conversation in my van, eh?"

Jo and Cindy helped the kids with the rest of their suitcases and the group followed Mike outside, Anne sticking close to Isaac. The kids recognized the news van parked in front of the hotel instantly and they could hardly hold back their excitement. They didn't expect all this support to arrive in New York City. They assumed they would have to solve this mystery and fight the Minotaur's on their own, but here was Mike Kelly, the man who knew everything that happened last summer and had helped them through it! But there was a hitch; although they had Mike, Amy had told no one of the powers they possessed, and Isaac wasn't sure how much his mother knew. He hadn't shared any of the details about the Eye of Horus either. That meant they had to be careful of what they said in front of Jo, Cindy, and Anne.

The inside of the van was lined with three rows of seats and an assortment of news equipment was scattered haphazardly: a hand-held recording device, piles of newspapers and notebooks and a portable typewriter. It was a tight fit, with hardly enough seating for everyone alongside all of Mike's tools of the trade. While the kids took in their surroundings Mike spun around in his captain's chair at the front of the vehicle.

"Well," he said. "As you can see from the size of things,

we couldn't take all your parents on this little road trip but rest assured that the gang we have was more than up for the task." His mouth broke out into a big smile, stretching from ear to ear, as did Anne's, Jo's, and Cindy's.

"Why are you guys acting so weird, with those creepy smiles on your faces?" Amy exclaimed.

Suddenly, the van erupted as the adults threw questions and exclamations at the kids, all of them speaking quickly and over each other. The curiosity of the three women was seemingly directed at everyone, someone, and no one all at once.

"—Why didn't you tell me about your powers?"

"—What attacked you kids last night?"

"—Are you okay? You could have been killed!"

"—We are so proud of you!"

It was obvious to the kids that the adults had been holding themselves back until this moment. Isaac quickly looked at Mike in the driver's seat.

"Good grief," Isaac glanced at Mike, still grinning back at them. "Did you have to tell everyone?"

Anne placed her hand lovingly on her son's cheek. With a glance at the others, she told him, "It wasn't Mike. I knew it on that day last summer when you came home with your grandfather's comic book, *The Katzenstein Kids*." She removed her hand. "I knew he was chosen by Horus. It didn't take much for me to realize all four of you had been given the gift... the *responsibility*. And of course, Mrs. Weatherbourne helped fill in the missing pieces."

"So when Anne called me, I called Jo and Cindy, and we put together a plan," Mike added matter-of-factly. He had turned back around facing the road, and the van started up with a low growl. "I knew what we really needed was a cover story!"

All four kids nodded in agreement, excited that they weren't alone in this anymore. Their last moments before falling asleep the previous evening had been spent worrying about the lies they would have to tell to hide their scrapes and bruises, fearing that someone might have seen them or figured out they were involved. Now that there were no more secrets between themselves and the adults, it felt as if a weight had been lifted off them. They relaxed, feeling their minotaur encounter in their aching muscles even as they did. Once a cover story was formed, they could get back to the Hideout, safe in a basement back on Cape Cod where they could try to figure out the location of the Was Scepter before the Minotaur's could.

Mike drove the van around the block before pulling into an alley next to the hotel. He jumped out of the van, leaving the others to follow after him in bewilderment. When they were all out, Mike handed Dez a large video camera.

"Okay Dez, just stand right there and when I say 'action,' you push that red button. Make sure to keep me in the frame," he smirked. Then he gestured for Amy's mom, Jo, and her girlfriend, Cindy, to stand by the entry to the alley. They did. "When I walk over to you, just tell the story we discussed on the ride to New York."

Both women nodded, excited. Mike then looked over at Anne and gave her a wink. She smiled, her eyes twinkling with a silent understanding. Amy, Isaac, and Will watched on in confusion.

"What the heck are they doing?" Will wondered aloud, only for Isaac and Amy's ears. They shrugged.

In a hurry, Mike grabbed a corded microphone from within the van, took a deep breath and began speaking to the camera in Dez's hands. "Hello, this is Mike Kelly of the Cape Cod Daily, reporting today from the Big Apple! Just twelve hours ago, students from our very own Wixon Middle School, who had been staying at the Roosevelt Hotel as part of their eighth-grade class trip, were suddenly awakened by a mysterious disturbance. School chaperone Thom Rice was brutally attacked in the hallways of this famous hotel, by what some have described as a *wild beast.*"

The kids could scarcely believe what they were hearing. They exchanged horrified glances. This wasn't going to help them at all! Mike was going to bring more attention to the events—was this his idea of providing a cover story? Dez gave the others a worried glance over his shoulder but didn't dare move the camera off the flamboyant reporter.

Mike went on, his sparkling grin bringing out the dimples in his cheeks. "Ladies, I was told you may have seen something. Can you share with us what that might have been?" Dez panned the camera along as Mike approached Jo and Cindy, microphone in hand.

"Well, yes sir, we sure did," Jo nodded seriously. "Last night, right about the time this mysterious disturbance occurred, we noticed a large, scary man dressed in a big black gorilla suit!"

Cindy jumped in with her own exclamation, putting on a great New Yorker accent. "That's right; he came running out the back door of the hotel and pulled off his mask!"

Behind his back, out of view of the camera's lens, Mike made a small gesture, a signal with his hand that the kids almost didn't notice. That was when Anne came running over. "Excuse me, excuse me," she called out. "Are you with the news?"

Mike looked up with pure confidence. "Why, yes, I am!"

"I want to report a man in an animal suit who just tried to steal my pocketbook," Anne told him in a panicked voice. "He ran that way!" She pointed her finger down the alleyway.

Dez pointed the camera down the alley before turning back to Mike, who stepped forward toward the camera with a twinkle in his eye. "Well, there you have it folks, live on camera, our very own students seem to have gotten a taste of the Big Apple they didn't expect. This was no mysterious beast rampaging the city, but rather a simple case of a petty thief looking for some quick cash dressed in a gorilla suit! I'm Mike Kelly of the Cape Cod Daily, signing off from New York City." He reached forward and clicked the stop button on the camera.

A red blinking light above the lens stopped as the feed came to an end, and everyone cried out in excitement, the parents and the kids alike.

"We did it, we did it!"

The kids were overjoyed, albeit astonished. Did that really all happen? Mike had a plan after all—the perfect cover story for all the supernatural events going on.

"Once I release this footage to the station, every

channel will pick it up," Mike told them.

"That's what I call a cover story," Dez laughed.

The kids thanked Mike excitedly as they all climbed back into the van to begin their journey back to Cape Cod, smiles on their faces.

CHAPTER 18
THE DOOR WITH THE LAVENDER WREATH

The van meandered through the Upper West Side of New York, its tires rolling smoothly over the pavement. Central Park West offered a brief respite from the towering concrete structures that defined the city skyline. As the vehicle traversed W 89th Street toward the parkway, patches of greenery peeked through the urban landscape, offering a glimpse of the massive park amidst the bustling metropolis. Inside the van the kids settled into their seats, relishing a moment of tranquility after the whirlwind of events they had experienced. Around them, the adults sensed the need for a brief reprieve and allowed them their silence. They didn't quite understand the weight of the challenges that lay ahead, but they were aware their kids were going through much more than the average teenager.

In many ways, the events of the past twelve hours had been nothing short of extraordinary. To the average person, the trials they had faced would seem unbelievable. Yet, amidst the chaos and uncertainty, a sense of purpose guided the thoughts of the Katzenstein Kids in finding the Was Scepter.

Suddenly, Amy's voice pierced the calm, commanding attention. "Stop!" she cried out, her urgency evident. Mike, the driver, reacted swiftly slamming on the brakes and bringing the van to a sudden halt. Jo, Cindy, and Anne exchanged puzzled looks.

"What's wrong?" Mike asked, his brow furrowed in concern as he turned to face the group.

"Pull over, now!" Amy shouted with even more urgency. She glanced through the window, giving the others the impression, she had seen something. "I need to get out."

"Did you see something?" Dez asked, glancing out the same window. He shrugged at the others when he couldn't see anything of note.

The van had barely come to a stop when Amy leaped out of her seat, her hand already grasping the door handle and pulling it open. Without hesitation she bolted out onto the sidewalk, retracing the path they had just traveled, running at breakneck speed. Will, Isaac, and Dez sprang into action, their instincts kicking in as they followed Amy's lead. Each of them clutched the trinket hanging from their necks, ready for whatever might await them. Behind them, the adults looked on in shock.

"What's happening, Amy?" Jo called out; her concern evident as she watched Amy's retreating figure. She turned to Mike hurriedly, "We have to back up."

The van began traveling backward up the road, humming as it did. With the door open, Jo fell back into her seat while the vehicle moved and eventually stopped along the curb near where the kids had gathered.

Amy came to a breathless stop in front of a three-story brownstone house, her wide-eyed gaze fixed on the entrance. As the boys caught up to her, they realized that it was just an ordinary house, nestled among the row of large homes lining the quiet street. But the recognition was clear on Amy's face as she pointed to the door directly in front of them, the one adorned with a lavender wreath.

"It's the door with the lavender wreath," she exclaimed, her voice tinged with excitement and disbelief.

Gathering around Amy, Will, Isaac, and Dez exchanged a surprised glance. They understood the significance of Amy's vision, even as the adults looked on with uncertainty.

"Love?" Jo called, stepping out of the news van.

Amy turned to face the van, her eyes alight with determination as she recounted the visions she had seen through the Prophecy Gem—the meaning behind the door with the lavender wreath. "I've been dreaming about this door for months, but every time I came close to opening it, I would wake up. I was supposed to come here; I know it. Maybe we all were. Maybe I couldn't open the door, or it wouldn't open for me because I was supposed to be here with you, with all of you."

Her mom, noticing the glow emanating from Amy's Prophecy Gem, pointing it out to the others. "Your ring is glowing," she observed, her voice filled with wonder.

Amy nodded, her resolve firm. "That just proves it!" She turned back to the boys. "We must go up those steps together and uncover the truth behind this mystery."

Will offered Amy his hand and she took it. Then, hand in hand, they ascended the stone steps leading to the door with Isaac, Dez and the group right behind them, their hearts pounding with anticipation. As they reached the top landing Mike's voice piped up from the back of the group.

"Darn, I left my camera in the van!"

Undeterred, Amy raised her finger and pressed the ornate doorbell. A melodious chime resonated from within the house, signaling their arrival. After a moment's pause, the door creaked open to reveal a woman in her late thirties, her appearance striking yet welcoming. She stood tall, her long dark hair softening her features.

"Well, hello. How can I help you?" The woman greeted them, her curiosity piqued by the unexpected visitors.

Amy stepped forward; her voice steady as she explained their unusual circumstances. "This may sound like a strange story, but I assure you it's true. I've seen this very door with the lavender wreath in my dreams. I don't know what it means, but I believe there's a reason we're here and I… well, I hope you'll let us explore what it might be."

The woman regarded them with a mixture of skepticism and intrigue. "In your dreams? I don't understand. Have you been here before?" She inquired; her brow furrowed in confusion.

"No, none of us have," Amy replied earnestly. "We're visiting from Cape Cod, Massachusetts and as we were driving by, I saw your door, a door that I've been seeing for months whenever I go to sleep at night." She gripped Will's hand tighter in her nervousness, worried she might be scaring the woman. "I know it means something. I know there's a reason we're here; it feels like it was meant to be."

The woman hesitated, uncertain how to respond to the unexpected revelation. "I'm not sure about this," she admitted, her apprehension evident in her voice.

Just then, an elderly woman's voice echoed from within the house, tinged with an accent. "Liz, who's at the door?" She called out, drawing closer to investigate the commotion.

The woman, now identified as Liz, opened the door wider, revealing the group gathered on her doorstep. "This young lady believes she was destined to..." Liz hesitated as she looked at all of them. "She was destined to meet us," she explained to the elderly woman. "She said she saw our door with the lavender wreath in a dream."

The elderly woman stepped forward, her eyes scanning the faces before her with a mixture of surprise and recognition. The corners of her eyes crinkled with amusement. "Well, look at all of you. Did you all have the same dream?" She mused aloud, an equally curious look on her face as she took them in.

Amy shook her head. "No, ma'am, just me."

The elderly woman's eyes flitted from Amy's face to Will's, to Dez's, and seemed to linger a bit longer on Isaac's face before she moved on to look at the adults behind them. Her expression softened when her gaze landed on Anne, whose eyes were already brimming with tears. A sense of recognition dawned on her face, and within seconds the elderly lady's eyes welled up too.

"My goodness, Sofia," she gasped, both her voice and the hand she used to cover her mouth trembling with emotion. "I never forgot your face!"

Anne rushed forward through the bodies on the steps, enveloping the elderly woman in a tight embrace. "Mother, oh Mother, I can't believe it's you!" She cried out, her heart overflowing with emotion.

As they watched the heartwarming reunion unfold, the others gathered on the landing felt a sense of awe and wonder. Goosebumps covered Amy's skin, and Isaac's mouth had dropped open. After all the horrors the Goffman family had faced in their past, it was astonishing that Anne's mother had survived the holocaust, defying the odds and reuniting with her daughter after so many years through the power of a vision.

"It's incredible," Jo whispered, echoing Amy's thoughts, her eyes shining with tears of her own.

But Will, Isaac, Dez, and Amy knew better. They understood that it was the Prophecy Gem that had led them here, guiding them toward this momentous encounter. And they were certain that there was more to uncover, more secrets waiting to be revealed.

"I think you all had better come in," Liz said, a tear running down her cheek as she stepped aside.

The elderly woman pulled back from her daughter's

embrace but kept her arm wrapped protectively around Anne as she led them inside. With Liz's invitation the others followed them into the house, entering a world of opulence and elegance. The living room was adorned with original artwork, ornate Victorian-style furniture, and luxurious furnishings—a testament to the wealth and taste of its occupants. Finding seats amidst the plush armchairs and sofas they settled in, their minds buzzing with anticipation. Anne and her mother clutched one another close, seeming unwilling to let go now that they had found each other again.

"I can't believe it's really you," Anne told her mother. "I never thought I would see you again."

"And I you, my child. For all these years I thought you were gone, but deep down I had hoped for a miracle. And now this," Anne's mother faced Isaac with a knowing smile, even as tears rained down her face. "This must be my grandson. I'd recognize those eyes anywhere."

Isaac leaned into his grandmother's hand as she cupped his cheek, shutting his eyes. It was clear this moment was just as emotional for him as it was for his mother, even if he didn't cry.

"You're right," he told her. "I'm your grandson!"

"Come here, my child," she told him, and Isaac threw himself into the outstretched arms of his grandmother. The three of them embraced tightly in the luxurious living room. "I never thought it possible."

The only person who wasn't comfortably seated was Mike Kelly. The news reporter was standing in front of the fireplace, picking up and looking at one framed photo after the other before setting them back down among an impressive collection. "This is incredible," he said. "All these important people!"

Jo and Cindy went over to join Mike, gasping. Not only were there framed photos of Liz and a handsome gentleman with graying hair, but they were standing beside many notable people, from a former governor to a popular jazz singer of the 70's. It seemed that in the time she had been in America, Isaac's grandmother had met a number of important people and had a bevy of interesting stories to tell.

"Indeed, it is," she said with a chuckle. "And my second husband, of course. He was a Wall Street investor; peace be upon him. It's because of him I was able to meet all those wonderful people and because of him that we have such a lovely home."

"Yeah, Dad wouldn't have had it any other way," Liz smiled demurely. At Isaac's surprised expression, she nodded. "That's right. Your grandmother is my mother, which means I'm your aunt... and," she turned to Anne, "I guess that makes us sisters too. I'm Liz."

"Liz," Anne breathed with a smile. Then, she broke away from her son and mother to embrace her sister tightly. The two laughed as they hugged, wiping at teary eyes.

"Well, since we're introducing ourselves," Jo said lightly.

"My name is Jo, and this is my girlfriend Cindy. Amy, the lovely young lady who came knocking on your door with all of us strangers in tow, is my daughter."

"She's one of my best friends," Isaac told his grandmother. He gestured to the boys. "And so are Will and Dez. We call ourselves the Katzenstein Kids."

"The Katzenstein Kids? Now, that is a name I haven't heard in a long time. It's a pleasure to meet all of my grandson's best friends. You can all call me Helen," she said with a laugh. "Although I hope you'll call me *Grandmother,*" she added to Isaac, who beamed at the sound of that.

With that, Helen stood and joined Jo, Cindy, and Mike at the mantelpiece picking up a photo of herself and Liz at a graduation ceremony. "Now, this looks like a simple picture of Liz graduating from Cornell University—a feat well worth celebrating on its own—but the real gem of the story is how she worked with the university for recognition of what happened during the war, to prevent such things from ever occurring again." The photo was passed around. "So how did we get here, to the Upper West Side of New York? Stories, stories to tell!"

"Mom always says stories should be told over a steaming hot cup of tea," Liz said with a grin. "And of course, pop for the kids," Liz added with a wink.

"That I do," Helen nodded enthusiastically. "So, who is up for one?"

Helen's movements were graceful and deliberate, a testament to her elegance. She moved through the room, taking orders and then disappeared with Anne into the kitchen for what seemed like only seconds before they reappeared with a tray of drinks and another laden with treats. It seemed Helen didn't let her age get in the way and was quite content to be the hostess, serving everyone their beverages and butter cookies. They all sipped their drinks while Helen regaled them with tales of her life in New York and all the twists and turns that had brought her to this moment.

"My new life here began when I met my husband. He reminds me a lot of Herman sometimes, my first husband and Sofia's father. But of course, when I met him, there were a lot of things from my old life that I wanted to forget," she told them honestly. "When I first came to America, I did not trust anyone for a long time. I stayed not far from here, in housing used for refugees of the war. I was on a list, waiting for a kind American couple who gave me a home and told me it was safe again. It was a lonely time filled with dread and worry, never knowing if I would see those I had left behind again. Many months passed, I learned to speak English, growing more independent until I was able to make it on my own. The family that took me in provided a safe haven and helped me find work.

"You must have felt so alone and scared," Anne said.

"Almost all the time," Helen nodded. "The hardest part of it all was the quiet. Though I was far away from the war in Europe and the atrocities being reported in the newspapers, I remained terrified. Afraid of being all that remained of our family, I spent a lot of time reading books. Some weren't so lucky as to stay in a refugee sponsored home." She paused, and the haunted look in her eyes told them she was remembering. "As the years passed and the war came to an end, I ended up as a receptionist in a highly sought-after stock firm. My late husband became one of our first investors. For some time, he was my only friend here in America and eventually, we fell in love. I wouldn't have been blessed with all the beautiful things I have, not least of all my daughter Liz, if it weren't for meeting him. Liz is the one who chose to put that lovely lavender wreath on the front door that led to me being reunited with my darling Sofia!"

"I go by Anne now," Anne told her mother. "It was the name I took on when we left... well, that place. It's who I am now."

Helen smiled. "And I can only imagine all you had to go through to choose to be Anne."

"To tell you the truth," Anne glanced at her son, eyes sparkling with wonder. "I only really came to terms with everything last year, with the help of my son."

"Oh?" Helen looked at Isaac. "Do tell me more."

The air in Helen's living room hung heavy with shared secrets and the weight of history. It was a warmth born of newfound trust and a deepening bond between the room full of souls who had stumbled upon each other through the twists and turns of fate.

Thus, it was Helen's turn to listen to their stories: the tale of how Sofia had come to be Anne, a young woman with an extraordinary past and an even more extraordinary story of survival. And the tale of Isaac, the boy who had rediscovered the comic book *The Katzenstein Kids,* a relic from his own hidden heritage, along with a set of four very special Cracker Jack trinkets.

As the sun began to set outside, casting long shadows

across the room, Helen turned to them, her eyes twinkling with excitement. "Well, after hearing all about your wild adventures, do I have a story to tell," she announced, taking a deep breath as she prepared to share her most precious memory. "This is the amazing story of the night I escaped from Auschwitz."

A hush fell over the room as Will, Isaac, Dez, and Amy leaned forward, their hearts pounding with anticipation. They knew they were about to hear something profound, something that would forever change their understanding of courage, resilience, and the indomitable human spirit. And as Helen began to speak, her voice soft but steady, they were transported back to a dark time in history, a time of unimaginable horror, but also a time of extraordinary bravery and hope. For destiny had brought them together, guiding their paths toward a future fraught with mystery and adventure. And it had all started with Herman and Helena Katzenstein.

CHAPTER 19
BUNK 18
Auschwitz, Poland - 1943

Helena, a middle-aged woman at the time, lay back on a straw-covered wood bunk, filled with worry and disbelief at her situation. Of course, that was her state most days since she'd been placed in this dark, damp place. Stacked above her were two more bunks, and in them two other women she barely knew. She rolled to one side to ease the deep ache radiating in her lower back, tucking her dry worn hands under her head. There, she stared into the darkened room at the other women climbing into their bunks around her. Her eyes narrowed in on the wood post that supported the three-tier bunk she lay in, engraved in the wood was the number 18.

Bunk 18, she thought.

Of all the bunks, sixty perhaps, that filled the wood barracks she was in, she had been assigned to the bunk numbered eighteen. *The irony, she thought.* Being Jewish, the number eighteen was symbolic of giving "chai" or life. There didn't seem to be much life in the barracks, though. More fear than anything else, hopelessness.

Tired thoughts rambled through her mind, a mantra she told herself before sleep could steal her away, to remind herself to be strong the following day. *I must walk without dragging my feet, so my Nazi captors will not see me as weak or sick. That would certainly get me sent to the other line. The line that led to the little red house, a place no one returns from. I must remain alive, even in this place.*

Whispers began to flow like a wave through the barracks, soon washing upward and falling onto her ears, bringing with it the dreadful news. "Did you hear? There were two Kapos talking about clearing out our barracks at sunrise. They are making room for a large number of Hungarian Jews arriving by train."

A low roar of desperation filled the barracks as the women of many ages began to come to grips with the news. Helena caught the panicked whispers but didn't add her voice to the noise. It would be the death of them, the others said. They had seen it before just days ago; the barracks to the north had been herded out in a long line and were stripped of their striped pajamas, hats, and wooden clog shoes. Each entered the little red house one after the other, never to return. And yet, her greatest fear was the smokestack buildings; there, you didn't have to be sick or weak. There, the towering smokestacks would rain down ash as if it were snow falling from the sky.

She lay back and tried to keep her eyes open, afraid that if she fell asleep the morning would come too fast and the end of her life would soon follow. But her eyes would not cooperate, the weight of her lids pressed closed and shut out the world and the whispers of the women around her. Soon she felt her mind wandering, seeing her little Sofia dancing in her mind. Memories of a better time, when she and Sofia would laugh on their way to school. A time when she shared a quiet dinner with Sofia and her beloved Herman. In the dead of night, she could count on the thoughts of her loved ones to return to her, far easier than they did in the discomfort of daylight.

Suddenly, her lids opened wide. *My God*, she thought; *she had fallen asleep despite her efforts!* Her eyes, already used to the darkness could see a dark-skinned boy, a young boy, standing beside her bunk. If she had to guess, she would say he was around eight years old. He was barefoot and wore a long cloth garment.

She glanced around the barracks, but no one else seemed to be awake. In a whisper, she asked the boy, "Who are you?"

But the boy simply looked on silently. After a moment, he offered her his small hand and without thinking, she took it. The boy's touch was soft and kind; he took her hand and gestured with his head. It occurred to her that he wanted her to follow. She gulped, her throat feeling tight and glanced around once again. But still, none of the other women woke, none of them showed any awareness of the strange boy visiting them in the middle of the night. After some hesitation Helena dropped her feet to the floor and allowed the boy to guide her away from her bunk, walking with her through the barracks to the door at the far end. Helena was confused and even more so scared. The closer they came to the door the faster her heart raced, pounding hard against the inside of her chest. She knew once they opened the door an armed Nazi guard would surely shoot them both.

The boy reached for the knob and Helena stopped him, tugging his hand back with her free one. "No, "she whispered frantically. "We will be seen!"

The boy reached into his garment and removed a green gem, holding it open in his left hand. In his palm was a birthmark forming the shape of a crude eye with a large pupil, a curved eyebrow above it and a curved teardrop below. Unfamiliar to her, it was the symbol for the Eye of Horus. Helena did not understand who he was, why he was there, or what he was doing. But she felt a power coming from the green gem in his hand, a power she couldn't explain. Part of her grew more frightened and she resisted the boy and his desire to open the door—until she heard a voice speaking clearly inside her mind.

"You must leave this place," the voice stated.

Helena gasped softly at the sound of the voice in her head and suddenly the green gem began to glow in the boy's hand. The boy placed the glowing gem into his right hand and clasped Helena's hand over his. The glowing green gem brightened and illuminated from both their hands.

With that the boy opened the door to the barracks and

they stepped out into the night. As they turned the corner, a uniformed Nazi guard saw them and hollered, "Halt!"

The boy calmly walked forward as if undeterred by the armed guard. Helena felt a rush of fear, then like a switch, a sudden calmness. In her head the voice returned, "As the holder of the Protection Gem, no harm can come to you!"

The guard didn't miss a beat. He raced toward them angrily, raising the butt of his rifle to strike at the boy's head violently. But just before impact the butt of the gun was repelled, the energy forcing the guard backward and onto the ground.

He stood in frustration and anger and hollered once again, "Halt! Halt, or I will shoot!"

The boy ignored the guard. One hand still clasping Helena's, he calmly walked across the dirt ground barefoot and steadfast. Helena could hardly believe her eyes as she watched the child, could hardly believe her feet as they followed him, but a sense of calm had come over her as well. They were heading for the main gate. Behind them, the guard took aim and began firing his rifle. Helena's heart skipped a beat; she flinched and squinted from the flashing muzzle. Her shoulders tightened as she waited for the impact of the bullets, only to see them ricochet in every direction without ever hitting their intended mark. No harm came to either her or the boy just as the voice in her mind had foretold.

Gunfire had given them away however, and overhead searchlights mounted on a pair of watchtowers lit into action. From the high position Helena could see the shadow of a large figure taking aim behind a large machine gun mounted to the railing. Then another figure appeared behind a large machine gun on the other side. In a furious expulsion of sounds that broke through the night— clicking metal feeding through the belts of the large-caliber machine guns—rounds of ammo sprouted into the guns' firing chambers.

"We must run, they're going to open fire!" Helena cried out to the boy.

But the boy barely acknowledged the danger, simply raising his left hand up to the searchlights exposing the Eye of Horus birthmark upon his palm. He persisted toward the main gate with Helena hot on his heels.

From all around them they could hear the Nazi guards hollering to each other.

"Hitler's buzzsaw awaits you my young Jew!"

The word "Fire!" ripped through the air sending a shiver down Helena's spine. Fear gripped her heart, threatening to send her crumbling to the ground. But she clung to the boy's hand, her lifeline in the chaos.

A deafening roar erupted as the machine guns unleashed their fury, raining bullets down upon them. The earth before their feet exploded, a cloud of dirt and debris billowing outwards. A symphony of light and sound filled the camp, each bullet sparking a burst of color as it struck the ground. The assault seemed to stretch on for an eternity, a relentless onslaught that threatened to consume them whole.

Finally, with a bone-jarring click, the machine guns fell silent. The only sound that remained was the crackling of flames and the acrid scent of smoke. From all around them the shocked cries of Nazi guards pierced the air. They couldn't believe their eyes – the boy and Helena still stood, miraculously unscathed.

A frantic chorus of orders filled the void. "Reload! Hit them again!" The sound of metal feeding through belts echoed through the camp. Helena's grip tightened around the boy's hand; their eyes locked in a silent pact of defiance.

Then once more, the command "Fire!" rang out. The ground before them exploded anew, a maelstrom of dirt and light. The camp was engulfed in a blinding inferno, the colors of destruction painting a horrific mural on the night sky.

Again, the assault ended with a chilling click, the machine guns falling silent. The air was thick with smoke, the ground littered with spent shells. But amidst the chaos two figures remained standing, the Protection Gem had shielded them both from harm. Around them the Nazi guards stood in shock, doing little but watching what was an unbelievable event unfold before them.

At the gate the boy pushed his hand forward and the electrified wire fencing sparked in every direction. Helena flinched as white-hot sparks flew around them; she could smell the smoke and burning electricity. At its center the metallic gate melted and fried until a hole appeared in the wire mesh. The boy and Helena stepped through the opening and made their way to the tree line without ever looking back. Helena expected to hear the haunting sounds of guards and dogs trailing them, yet for some reason things seemed unusually quiet.

It was as if the guards themselves had questioned what

they witnessed, as if it was all as unreal as it must have appeared, and Helena wondered for a moment if perhaps this was all a dream.

The pair walked for what seemed like miles through

marshlands and hills into a deep dark forest, finally arriving at their destination. The boy never speaking a word, simply stopped, and gestured for Helena to sit and wait on a log. Then, the boy walked off and disappeared into the darkness, leaving her there.

After several minutes an elderly man approached with a horse and cart. He wore a hooded wool coat and mumbled some words as he approached. Helena stood up, not in fear but in expectation, for in her heart she felt he was coming for her.

The man stopped and looked up. "Helena Katzenstein?" he asked. She looked up and nodded, noticing that he only had one eye. "Climb aboard, we have a long journey," he added.

The one-eyed elderly man and Helena traveled for days. In the most unusual of circumstances, they traveled openly along the back roads, through small towns, and villages. She didn't see the boy again and she wasn't sure what had happened to him. The man didn't say very much, and she was too tired to ask too many questions. Simply grateful for the fact that she was no longer sleeping in bunk 18, no longer trapped in the barracks she had escaped from. On occasion they crossed paths with uniformed German soldiers. The first few times had Helena terrified on the back of the cart, practically tempted to dive under the wool and blankets to hide. Each time, however, the soldiers would continue on their way without a single moment of questioning or suspicion. The fear at seeing the soldiers pass them by never went away. But Helena stopped jumping at the sight of them, stopped feeling the need to hide, until eventually, she accepted that she was somehow safe with the one-eyed elderly man and his cart. It was then that she began sleeping; most of the journey through the country was spent sleeping away horrors and resting in a way she was never able to back in the barracks on bunk 18.

Soon they entered France, and then to her horror, she learned it was time to leave the safety of the horse's cart. They were going to charter a small fishing boat to take them across the English Channel to England. She kept her head low as the one-eyed elderly man spoke to a fisherman, not meeting anyone's eyes and watched as he handed over a few coins to pay for their journey across the water.

Perhaps the one-eyed elderly man had a glowing gem in his pocket the entire time, she thought.

When Helena tried to have a conversation with the one-eyed elder, he was of few words and those words often didn't have much meaning for her. He told her stories of his travels, and it was hard to believe that this man had been to as many places as he said he had before the war. "I was once a performer," he told her. "Before the world was overtaken by violence and evil, I would travel across the land with a box filled with puppets, performing shows."

"But how did you get here?" She'd ask him.

"I was once a man from Thebes. My feet took me places first, then horses did and then boats like this one," he'd sat calmly as he spoke.

"What about my rescue? Why was I saved? There were many others back there. Why me and not one of them?"

It was when she asked this question that the elderly one-eyed man would grow quieter. He would never fully answer her question, only stating words such as, "One day, you will know why you met the one-eyed man from Thebes."

Then he would stop talking, sometimes for days at a time. Helena was frustrated that she didn't know more about her rescuers, didn't know more about why she was saved, and she felt some guilt at having left the other women in the barracks. Nevertheless, it felt like a true miracle that she had gotten away.

Soon enough they arrived in England and Helena accepted that she was safely in allied hands. When their boat arrived on the shore, another horse and cart awaited them, but this time the trip was a short one as they navigated to a refugee shelter.

Once there, Helena allowed herself the first emotion in days, her eyes welling up as she thanked the one-eyed elderly man. Before he left, she asked him one last question. "Where are you heading?"

"To join a friend at the opera," he replied with a smirk and a glint in his eye.

◆ ◆ ◆

In the coming weeks, Helena often felt as though she was dreaming. Warmth and enjoyable meals seemed like they weren't real, and it occurred to her that was because she never expected to be granted a semblance of normalcy again. More surreal still than the safety she found herself in was that she was offered a way out of Europe and was given passage on the Queen Mary. The ship was being used to transport troops from and to America, as well as a small group of refugees headed to New York, and Helena was part of that group.

Helena was astonished to be enjoying the serenity of normalcy. Just weeks prior, she was in fear of the "little red house." Since then, she had been shot at by machine guns, had traveled hundreds of miles through war-torn Europe, and had taken a boat across the channel to get to where she was. Ever since coming to England life had been cautious and quiet, a far sight from the violence and noise she had experienced in the camp. But it wasn't until she made her way onto the massive ship that she finally allowed herself to accept that she was safe. With safety came exploration, and on her first day aboard the ship Helena was pleasantly surprised to find a synagogue on the Queen Mary's B-deck, behind a door labeled The Scroll Room.

What a beautiful gift, she thought. *To build such a magnificent ship and provide this secret place, especially in a time like this.*

There were other Jewish people in the synagogue, and she joined them in worship for some time, feeling a peace deep within her chest. None of the others exchanged words with her that first day, only giving her a knowing nod as she took her seat among them in this holy place. Many of the refugees were in tears, mourning their losses even as they thanked God for saving them and bringing them here.

Helena soon returned to her bunk with thoughts of seeing the Statue of Liberty when she arrived in New York. Oh, to have such an experience! To be able to see new things! Still, she wished that she were not alone on the Queen Mary, that her beloved Herman and her beautiful Sofia could be with her. Thinking about them brought on an unpleasant twinge in the pit of her stomach, and she tried her hardest to block out the horror of what had become of both of them, finding it too difficult to bear.

Tears fell from her eyes, old tears that had been waiting for so long to finally spill from her lids. Within her salvation and newfound peace came a long-awaited release of pain and heartbreak, caused by the loss of her family, Herman, and Sofia.

It was as her eyes began to close on that first night that Helena noticed one final thing: a brass tag with the number 18 engraved into the wood of her bunk.

"*Am Yisrael Chai!*" She whispered to herself. "The people of Israel live!"

CHAPTER 20
CLEOPATRA'S NEEDLE
Manhattan, New York – 1980

All eyes in the living room were on Helen. Outside, night had fallen upon the city streets, though they were still bustling. Even here on the Upper East Side, New York did not sleep. Will, Isaac, Dez, and Amy looked on in excitement and anticipation, impressed by the strength of the woman before them and amazed that they had met the one-eyed elderly man not once, but twice, confirming his importance in all that had happened and all that was happening now.

Jo, Cindy, and Mike looked on in amazement at the chilling tale. The children could tell they were at a loss for words. None of them had expected to hear this story today. Anne held back the tears that welled in her eyes at the miraculous story of her mother's survival and escape from Auschwitz. Anne, most especially, could relate to the glowing green gem in her mother's story. After all, it reminded her of her own story, of how she had survived the horrors of the war at a young age and had been led to safety by the glowing green gem.

Helen's words slipped off her lips as if she had told the story a million times, but the truth was that she had not. None of what she had just shared had ever journeyed from her painful memories to find her lips. Rather, like all trauma, it remained locked deep inside her memories. She had kept the tale to herself since 1943. Now, 37 years later, she felt like a page from destiny had knocked upon her door, beckoning her to share her experience. As she completed her amazing tale, the room was full of kids and parents alike who had intensely listened to every word, as if a greater meaning was hidden between the lines or perhaps a clue or two that filled in some of the missing pieces.

"I could not have imagined I would ever have to relive that memory again," Helen quietly confessed, once she had finished the story. "Then again, I could not have imagined living in a world where a group of kids would one day appear at my door, with a name they had adopted from my late Herman's comic book, the Katzenstein Kids. I have always believed, however, that our paths are chosen, that they are pre-destined."

Dez jumped up in excitement at this point, "That's it, that's it! The one-eyed elderly man that saved you—it must be Horus himself. He helped you escape Auschwitz, and he helped Anne, I mean Isaac's mom, escape as well. I think he was in the subway tunnels last night and helped us find Amy!"

"Find Amy! What happened to Amy last night?" Jo cried out in disbelief.

Amy glowered at Dez, shifting uncomfortably next to her mom. The last thing she wanted was for her mother to find out that she had been kidnapped, and truth be told, it was an event they simply hadn't had the chance to share yet. She tried to change the subject; "Hold on, Mom. I think we need to recognize that the green gem, the Eye of Horus, is the one thing that is connecting all of this—all of us—together. It was used to save Helen, Sofia... I mean *Anne*, Will, Isaac, Dez, and me! This clearly is not a coincidence."

"Like I said earlier, our paths are already chosen!" Helen replied. "It is destiny that brought you all to my doorstep today."

"Yes," Amy added, continuing, "Horus has spoken to all of us. He told us that we have been chosen and that my ring, my Prophecy Gem will tell all that was, all that is, and all that will be! And now look, it brought us here... it led the way to Helen. The question now is... What is it trying to show us?"

Will, who had been watching Helen closely, nudged Isaac with his elbow before gesturing at a faint mark peeking from the sleeve of Helen's left forearm. Isaac's eyes widened at the sight of it. Dez, catching the interaction, looked at his friends with a bewildered expression, causing Will to lean in and whisper to him.

"The mark on Helen's forearm," he said quietly.

Dez's eyes found the mark and they widened too. He whispered back, "That's it. That's the clue. It must be the location of the Was Scepter!"

Helen took notice of the boys eyeing her strangely. "What seems to have riled you boys up?" She arched her brow, but the boys simply shifted, Will's cheeks deepening in color. "Come on now, we are all a part of something much bigger here. If you have something to add, please do!"

Will and Dez looked to Isaac to break the news; after all, it was his grandmother. He nodded. "Well, Helen... I mean... Grandma... Grandma Helen, it's just—we noticed your Holocaust tattoo."

Helen looked down at her arm and pulled back her sleeve to reveal a six-digit number tattooed into her skin. "Oh yes, I often thought about having it removed, but then decided that it's best to let it serve as living proof of having survived Auschwitz." Her expression softened. "Not everyone could say that."

Since she revealed the tattoo to them, Will, Isaac, and Dez jumped up and walked over to Helen to take a better look. Bemused, Helen twisted her arm to show them the full mark. Faded and muddled from time and age, the six-digit number was hard to read but clear enough to make out what they once were: 151745.

"Do you think it's possible?" Will asked Isaac. "Could it be a longitude?"

"Could be, hard to know for sure," Isaac suggested.

"May I?" Isaac met his grandmother's eyes and she

gave a nod. Isaac took his grandmother's arm and ran a finger along the numbers. They stuck out slightly on her skin, raised bumps. Isaac pondered, "If it is a longitude, we will at least have one-half of the coordinates! Grandma, do you have a globe?"

Helen pointed to an adjacent room and Dez, Isaac, and Will hurriedly ran into it without another word. It was set up much like a study with bookshelves lining the walls and a big wooden desk in the middle. On it stood a 12" diameter Bingham Globe. Will grabbed it with both hands, and the three boys left the study, rejoining the others in the living room.

The boys set the globe down on the coffee table in the middle of the room and Helen leaned forward in excitement, as did Jo, Cindy, Mike, Anne and Liz. Amy joined the boys as they began running their fingers across the longitude lines and spinning the globe in one direction and then another. Each of them called out the six-digit number as they did: 1-5-1-7-4-5.

The parents looked on intensely, yet not without confusion, their brows furrowed as they watched the kids.

"What are you guys looking for?" Cindy asked them, peering over Amy's shoulder.

Dez waved his hand in the air as if to wave the grown-ups off. "Stay back, we've done this before. We're professionals!"

Helen, amused by all the youthful excitement in the room waited patiently for the next thing that would come out of their mouths.

"Here!" Isaac yelled out suddenly, his finger pressed to

a specific location on the globe. "Here it is... it intersects with this tiny island in the middle of the Pacific Ocean... Bora-Bora!"

Amy couldn't keep the confusion off her face, nor from her voice. "Bora-Bora? That makes no sense."

Dez fell back on the floor in disgust, heaving a sigh. "Not in the middle of the ocean! Why did it have to be the ocean?"

Will looked up at Helen, explaining apologetically, "We're kind of afraid of sharks."

Helen nodded understandingly.

"Doesn't Bora-Bora seem like a strange place for our journey to lead?" Amy asked the boys. "And let's say this is longitude, where is the latitude? It could give us an entirely different location."

Will, Isaac, and Dez felt a bit deflated and it could be seen as their faces fell; Amy was correct, this was not necessarily a valid clue.

Jo and Cindy looked on with bewilderment, and when it seemed the kids weren't going to add more, Jo returned to her previous question. "Enough about Bora Bora. Can someone tell me what happened to Amy last night?"

At this, her daughter met her eyes with some concern and more than a little frustration. "It's okay Mom," she started. "We didn't want to tell you this, but I was kidnapped from the hotel by a minotaur. But Will, Isaac, and Dez rescued me. I'm okay, I promise."

"A minotaur! So, the beast was a real minotaur? Like half-man, and half-bull?" Jo cried out.

"We all heard what happened and we know what you

kids are involved in, the kind of great powers you possess, but I'm not sure any of us expected to hear *this*!" Mike added. Cindy and Anne nodded in agreement, while Jo continued to look on dumbfounded, as if she had been slapped by the information.

Dez cried out, "I know all of this is hard to believe, but trust us, it's real. Minotaur's, the ancient Egyptian deity Horus, the powers we have been granted with his eye, and the rise of the evil deity Set! It's like the stuff that comes straight out of one of our comic books."

"Yeah, only these pages are coming to life," Isaac added.

Helen sat back in her armchair and cleared her throat pointedly. "If I may, did you say half-man, half-bull? Well, now things are beginning to make much more sense," she told them with a nod. "You should have mentioned the bull sooner."

All eyes, wide, turned to Helen, and complete silence filled the room.

Helen told them, "There is one place in all of New York City where the words 'Bull' and 'Horus' are used together. I remember seeing it a long time ago; it left an indelible mark. Now, after hearing your tales, it may be the clue you're looking for."

Her eyes brightened. "Cleopatra's Needle! It's an ancient Egyptian obelisk that stands almost seventy feet tall. If I'm not mistaken, along the top banner, written in hieroglyphics, are the words: *The crowned Horus, Bull of Victory Arisen in Thebes.*'"

"That must be it!" the kids cried out, their excitement

overflowing. They all jumped up from the floor, exchanging enthusiastic glances.

"What are the odds of an ancient Egyptian obelisk being here in New York, the same place the Minotaur's are located?" Will exclaimed.

Mike's eyebrow shot upward. "Did you say… Minotaur's? As in, plural?"

Dez slapped him on the shoulder, grinning. "Oh yeah, we saw at least three of them!"

"Yeah, and if hieroglyphics refer to Horus, Bulls, and Arisen…" Amy redirected the attention to the more pressing issue, "it must have something to do with Set's attempt to resurrect himself."

Dez furrowed his brow, remembering a detail. "Wait, isn't an obelisk tall and narrow? Do you think it could be the hiding place of the Was Scepter?"

The kids looked at each other in realization. *It must be!*

Suddenly, Amy's Prophecy Gem began to glow brightly. "Look!" she called out. "The Prophecy Gem is glowing! It must be a sign… it must be trying to tell us that we are on the right track. The Was Scepter must be hidden within the obelisk."

Helen interrupted the excitement, musing over the past. "One day you will know why you met the one-eyed man from Thebes. That is what he told me back in 1943, the one-eyed man who rescued me. That is why I never forgot those words engraved on the top banner of the obelisk. The first time I came across Cleopatra's Needle, many years ago, I didn't think too much of it. Until I read those words, *The crowned Horus, Bull of Victory Arisen in Thebes,*' I thought it must be a strange coincidence." Helen looked over at Liz. "But what do I always say…"

Liz smiled at her mother. "Our destinies are predetermined." As she finished the rest of the statement, the kids spoke with her in unison, "Our paths are already chosen!"

"Just like Mrs. Weatherbourne always says," Isaac added.

The room fell silent for a brief moment, a buzz of anticipation in the air as they all took in each of the puzzle pieces that made up this incredible story of all their destined paths converging upon this very moment.

"Where is Cleopatra's Needle?" Isaac asked suddenly.

Helen smiled. "It is located in Central Park, right behind the MET."

The kids all looked at each other again, and the parents too.

"THE MET? Holy Calamity Batman," Dez cried out.

"We must have walked right by this thing and never even realized it," Will added.

Mike stood up. "I will take you there!"

"Whoa whoa whoa," Jo stood. "Let's not get ahead of ourselves."

Cindy and Anne began to object, voicing their fears of how dangerous it could be, until Helen stood from her armchair and took Jo, Cindy, and Anne by the hands. With a stern voice, she addressed everyone in the room. "Each of you has been chosen. These four kids are holders of the Eye of Horus, protectors of the children of men and women. Our destinies, their destinies, were set a long time ago, written into the fabric of our lives long before any of our paths ever crossed." Making eye contact with Jo, Cindy, and Anne, she told them gently, "I know you are afraid for them, but Horus is watching over all of us. This is what they must do!"

Jo looked down at Amy, and Anne at Isaac, both nodding slowly in understanding.

"She's right," Cindy told Jo, feeling Helen squeeze her hand reassuringly.

"We have to go there. We don't have a choice," Will spoke. "We have to go to Cleopatra's Needle in Central Park."

"It has to be tonight," Amy told them. "I heard the Minotaur's talking about the power of the Was Scepter, how it will be a weapon of great power for Set when they held me captive. It must be tonight; we must not let the Minotaur's get it before us; it will only help their mission to resurrect Set."

"And it's up to us to stop them," Isaac nodded resolutely.

"Katzenstein Kids," Dez held out his fist.

The others added theirs, and the kids cried out, "Unite!"

The room erupted in hugs, and each of them now knew what they must do. Dez, Isaac, Will, and Amy would go to Cleopatra's Needle in Central Park at midnight under the cover of darkness. And Mike Kelly would be the one to drive them.

CHAPTER 21
THE 12 MINOTAURS

Driving through New York City in the dead of night was exactly as one would expect: the roads, typically lit up by sunshine, were ablaze with the flashing colors of streetlights, car lights, and bars and pubs teeming with lines of people waiting to enter. The usual level of quiet was nonexistent. The kids took in the nightlife from behind the dirty windows of the news van as it traveled through the streets, absorbing the lights, colors, and noise while trying to calm their frayed nerves. It was nothing like driving through the quiet and abandoned streets of Dennis Port in the evening, where everything would be closed, and no one would be out and about.

Before they knew it Mike was slowing down the van

and pulling over along 5th Avenue and Central Park East. Dez, Isaac, Will, and Amy readied themselves.

"The MET is just ahead," Mike pointed his finger forward, directing them through the windshield. "If you enter the park over there and follow the path, you should find the obelisk somewhere behind the museum. You can't miss it." He glanced over the driver's seat at all of them, their jaws set with determination. "I will wait right here for your return and good luck!"

With that, the kids slid the door open and jumped out of the van onto the streets of New York, the boys' hands clutching their necklaces tightly. They looked both ways and began walking toward the dark, moonlit paths that led deep into Central Park.

As they entered the wooded space, the urban symphony of the city beyond faded into a muted hum. The tranquility of Central Park at night was almost deafening, a stark contrast to the vibrant energy they'd left behind. The cool air, a refreshing change from the summer's warmth, washed over them, carrying with it an undercurrent of apprehension.

It was darker here, without the reassuring glow of streetlights or the sweeping beams of car headlights to illuminate their path. Each step was guided by the dim moonlight filtering through the canopy of leaves above, and the rhythmic crunch of their footsteps on the gravel path served as a constant reminder of their isolation.

They walked under Greywacke Arch, its imposing stone structure looming over them, and rounded a corner, leaving the familiar sights of the park behind. The towering trees, their silhouettes stark against the night sky, closed in around them, their gnarled branches reaching out like skeletal arms.

The initial alertness to every rustle and shadow gradually gave way to a hesitant acceptance of the natural symphony of the woods. Leaves whispered secrets in the gentle breeze and the occasional chirp of a cricket pierced the stillness. It was a reminder that they were not alone.

Their pace quickened as they pressed deeper into the wooded path, their eyes scanning the shadows for any sign of movement. A shared sense of purpose propelled them forward, fueled by the urgency of their mission.

Suddenly, a clearing emerged from the darkness and their breath caught in their throats. There, bathed in the ethereal glow of the moon stood a massive obelisk, its towering presence a stark contrast to the natural world around it. Its weathered, ancient stone seemed to whisper tales of forgotten times and long-lost civilizations. Cleopatra's Needle, their destination, their beacon in the night, had revealed itself.

"There it is!" Will cried out.

They quickened their pace, approaching the base of the obelisk. Looking up at the tall four-sided monument with its pointed top reaching towards the sky, they couldn't help but be impressed. Carved in red granite and engraved from top to bottom with hieroglyphics, they knew it was what they were looking for.

"Now what?" Dez muttered, voicing their shared concern. If the Was Scepter was hidden within the obelisk's structure, how could they possibly retrieve it?

Before they could ponder further the boys' necklaces and Amy's ring began to glow, bringing with them an unsettling feeling of an ominous presence nearby. The kids felt a prickling sensation on the back of their necks, the undeniable feeling of being watched. They spun around, their backs to the obelisk, scanning the darkness for the source of danger.

From the pitch-black shadows a deep voice shattered the night's tranquility. "You may carry the powers of the Eye of Horus, but your lack of strategy eludes you. "The lead minotaur, Draconis, emerged from the darkness. "We planted the seed of the Was Scepter in the girl's thoughts, knowing you would seek it out and lead us to its hiding place."

The ground shook as another minotaur leaped from the shadows, followed by another, and then another. The kids stumbled as the earth trembled beneath the weight of the beasts, encircling them from all sides.

Dez, Isaac, Will, and Amy froze in horror. Twelve giant Minotaur's surrounded them. They could fight, yes, but they had never faced such a formable threat before this night, let alone the power of twelve of them.

"Kill them all and give me the four pieces of the Eye of Horus!" Draconis roared. "Then we can tear down this obelisk and retrieve the Was Scepter."

At this, the kids leaped into action, each taking their defensive positions just as they had in the tunnels beneath the city. Isaac took point, his hand outstretched and ready to deliver a powerful burst of energy. Will interlocked his free arm with Isaac's, offering a shielding connection to

anyone he touched. On the other side, Dez interlocked his free arm with Will's, offering a healing connection to anyone he touched. This time, Amy staked out the rear of the group. Together, they were as prepared as they could be, with no time to waste on fear.

"Draconis!" Isaac cried out. "You and your Minotaur's are nothing but beasts from the underworld!"

"Yeah," Will added. "You are powerless against the Eye of Horus!"

Draconis erupted into a thunderous laugh that seemed to make the air around them tremble. Then he seized the wrought-iron fence bordering the walkway into the park and with his bare clawed hands, tore off a spiked-tip picket, raising it above his head. He swung the makeshift weapon like a battle spear, roaring once more. Following his lead, each of the monstrous beasts ripped at the fence, grabbing iron pickets to use as weapons.

"Well, so much for hand-to-hand combat," Dez muttered as the Minotaur's made quick work of the fence.

"We need to take these guys out before they close in!"

"Katzenstein Kids, Protectors of the North, South, East, and West!" Amy cried out from behind them. "Unite!"

"Unite!" Dez, Isaac, and Will shouted in unison.

The Minotaur's charged from every direction as Isaac took aim. He called on Horus from deep within, throwing a left and then a right fist at two approaching Minotaur's. Huge radiating beams of energy blasted from his fists like cannons, hot and smoking, each strike distorting the air around the kids like a wave. Two Minotaur's were thrown back like ragdolls, landing with hard thuds. But more took their place. Suddenly, Isaac was flailing his arms in every direction, shouting as blast wave after blast wave burst forth from his fists. Three more beasts flew back with deep growls, but it wasn't enough. As soon as the beasts landed, the others bounced back, strong and unhurt by the impact of Isaac's energy. They came in waves, able to continue their assault by following one after the other. Will held on tight, hoping the shield he projected would keep them safe even as Isaac continued his attack.

With each wave, the beasts got closer and closer, until a crack whipped through the night as one of the iron spears flew into and bounced right off the shield cast by the Protection Gem.

"I don't know how much longer we can take this," Will called out. "There are too many of them!"

The ring of attacking Minotaur's tightened around the four kids, their monstrous forms a blur of muscle and rage. Will, channeling the power of his Protection Gem, to deflect their blows with a shimmering shield of energy. Each strike of an iron spear against the shield sent shockwaves through the air, followed by a retaliatory blast from Isaac's Power Gem, hurling the Minotaur's back momentarily.

Yet, they rose again and again, their relentless assault a testament to their unwavering determination. The four gems, worn by Dez, Isaac, Will, and Amy, crackled with power, a visible manifestation of their combined strength. But the strain of maintaining this magical barrier was beginning to take its toll.

Dez could see the fatigue etched on their faces, their movements becoming sluggish as their energy reserves dwindled. The gems demanded a tremendous amount of willpower and focus and the longer the battle raged the more difficult it became to hold back the tide of Minotaur's.

Will's shield flickered, a sign of his waning strength. A Minotaur, seizing the opportunity, lunged forward its spear aimed at his chest. Dez gasped, his heart pounding in his chest. But before the blow could land, a bolt of green energy shot out from Amy's gem, striking the Minotaur's arm and sending the spear flying.

Isaac, sensing Will's vulnerability conjured a whirlwind of sand and fallen leaves, momentarily blinding the Minotaur's, and giving Will a chance to recover. But it was only a temporary reprieve. The Minotaur's, enraged by their thwarted attacks redoubled their efforts, their roars echoing through the night.

Dez knew they couldn't hold out much longer. They needed a new strategy, a way to turn the tide of the battle. But with their energy fading and the Minotaur's closing in, time was running out. The fate of the Was Scepter and perhaps the world hung precariously in the balance.

Suddenly and unexpectedly, they heard the voice of a young girl. "Hey, Minotaur's!" she called. "Why don't you pick on someone your own size?!"

The Minotaur's halted their attack on Dez, Isaac, Will, and Amy, turning their attention toward the new voice. At the edge of the walkway, each standing in their own defensive stance were Daria, Myra, and Olivia. One at a time, each of them raised an iron picket from behind their back and held it outward with both hands on the hilt, as if it were a sword.

One by one, they called out: "I am the grip... from this

place, I stand! I am the guard... from this place, I defend! I am the blade... from this place, I attack!"

The tide of the battle shifted abruptly as the Minotaur's, their attention drawn by the sudden intrusion, turned their wrath towards the three sisters. With a guttural roar the beasts charged, their hooves pounding the earth, their iron pickets raised high.

For a moment the kids were frozen with fear, expecting the delicate figures of Daria, Myra, and Olivia to be overwhelmed by the sheer brute force of the Minotaur's. But to their astonishment the sisters reacted with lightning speed and grace.

Moving as one they formed a triangle, their bodies weaving and twirling in a mesmerizing dance of combat. Each minotaur strike was met with a perfectly timed block, followed by a swift counterattack. Their movements were fluid and precise, like a deadly ballet choreographed for war.

Olivia led the charge, her spiked picket deflecting blows with deceptive ease. Myra, followed closely, her spinning picket flashing like silver lightning, finding gaps in the Minotaurs' defenses. Daria, was a whirlwind of motion, her smaller stature allowing her to dart between the larger beasts, her spear a constant threat to their flanks.

The Minotaur's used to overwhelming their opponents with brute strength found themselves outmatched. Their clumsy attacks were easily parried, their defenses breached by the sisters' coordinated strikes. One by one, they were sent sprawling, their bodies hitting the ground with heavy thuds.

The clearing became a chaotic whirlwind of motion, a symphony of grunts, clashes of metal, and the enraged bellows of the Minotaur's. Yet, amidst the chaos the three sisters remained a beacon of calm, their movements a testament to their years of training and their unbreakable bond.

"Holy cow, they know how to fight!" Will cried out, an almost giddy feeling washing over him sending a new surge of energy through his gem. "Let's join them and kick ass!"

The minotaur leader, Draconis, looked on in obvious frustration. He angrily pawed at the ground with his hooves, scraping them against the hard concrete, before charging toward the 200-ton obelisk and crashing into its base with all his might. A whipping noise rang out, so loud it hurt the kids' ears. The towering structure shook slightly but continued to stand tall and strong. Beneath it, Draconis began to grunt and bellow, his angry roars reverberating across Central Park. With a deep grunting breath that flared his nostrils, the beast pawed his hooves against the ground again, preparing to strike the obelisk's base once more. A huge crack whipped through the air as Draconis crashed into it again as hard as he could. This time, the obelisk began to tilt unsteadily, and the other minotaur's took notice.

As the kids watched, another minotaur joined Draconis, and then another. Muscles bulging across their shoulders, arms, and backs. The other Minotaur's followed Draconis' lead scraping their hooves against the concrete in preparation. Then, they all rammed forward into the obelisk at once, their ferocious strength bringing the huge monument crashing down. The noise was deafening, and the earth shook again as if an earthquake had struck Central Park. Blocks of red granite and dust billowed all around them bringing the epic battle to a sudden halt. The twelve Minotaur's cheered and cried out in victory.

Dez pointed at the remains of the obelisk and called out to Myra who was the closest to the destroyed monument. "They're after the Was Scepter! We must stop them."

Before any of the other beasts of the underworld had a chance to move, Dez, Isaac, Will, and Amy were attacking them once more, joining forces with Daria, Myra, and Olivia. The battle raged as if it had never stopped, but the lead Minotaur no longer seemed to care about the fight. Draconis began digging through the rubble in a hurry, disappearing into the plumes of dust. Then, in a matter of moments Draconis rose from the top of the pile of red granite, the Was Scepter held high above his head.

The battling Minotaur's paused to glance back at their leader, the battleground fell silent, giving the exhausted kids a small reprieve. The clash of weapons replaced by an unwelcoming stillness. Draconis, his imposing figure silhouetted against the moonlit sky, stood atop a mound of red granite rubble, his eyes burning with an unholy fire.

He raised his arms, his voice a thunderclap that echoed through the park. "I call upon Set!" he roared, the sound reverberating through the trees and across the still waters of the pond. "I call upon the God of War and Chaos, Ruler of the Desert, Power of the Lands, the Sun, Thunderstorms, and Earthquakes! I call upon you to claim the Was Scepter!"

CHAPTER 22
THE CHILDREN OF QUSEIR

An eerie silence filled the air, seconds feeling like hours. Then from the direction of Central Park's Great Lawn, a crackle snapped across the sky. A sonic boom and a flash of lightning descended, electrifying the air and raising the hairs on the kids' arms and necks.

At the impact point a strange mist of smoky light appeared, altering the saturation of everything nearby. Trees, grass, and the cityscape beyond the mist appeared like negatives on film, casting an eerie glow. The presence of darkness, of a dark soul, filled them with an indescribable fear.

From within the mist emerged a silhouette—a half-man, half-beast figure resembling no known creature. It was unmistakably Set, the God of War and Chaos, though not yet fully formed. His body was pure blackness with muscular arms ending in long sharp claws that scraped the ground. A surge of power radiated from him, yet the rapidly dropping temperature suggested a soulless creature.

"It must be Set," Amy whispered, her voice trembling. "Not yet fully resurrected, right?"

The boys nodded, remembering Horus's immense size. "No, not fully resurrected," Will agreed, his voice shaky. But pure evil without a doubt."

Set approached and the kids held their battle stance. Dez and Will interlocked arms with Myra and Daria, providing healing and shielding from their gems, with Isaac at the front and Olivia and Amy at the back. The Minotaur's knelt before their ruler, Draconis offering Set the Was Scepter like a gift.

Tendrils of black smoke snaked from Set's claws, wrapping around the scepter before his hand closed around it. He raised his head, his eyes as empty as the rest of him, and spoke in a voice that could shake the heavens.

"Children of Horus, holders of the Eye, do not fear me. For upon my resurrection, I shall crown you in victory against every land. I will turn this world to sand, and from it, I will return our great dynasty from the darkness of the underworld." He twirled the scepter effortlessly. "We will rise again. People of the sun will shine on every horizon under Ra. The chosen Set, who giveth all life, forever shall be the sole ruler."

Olivia broke from the group, severing the connection with her sisters and the boys. Unable to accept defeat, she cried out, "Sisters, we must stop him!"

With all her might, Olivia took several steps forward pulled her arm back and launched the spike-tip picket like a javelin spear. It flew over the kneeling Minotaur's, aiming straight for Set's black head only to be deflected at the last moment. Draconis stood quickly, blocking the spear with his arm before it could strike Set. The Minotaur leader grunted in pain as the spear's tip sliced a gash across his bicep.

Set's eyes looked down on Olivia and he tilted his head as he cried out in a thunderous voice. "All your skill and training, your courageous battle against my Minotaur's, and your willingness to give your life... for what?" He tilted his head mockingly in the other direction. "To stop the inevitable. What have you accomplished?" Glancing at Draconis, who acted unfazed despite the blood dripping from his arm, Set bared his teeth. "A scratch and a drop of blood." He then raised the Was Scepter and pointed it at Olivia. A bolt of electricity shot out striking her in the chest. She crumpled to the ground, killed instantly.

"Nooo!" Amy screamed in horror, breaking away from the group and moving toward Olivia's body. "You killed our friend!"

"Amy, take my hand!" Will cried out, knowing she needed to stay connected to him. The Protection Gem was their only defense. But as Will reached for Amy, Set pointed the scepter at her, and another bolt of electricity struck her down. "No! No!" Will screamed.

The remaining kids stared at Amy and Olivia's bodies, shocked. They remained frozen, except for Isaac. While staying connected for protection, he attacked, launching a barrage of energy at Set. Dez, Will, Daria, and Myra watched as blast after blast flew forward, only to be absorbed by the Was Scepter.

"My powers are having no effect on Set!" Isaac cried out, throwing his arms down helplessly.

Daria and Myra screamed in anger and grief, tears welling up in their eyes. Dez and Will struggled to hold onto them as they faced their inability to protect themselves.

"Children of Horus, Holders of the Eye," Set stepped forward, his voice booming. The Minotaur's rose, heads held high in victory. "You chose the Underworld rather than join us in our glorified resurrection." Set raised the scepter, aiming it at them, intent on casting their souls into the underworld.

Suddenly he paused, glancing beyond them into the trees. From Turtle Pond a mob of silhouettes emerged from the darkness. Their footsteps echoed from all around. They weren't adults, but children—perhaps twenty of them. Steadily, they approached, surrounding the kids who stood facing Set and his Minotaur's. Each child held up their left hand, revealing a birthmark in the center of their palm shaped like the Eye of Horus. Just like the boy who had led Helen to safety from Auschwitz all those years ago.

Set, looked down on the fortified barrier of children surrounding the kids. His eyes narrowed with malice as he aimed the Was Scepter, with a flick of his wrist he unleashed a barrage of electric bolts from the scepter's tip at the protective circle.

The bolts crackled and hissed through the air, each one radiating an ominous glow as it descended like a miniature lightning strike. The deafening crackle of electricity echoed.

But as each bolt struck the barrier, something extraordinary happened. The children's palms, adorned with the Eye of Horus symbol, began to glow. The light intensified with each impact, reflecting off the symbol like a beacon in the night. Then, as if absorbed by their very skin the energy of the bolts dissipated harmlessly leaving the children untouched. Set's face twisted in frustration and disbelief. His powerful weapon capable of leveling towns, was being thwarted by the group of mysterious children.

Set drew the Was Scepter back, placing it by his side with the staff's hilt touching the ground. "He who called upon the Children of Quseir," Set spoke into the darkness of the park. "The inevitable awaits you, my brother! All that has happened before will happen again." Then, turning to Draconis he whispered something the kids couldn't hear. After receiving the verbal direction Draconis raced off with two other Minotaur's, disappearing from sight. "As for the Holders of the Eye and the Children of Quseir, your fates await you. Once I am resurrected, nothing can stop me... your efforts to resist the inevitable will be futile." Set and the remaining nine Minotaur's gave them one last look before turning on their heels and walking back to the Great Lawn, fading into what remained of the lingering black smoky mist and vanishing from sight.

Without a word, the Children of Quseir dispersed,

giving the kids room to assess their losses.

"Dez, hurry," Will turned to his best friend. "We need the Health Gem to save Olivia and Amy."

Breaking away from the group, Dez rushed over to where Olivia and Amy lay on the ground. He took each of their hands into his own, cupping his hands together and closed his eyes tightly. As he did, the Health Gem hanging from his necklace began glowing immensely and the same green glow radiated from both girls, casting a warmth over them.

Dez and the others began pleading, "Wake up, wake up. Come on, Olivia and Amy, stay with us!"

A moment later Amy's eyes snapped open and a deep gasp of air flowed into her mouth, causing her chest to rise as she gasped herself awake. Tears in their eyes, Daria and Olivia cried out, "Olivia! Don't give up, Olivia!"

Now that Amy was awake Dez released her hand and clasped Olivia's in both of his hands. Turning all his attention to her, he quietly pleaded for her to awaken, practically praying for her to open her eyes. Thought, he couldn't deny how cold her hands felt in his and soon the Health Gem began to fade, its glow subsiding altogether.

From behind them one of the Children of Quseir stepped forward putting a gentle hand on Dez and pulling him to his feet, away from Olivia. In a low voice, he told the kids, "The Eye has the power to heal, but not to resurrect. I'm sorry. The scales now await her in the Hall of Two Truths."

Daria gave a sniffle as Myra asked, "What is the Hall of Two Truths?"

"It is the place of judgment," the boy continued, "where Maat will weigh her heart against the feather of truth. Those absent of a heavy heart are given passage to the afterlife. Those who fail are given a door to the underworld."

"She gave her life to stop Set, to save us," Isaac told the sisters, comforting them. "Her heart is pure, good, and carries no heaviness. She will be okay she will be given passage!"

"Thank you for your kind words, Isaac," Myra said, her voice devoid of emotion.

Meanwhile, Will helped Amy get back onto her feet. She was slightly disoriented but seemed fine overall. "We almost lost you, Amy!" Will told her.

Amy glanced over at Olivia's body sadly, "Remember my vision? It came true, someone did die, only it wasn't me on the ground, it was Olivia."

"I'm sorry to ask," Dez said, stepping toward Myra. "But how did you know we were here?"
Myra looked down, contemplating her reply.

"You followed us, didn't you?" Amy pressed, frustration in her voice. "We know you're lying to us; you were looking for the Eye of Horus. You wanted our gems, right?"

Myra looked up, meeting her eyes. "Yes, we haven't been honest with you."

"Great," Dez sighed. "So, you only pretended to like me?"

"No, Dez," Myra shook her head. "I do like you; we like all of you... but we were on a mission to track down the Eye of Horus. It had nothing to do with you personally."

"And stop Set as well!" Daria added.

"Who do you work for?" Amy asked them.

"We are known as the Matryoshka Dolls," Myra told her.

"Russians! I knew it," Isaac said. "They're probably related to Gorska Maika, the Russian Boogey woman!"

"Gorska Maika? Never heard of her," Daria shrugged, wiping the tears away from her cheeks. "It's a long story, but we're here to help. I know you don't trust us, but our primary mission is to stop Set!"

Dez looked back down at their sister before responding. "Olivia died trying to stop Set, so I believe you."

The girls seemed relieved.

"I don't understand how Amy survived and Olivia didn't?" Will asked. He glanced over at Amy's burn mark on her chest; the strike from the Was Scepter had burnt a hole through the material, leaving a singed circle behind in her top pocket. "Set struck you right in the chest!"

Amy reached into the top pocket of her shirt, a pocket charred and burned from the bolt of lightning of the Was Scepter and removed the 24-Hour AA Chip Will had given her a few months ago. "Your dad's AA chip," she whispered as she looked down at it, running her fingers along its rough surface.

"Holy cow!" Isaac exclaimed. "You had a bronze AA Chip in your pocket! That thing must have absorbed most of the energy; you know, bronze is an excellent conductor of heat and electricity!"

"Ha," Will smiled. "Looks like I'm not the only one paying attention in science class."

The others looked at Isaac with raised brows, and Dez added, "Okay, okay, Isaac Newton, we all know you're an A student in science."

Isaac blushed and mumbled under his breath, "Gee whiz, I was just saying!"

The kids gathered around Amy. She held the chip out on the palm of her hand and read the words on the front side out loud. "It reads: Unity, Service, and Recovery, and has the symbol of a triangle or pyramid. My friends, this is just another sign; we have been chosen." She looked up at Daria and Myra. "All of us have been chosen. We must listen to the signs; we have been unified and we must be united, too. We are here to serve Horus and save the world from Set, and..." She looked down at Olivia's body, "we must recover from our defeat!"

"We know you don't trust us," Myra started, wiping the tears from her eyes, "but we must join forces... Besides, if there's nothing else that you can trust about us, you know for sure that we have a common interest in stopping Set. We want to avenge our sister."

Daria nodded emphatically. "Sometimes those you may least expect, even a tiny mouse can make a difference. We all bring value even in the smallest and least of ways."

"The enemy of my enemy is my friend," Dez added. "I heard it in a movie once."

"Actually, that quote dates back over 2,000 years," Isaac corrected him.

"Oh my..." Dez shook his head, but Will interrupted before he could complete the statement.

"Okay, enough," he said. "Myra is right. They lost their sister, and they are good fighters—really good fighters. We need to work together."

As he stopped talking the Children of Quseir began walking back into the darkness from whence they came, back toward Turtle Pond, disappearing the same way that Set and the Minotaur's had. Behind them, Daria and Myra placed their hands over Amy's outstretched fist, followed by Dez, Will, and Isaac.

Myra cried out, "Unity!"

When the kids all threw their hands into the air, they could hear clapping coming from the shadows. They looked over to see who it was, squinting into the darkness, and Rurik appeared dressed in a sleek black suit and wearing his fedora hat with the long feather.

His hands clapped together in a slow applause.

"Dollmaker!" Myra called out to him.

The man's voice, a deep rumble tinged with sorrow, cut through the silence that had settled over the battlefield. "I heard what you all said," he addressed the group, his gaze lingering on Daria and Myra, "and I witnessed the power of Set for myself."

He moved towards Olivia, where she lay still and lifeless. With a gentle touch he closed her eyes, a single tear tracing a path down his weathered cheek. "I'm sorry about your sister," he whispered, his voice thick with emotion. "I, too, am hurt by the loss of Olivia."

The weight of his words hung heavy in the air. It was

clear that he shared a deep bond with these young women, a connection that went beyond mere guardianship. "You are not just my Matryoshka Dolls," he continued, straightening up and addressing the entire group, "but my daughters as well. We must work together to destroy Set before it is too late."

His gaze swept over each of them, a flicker of determination igniting in his eyes. "I can help you," he declared. "I have many resources at my disposal and perhaps I can help track Set's location. You are not alone in this quest."

A glimmer of hope flickered in the eyes of Daria and Myra. They had lost their sister, but they had found unexpected allies in Will, Isaac, Dez and Amy. This revelation brought a new dimension to their mission, a sense of unity and shared purpose that transcended the boundaries of blood and ancient powers.

CHAPTER 23
THE BOOK OF THE DEAD

Suddenly, alarms began blaring nearby, emanating from the MET.

"That can't be a coincidence," Dez said, looking towards the museum. "Something's happening! We need to go check it out!"

"Hurry!" Will urged.

"I'll take care of Olivia," Rurik assured them as they sprinted towards the museum. Daria and Myra looked back to see their adoptive father gently lifting Olivia's body. Adrenaline pumping, the kids navigated the wooded path through Central Park. The MET's imposing facade grew larger with each step, its grand rear entrance a scene of chaos. A gaping hole shattered the glass doors, shards glinting in the moonlight. They scanned the area for any sign of the Minotaur's. Will gasped, pointing to a manhole cover. Three hulking figures were descending into the darkness below. The last, Draconis, clutched a bulky object.

"Did you see that?" Will exclaimed. "They stole something!"

The realization struck them. Set's Minotaur's had breached the MET and escaped with something valuable. What could it be? And what did it mean for their quest? Without hesitation, they rushed towards the museum's rear entrance. Shattered glass crunched underfoot as they burst through the doors, alarms shrieking. They followed the trail of destruction left by the Minotaur's. Deep gouges scarred the marble floors, leading to the Egyptian wing. It was clear they had been searching for something, leaving a path of shattered display cases and scattered artifacts. A sense of urgency propelled them forward. They had to discover what the Minotaur's had stolen and stop them.

"Guys," Isaac's voice was panicked. "Imhotep's ancient Book of the Dead!" The others rushed to where Isaac stood, the same spot where he had read from the book just a day before. The display case was smashed, the papyrus scrolls inscribed with black ink missing. "It's gone," Isaac said. "They took the pages and the ancient scrolls." The realization hit the kids hard - the Twelve Minotaur's had come for more than they knew. They now possessed the Book of the Dead, containing spells that could resurrect Set to his full power. "We failed to stop them completely. We failed to protect the world from Set," Amy lamented.

"We lost the battle against the Twelve Minotaur's," Isaac added.

"We lost the Was Scepter," Will said.

"We lost Olivia," Myra's voice trembled.

"And now we've lost the Book of the Dead," Dez finished, defeated.

Rurik's voice echoed into the room, interrupting their despair. He stood in the entryway. "Olivia's in the car, we must go, police sirens are approaching."

The kids started towards the exit, dejected. But Daria noticed a small wooden artifact on the ground, discarded from its case. "Maybe something was meant to be found," she mused, picking up the glowing red wooden bird. "It's tingling in my hand," she said, showing Myra. "It's a small red bird, like the one in my dream." Myra's eyes widened. "All that has happened before," she whispered, "will happen again."

"In my dream, the stampede of bulls killed the young woman, while the red bird tried to save me," Daria recalled.

"Yes, perhaps your dream was symbolic. The young woman must have been Olivia, murdered by the Minotaur's," Myra confirmed.

Rurik approached, his mismatched eyes meeting theirs. "The young woman in your dream was not Olivia. She was your mother."

The girls were stunned. Daria screamed at her adoptive father, "Our mother? How would you know? What haven't you told us?"

"I'm sorry, I should have told you sooner. I couldn't have known what would happen, but you deserve the truth. I didn't find you three in that orphanage by chance. I discovered your identities through a Top-Secret file regarding the Petrozavodsk Phenomenon. Your mother was an agency secretary at a secret underground facility in

Petrozavodsk. Your father was a physicist there. The Petrozavodsk Phenomenon occurred because of Set, when he was released unto the world, when he escaped. There was a thunderous light from the sky that struck the facility, destroying it. Both your parents perished." "Why didn't you tell us the truth?" Daria's voice trembled as Myra hugged her. "Set killed our parents! We deserved to know! He killed our mother, our father, and now our sister!"

Rurik knelt before Daria. "I am so sorry I didn't tell you, "He said sincerely. "I'm even more sorry this happened at all. The KGB is responsible for the loss of your mother, father and now your sister. Our agency inadvertently released Set," Rurik confessed, his voice heavy with regret. "It's why we're trying so hard to stop him, to right our wrongs."

Amy interjected, "Nothing can stop him if he resurrects. He has the Was Scepter. If he rejoins his soul using the Book of the Dead, he could destroy the world!" Outside, sirens signaled the police's arrival. "We must leave before they get here," Rurik urged, standing back up.

As Dez, Isaac, Will, and Amy headed for the door, Myra and Daria followed, Daria clutching the red wooden bird.

Suddenly, Myra stopped. "I feel something."

She walked to a broken display case containing a Khopesh Sword. Inexplicably drawn to it, she touched the hilt. A tingle ran through her fingers and down her spine. Something about this felt important and the others watched with anticipation.

At that moment, Horus's unmistakable voice filled their minds, resonating from Amy's Prophecy Gem.

"Daria, Protector of the Sky, Holder of the Saqqara Bird. Myra, Protector of the Land, Holder of the Khopesh Sword. These weapons have chosen you, and you have chosen them."

Amy's eyes rolled back, revealing only the whites, as her mind was pulled away from the museum. The sight of the kids and Rurik grew smaller as Amy felt herself being drawn away. She recognized the feeling; the same pulling sensation she felt last summer when Horus called upon her. It felt as though it was all in her head, but she knew her consciousness had somehow separated from her body and she was moving through time.

Suddenly, she was in a strange office, witnessing a conversation between Rurik and another man, a heavyset man. There was a strange static noise in the room. The man sitting across from Rurik handed him a file and Rurik began flipping through its pages and laying out photos as they spoke.

"You didn't miss any clues during our time in Egypt," the heavyset man stated. "No, I did not," Rurik replied. "Which is why I must ask, was the item you were really searching for in Egypt retrieved?"

"Damn you, what are you insinuating?" The heavyset man rose in frustration, abruptly walking over to a box and toggling a dial, intensifying the static. Then, he walked over to Rurik's side of the desk and leaned over to whisper something in his ear.

The whispered words radiated loudly in Amy's head: "Nikolai Yurchenko was carrying an RN-28 nuclear bomb, which still remains missing."

Amy felt the pull lead her out of the office and back inside the museum. She opened her eyes to find Will, Isaac, Dez, Daria, Myra, and Rurik speechless. "Did you all hear that? I had another vision; a nuclear bomb is missing in the sands of Egypt!" Amy cried out. The kids nodded, acknowledging the dire news.

Suddenly, she felt her mind pulling away again. "Everyone, quickly grab my hand, I'm having another vision!" Each of the kids took Amy's hand, her Prophecy Gem glowing brighter than ever. Daria reached for Rurik's hand, making sure he wasn't left out.

They all felt the familiar pull. Once again, their minds were drawn into a shared vision. This time, they saw a desolate desert, its sand dunes shimmering under a relentless sun. In the distance, a figure stood silhouetted against the blazing horizon. The figure turned, revealing the chilling visage of Set.

A cold dread washed over each of them. Laying before Set, gleaming ominously in the sunlight, was a nuclear bomb. Set's lips curled into a cruel smile as he raised the Was Scepter. "Behold the power of Ra!" Set's voice boomed through the desert, its echo chilling their souls. The next moment, he struck the nuclear bomb with the Was Scepter, and a blinding light engulfed the horizon.

The vision faded, leaving them in stunned silence. They all understood the implication. Rurik was the one who knew about the missing nuclear weapon. The pieces were falling into place. Rurik's actions, his mission, it all made sense now.

"Your destinies were set long ago," Horus's deep voice spoke to them all. "The Prophecy Gem has shown all that was, all that is, and all that will be. Will, Protector of the South and Holder of the Protection Gem; Isaac, Protector of the East and Holder of the Power Gem; Dez, Protector of the North and Holder of the Health Gem; Amy, Protector of the West and Holder of the Prophecy Gem; Daria,

Protector of the Sky and Holder of the Saqqara Bird; and Myra, Protector of the Land and Holder of the Khopesh Sword. Humans have harnessed the destructive power of Ra. These weapons must never be used. Set must not prevail."

Around the circle, their eyes widened in surprise. "We all saw the vision," Amy said, her voice shaking with a mix of fear and anger. "We heard Horus's warning. If Set gets his hands on that nuke, he'll use it. He'll turn the world to sand." The kids nodded, grim determination settling over their faces. Rurik wrapped his arms around Daria and Myra's shoulders. "The task ahead is daunting, but we have been chosen for a reason. We have been given a glimpse into the future, a future that is not set in stone. We must do all we can to prevent this impending apocalypse."

Suddenly, a loud voice echoed from the hallway, "Why is everyone just standing there? The entire New York Police Department just entered the front door!" Mike shouted. The kids quickly focused on escaping the museum. Will, Isaac, Dez, and Amy followed Mike to the van, while Daria and Myra followed Rurik to his car. "We'll regroup when we're back on Cape Cod," Amy called out to Daria and Myra. The others agreed, nodding silently.

Mike and the kids bolted through the dimly lit corridors of the museum, their footsteps echoing against the marble floors. A wave of blue uniforms surged through the main entrance, their flashlights cutting through the darkness like frantic searchlights. The group ducked behind a towering statue, their hearts pounding in their chests. As the clamor of the police grew distant, they slipped out of a side exit, vanishing into the moonlit night. The cool air hit their faces as they sprinted across the park towards Mike's van, their escape a hair's breadth away.

Safely back in the news van, Mike saw Amy, Dez, Isaac, and Will sitting in the back. He didn't ask any questions. Instead, he pressed down on the gas and the van sped away from the park, heading back to the Upper East Side to pick up Jo, Cindy, and Anne.

CHAPTER 24
BITTERSWEET

Back in Dennis Port, the familiar salty air did little to soothe the raw ache in their hearts. Will, Isaac, Amy, Daria, and Myra returned to their homes not with the triumphant cheers they had hoped for, but with the silent weight of defeat. The battle against Set and his twelve Minotaur's had been a brutal one, leaving them scarred, both physically and emotionally. Most devastatingly, they had lost Olivia.

As they entered their separate houses, the emptiness echoed around them. The laughter and warmth that had once filled their shared home were now replaced with a chilling silence. The reality of their loss, the death of their new friend, weighed heavily on each of them. The weight of the pending danger solidified in each of their minds. Myra and Daria clung to each other, their sobs a testament to their grief. Will, Amy, and Isaac found solace in their own moments of somber silence, their faces etched with sorrow.

Each of them struggled to find sleep that night. They tossed and turned, haunted by the images of the battle and the final moments of Olivia's life. For Dez, the guilt of not being able to save her with his Health Gem gnawed at him, leaving a bitter taste in his mouth. Yet, even in their darkest hour, a tiny spark of hope remained. They knew they had to find a way to move forward, not just for themselves, but for Olivia and for all the Children of Men and Women.

As the days passed, the kids returned to school and their routines. The normalcy of their everyday lives felt jarring after the horrors they had witnessed, but they knew they had to keep going. A wave of relief, blossoming into genuine happiness, washed over the students' faces as they caught sight of Mr. Rice and Ms. Fleming amidst the bustling hallway between classes.

The sight was reassuringly ordinary, a stark contrast to the unsettling anxieties that had gripped them. It wasn't just relief that nothing *worse* had happened; it was a deeper, more personal thankfulness.

In the familiar setting of the cafeteria, the six of them finally had a moment to gather since their return from New York City. The weight of their failure hung heavy in the air, a palpable tension that threatened to suffocate them. But they knew they couldn't let the silence consume them.

"We can't let this be the end… we have a job to do,"

Will spoke, his voice hoarse but resolute. "Olivia wouldn't want us to give up... we are not allowed to give up, we are the Katzenstein Kids! We need to regroup, learn from our mistakes, and come back stronger."

His words pierced through the gloom, igniting a glimmer of hope in their eyes. They nodded in agreement, their resolve strengthened by the reminder of Olivia's unwavering spirit. They had to honor her memory by ensuring her sacrifice was not in vain. The first step was healing, and they all agreed. They knew they must support each other through the pain, finding solace in their shared grief.

That weekend, as the sun beat down on the small gathering, casting long shadows that danced with a gentle sea breeze, they came together to say goodbye. It was a day of mourning, but also of celebration, for Olivia, a brave warrior who had fallen in their battle against the evil Egyptian deity Set.

Olivia's sisters, Myra and Daria, stood hand in hand, their faces etched with grief yet tinged with the pride of knowing their sister's bravery. Beside them stood Will, Isaac, and Amy, Olivia's newest and closest friends, their eyes reflecting the deep bond they had formed with their fallen comrade. Rurik, Olivia's loyal caretaker and mentor since her days at the House of the Abandoned, stood a little apart, his shoulders slumped with the weight of his loss.

The casket, adorned with symbols of protection and bravery, rested on a simple bier. As per ancient Egyptian beliefs, it was positioned so that Olivia's head faced north, towards the afterlife. Her journey to Aaru, the Field of Reeds, had begun.

Will, the first to speak, recalled their shared adventures since their first meeting in the school cafeteria, his voice thick with emotion. Isaac, the quiet observer, shared his admiration for Olivia's strength and determination, his words slow and deliberate. Amy, always the compassionate one, offered words of comfort and hope, her voice soft and soothing. Dez, uncharacteristically had no words, he simply took Myra's hand in comfort.

Myra and Daria, their voices choked with emotion, shared childhood memories of their sister, their tales weaving a tapestry of love and laughter. Rurik, his voice strong and steady, spoke of Olivia's unwavering spirit, her thirst for knowledge, and her unwavering dedication to protecting the innocent, especially her sisters and new-found friends.

As the sun began its descent, casting a golden glow over the gathering, the final farewells were spoken. The casket was lowered into the ground, its north-facing orientation a silent testament to the kids' and Rurik's newfound belief in the afterlife.

The days that followed were bittersweet, filled with both grief and quiet determination. Olivia's friends and family found solace in their shared memories, their stories keeping her spirit alive. They knew they had a long road ahead of them, but they were united in their resolve to honor Olivia's memory by becoming stronger and preparing for the battles that lay ahead.

◆ ◆ ◆

As the warm days of summer quickly approached, signaling the end of another school year, the kids had all received invitations from Myra to a surprise birthday party for Daria. Amy, Dez, Isaac, and Will arrived at the girls' house early, where Myra met them outside. They parked their bikes against the side of the house.

"Come on," she grinned with excitement, waving them over before pressing a finger to her lips, gesturing for silence.

The kids followed Myra through a breezeway and into a double car garage with darkened windows. None of them had ever been there before. It was pitch-black, and they couldn't see anything. They were momentarily horrified that this was where their host had chosen to stop them.

"Okay, stand in front of the garage door. The room has already been decorated," Myra told them. "When Rurik arrives with Daria, and he opens the garage door we will all yell 'surprise.'"

Less than a minute later, they shuffled as a vehicle pulled up outside. They could hear Daria's voice speaking to Rurik when the garage door opened with a mechanical buzz, allowing daylight to stream in and light up the dark space.

All at once, Amy, Dez, Isaac, and Will cried out: "Surprise! Happy Birthday!"

Myra faced them with a huge grin. "Surprise," she said. "Turn around."

They looked on, confused, finding the same big smile plastered on Daria and Rurik's faces. Furrowing their brows, the kids turned around, their jaws dropping in shock. It was a trick! The garage wasn't decorated with birthday banners or cake—no, instead, the inside of the garage held the most amazing sight they had ever seen. It had been converted into a high-tech headquarters, like something out of a spy movie, with a sophisticated long-range radio, a weather station, and a television surrounded by lounge chairs. The walls were lined with maps of the globe, along with clocks displaying the times of various major cities around the world, including New York, Paris, Moscow, and Hong Kong.

"Wow," Isaac pointed at one wall, where six school-style lockers were labeled with each of their names: Dez, Isaac, Will, Amy, Daria, and Myra. He rushed over, fully intent on opening one, but got distracted by a VCR sitting on a nearby shelf, with a video camera atop it.

Will and Amy investigated a desk in the corner of the room with the coolest-looking 16-bit computer they had ever seen, their faces reflected back at them in its sleek black monitor.

Lined up neatly beside the lockers were six brand new black Puch mopeds, the chrome trimming shimmering in the sunshine. Dez whistled long and low, approaching them. "These things are primo! They go like thirty miles an hour."

While they investigated everything, asking a hundred questions about what the things were and what they did, Amy turned to Rurik. "What is all this stuff?"

"Well," the Dollmaker tilted his head. "Being an international spy does come with its advantages. I figured if we are going to attempt to locate Set and his Minotaur's, we are going to need a headquarters."

"That makes sense," Amy said, "I guess it beats a treehouse and a basement hideout." She and the boys nodded their agreement.

Rurik glanced around the room, adding, "I have already sent word to all my contacts to report anything out of the ordinary back to me."

"That's not all," Daria said. The kids spun around to face their friend in surprise. There was more. "Check this out."

Daria reached for her red Saqqara Bird from her belt clip and threw her arm out, snapping her hand forward. With precision, a glowing red Saqqara Bird flew out at high speed, emitting a high-pitched whoosh. It suddenly sliced a pinecone off a nearby tree before returning to her waiting hand like a boomerang.

"Holy moly, that is radical!" Dez shouted.

"I was just playing with it," Daria said, looking on with an open mouth. "I figured out that it's a high-speed boomerang."

"High-speed," Amy laughed. "More like lethal speed!"

"I still don't know what these symbols mean," Daria added looking at the hieroglyphs engraved along the side of the red Saqqara Bird.

Amy's brow furrowed in thought as she addressed the group, her voice laced with concern. "There seems to be a lot of things we don't fully understand about our powers. During our battle with the Minotaur's, did anyone notice my Prophecy Gem shoot a bolt of green energy at one of the Minotaur's, knocking the spear from his hand?"

Will, his eyes wide with a mix of surprise and excitement, chimed in, "I noticed! It was incredible! I think our gems have a lot more to offer than we realize."

Isaac, ever the analytical one, agreed. "I concur with Will and Amy. We need to learn how to focus our powers better. The gems seem to grow more powerful when we join them together."

Dez added his own perspective. "I agree with you guys. We got our butts kicked out there. If it wasn't for the Children of Quseir, we could have all been killed." He paused for a moment, then declared with newfound resolve, "So, we all agree we must refine our powers to meet the challenges that face us."

The friends exchanged determined glances, a silent pact forming between them. They would uncover the secrets of their powers and harness their full potential.

Myra grinned, then she reached for a brown leather carrying case at her side and swung it over her shoulder. From it, she drew the Khopesh Sword, holding it up while extending her opposite fist. Daria touched her fist to her sister's, followed by Dez, Isaac, Will, and Amy.

"Well, we all agree we owe it to Olivia, and we all heard the voice of Horus," Amy told them. "He has guided us this far. As he told us, it's up to us to stop Set and prevent his resurrection. We are no longer four. We are now six, and with our continued training and combined powers, nothing can stop us!"

The kids all gave a determined nod. In unison, they cried out: "Katzenstein Kids, unite!"

ABOUT THE AUTHOR

A.G. Sullivan

Award winning author A.G. Sullivan grew up on Cape Cod in the small town of Dennis Port, Massachusetts. Since his youth he loved the art of story-telling. He studied at the Boston Architectural Center and later at the University of Phoenix, earning his degree in 1999. He lives with his two children in Arizona.

Known for his **Katzenstein Kids Trilogy** as well as his phycological thriller, **Trypophobia**. His work has earned him 5-STARS from READERS' FAVORITE, as well as a FIREBIRD BOOK AWARD.

CONNECT ONLINE

🌐 www.agsullivan.info
f facebook.com/agsullivanaz1
📷 instagram.com/AGSullivanaz
✖ x.com/agsullivanaz

www.ingramcontent.com/pod-product-compliance
Lightning Source LLC
Chambersburg PA
CBHW070738180626
46818CB00007B/2901